"Smith peppers his story with chilling scenes ... [his] writing is full of evocative language ... A creature feature that earns its suspense by rigorously developing its characters."

— **KIRKUS REVIEWS**

"One of the year's best thrillers. Exhilarating and original ... Cerebral, complex and yet heart-pounding, HYBRID teeters at a full boil throughout. A Finalist for the 2017 William Faulkner-Wisdom Novel Award, HYBRID is a must-read."

— **BESTTHRILLERS.COM**

"... a compelling thriller when mixed together in a vivid story backed by James Marshall Smith's science savvy and attention to crafting exquisite tension and detail into his story."

— **MIDWEST BOOK REVIEW**

"HYBRID is a taut, suspenseful tale of vengeance, deceit, and man's folly in believing that humanity is top of the food chain ... in the vein of JURASSIC PARK ..."

— **MANHATTAN BOOK REVIEW**

"The plot was super fun ... a fast-paced, entertaining read that will keep you on the edge of your seat."

— **SAN FRANCISCO BOOK REVIEW**

"HYBRID is equal parts adrenaline rush, scary science, and page-turning action. James Marshall Smith picks up where Michael Crichton left off, then takes things to a whole new level."

— **JEFF EDWARDS**, bestselling author of *'Sea of Shadows,'* and *'Steel Wind Rising'*

HYBRID

A THRILLER

HYBRID

James Marshall Smith

Braveship
BOOKS

Aura Libertatis Spirat

San Diego

HYBRID

Copyright © 2017 by James Marshall Smith

Braveship Books
San Diego, CA

www.BraveshipBooks.com

Cover Artwork & Design by Slobodan Cedic
www.99Designs.com

Library of Congress Control Number: 2017919650

ISBN-13: 978-1-64062-020-9
Printed in the United States of America

To J.M., and what could have been.

Other Titles by James Marshall Smith

Silent Source

"... monumentally conceived and masterfully sculpted ... Smith is the master of suspense ... spiked with surprising turns that will send readers jolting or gasping at times."

— MANHATTAN BOOK REVIEW

ACKNOWLEDGMENTS

I am indebted to all of the participants in the Rocky Mountain Wolf Conference, held during a beautiful spring week in 1997 in Chico Springs, MT. There I learned from many of the world's experts on wolves and wolf restoration, including discussions with David Mech, Carter Niemeyer, Joe Fontaine, and Diane Boyd.

Many thanks Doug Smith, leader of the Yellowstone Wolf Restoration Project, who shared with me accounts of the historical wolf restoration in the Park.

Thanks to staff librarians who provided excellent research assistance at the Veterinary Medicine Library, University of Tennessee. I am also grateful to those who read parts of the manuscript and provided expert advice: Sue Mansour, DVM, Ziad Kazzi, MD, and Timothy Smith, MD. Helpful also were enlightening discussions with Addison Fischer, Tom Stover, Col. Don Sawtelle, US Army (ret.), and Antonio Lacy.

A group of keen readers made invaluable comments on book drafts at various stages of development, including Pat Minicozzi, Jane Santiago, Sue Tankersley, Lynda Miller, and Susan Potts Sloan, MD. Many thanks to John Paine for superb editorial assistance on early drafts.

Although all of those acknowledged above provided helpful comments and advice, responsibility for any errors in the text are mine alone.

I am especially grateful to Jeff Edwards of Braveship Books, who has shown continued enthusiasm and support for my work. I cannot express my gratitude enough for my Chief Editor and loving wife, June, who provided not only meticulous editing but also much needed encouragement from beginning to end.

James Marshall Smith
December, 2017

"Human reactions are so profoundly influenced by the individual past that they are usually unpredictable and therefore appear completely irrational."

— René Dubos, in *So Human an Animal*, 1968

"Um elfe kommen die wölfe, um zwolfe bricht das gewölbe."
(At eleven come the wolves, at twelve the tombs of the dead open.)

— German folk saying

ONE

October 1993
Fourteen miles south of Hinton, Alberta

The young farmhand sneaked outside the barn to shake off the reek of fresh blood. A full moon climbed from a blanket of snow that draped Whitecap Mountain, casting a feeble silvery light on miles of harvested grain. The isolation of the barn was perfect. Sounds of terror from within faded into the Canadian wilderness.

A sour taste squirmed at the back of the farmhand's throat. He took a deep breath in the freezing air, a long satisfying breath before he returned inside and crouched near the fighting pit.

A chest-high fence of Ponderosa pine bordered the square pit that was six paces on a side. Between contests, the old man raked pieces of hair and flesh from the dirt.

Qualifying for admission that evening took a full year of work on the Castille Farm. "Where's the big Jap?" the farmhand asked.

"Just got here an hour ago," the old man replied, rolling a cigarette. "They'll bring him out for the wash-down shortly." He jerked a thumb. "Take a look at the mother he's facing."

A man with a hunting cap led a pit bull on a chain. They bore similar expressions, ferocious and sad. The dog's slick coat was milk-white with brown splotches. The ears stood erect, except at the tips that

1

curled like dead leaves. Largest of its breed on the Alberta circuit, the pit bull weighed in at one hundred and eighteen pounds.

Two dozen men gathered around the fighting pit—local ranchers, sawmill workers, lumberjacks, drifters, farmers with hired hands. The men chatted in tight groups and shared hip-pocket flasks of cheap whiskey. In one corner, a pot-bellied stove burned pine. Heavy wool jackets hung along a wall above bales of hay.

The grand finale approached.

From a side entrance a massive dog hauled an Asian man by a rope. He leaned back as though headed into a Clipper wind. The rope linked to a chain that circled the dog's neck like a noose. The look of the animal demanded respect: a corrugated brow, bulky through the shoulders, taller from ground to withers than the pit bull. Heavier by a good fifty pounds.

"What the hell *is* that?" the farmhand asked.

"Tosa Inu," the old man said. The words slid from around the cigarette that dangled from the corner of his mouth. "More beast than dog. They shouldn't allow 'em in."

The sheen on the coat of the giant dog seemed to glow in the dim light of the barn. Its coloring was the most spectacular of the evening, shades of a deep crimson. "It looks almost red," the farmhand said.

"The color of old blood."

"How come I've never heard of the breed?"

"Bred for centuries in Japan. Fighting, guarding royalty and shit like 'at."

From across the barn the fight boss called out for bets. Spectators tossed cash onto a makeshift table, a battered door from a shed placed over two sawhorses. The pudgy boss climbed atop a folding chair. He carefully balanced himself and shouted above the crowd, but only with enough effort to avoid shifting his weight.

"Listen up, fellas. Last call on the final contest. Peter the Great, the Grand Champ-ee-un pit bull terrier from Edmonton, versus the Japanese Warrior . . . the towsa eenew from Seattle. Cloooosing out!"

The pit bull snarled and tugged at its chain. Piercing eyes glared from an egg-shaped head, staring down its opponent that stood frozen in place, a statue of itself.

The fight boss swaggered to the corner of the fence. After waiting for stragglers to lay down their money, he hoisted his arms to command attention.

"Action's closed. Handlers, are you ready?"

All stares fixed on the dogs.

"Face corners!"

The handlers grasped the prized animals around their thick necks and knelt into position. Each handler had a breaking stick tucked down his backside—a piece of hickory with bark gnawed to shreds. Dogs and handlers gazed at their corner posts while the gamblers clustered around the fence, yelling, swearing.

"Unchain!"

The handlers unhooked the restraints.

"Face dogs and release!"

The handlers retreated over the fence. As the dogs charged across the scratch line with erratic head thrusts, the fighters circled each other, growling.

The crowd jeered, waving arms and fists.

The dance continued until the Tosa withdrew, moving backward but still facing his opponent. The pit bull—Peter the Great—matched the stride, step for step strutting forward and snarling. Sensing victory, it bounded on the Tosa and sank gaping jaws into the Tosa's shoulder. As Peter the Great dangled by its teeth, the Tosa reeled about and catapulted the startled animal into the fence with a thud.

A roar burst from the crowd. Peter the Great staggered, then attempted to regain balance.

The Tosa attacked like a rattlesnake.

It buried its teeth into the pit bull's throat and ripped open its neck, exposing the windpipe and silencing its howls.

Peter the Great's handler leaped over the fence and thrust a breaking stick between the Tosa's teeth. The Tosa snapped the thick baton in half, then turned for the handler, who tripped as he backed away. He fell hard to the dirt and quickly covered his face with his arms and curled his knees into his stomach.

The Asian jumped into the pit and grabbed the Tosa by the neck with both arms. He quickly hooked the chain and yanked with the full weight of his body.

A tremor arose from above, the thumping of helicopter blades.

A lookout darted inside. "Mounties! Mounties!"

Pandemonium erupted. Everyone scattered, some dashing for the wall to snatch their coats. The young farmhand raced for the door before braking.

A dozen Alberta troopers—Royal Canadian Mounted Police—surrounded the barn's exit. A Comanche helicopter hovered above and beamed a searchlight onto the field. The troopers below aimed their revolvers straight ahead and yelled for the fleeing men to stop.

The farmhand ran back to the fighting pit as the Asian clutched the Tosa to his chest. Mounties spanned the area with their weapons. The Asian released the chain and shouted to his dog. "*Ike!*"

The Tosa vaulted the fence and bolted through the crowd. One trooper spun around, but too late to avoid the leap of the mammoth animal. A glancing blow knocked him to the floor and the dog's claws slashed the trooper's cheek as he screamed.

The Tosa darted through the center of gunfire for the open door.

                    *   *   *

The Japanese Warrior was free. The Tosa sprinted like a leopard along a path lighted by a metallic moon, throwing his rear legs out before his muzzle and stretching his front paws far beyond natural stride. After a while he stopped to thrash about in a patch of snow to soothe stinging from the open wound inflicted by Peter the Great.

The howl of a wolf arose from a distant valley. Another followed. Both melded with those from a pack, a feral chorus carried on an arctic breeze, the lament of his brothers and sisters. He resumed his lope among spruce and fir dusted with snow.

Deep within Alberta's wilderness, the Japanese Warrior would soon find his new home.

TWO

Four years later . . .
Colter, Montana

She lay on the ground in the soft light of a lantern and sheltered from the wind by the tall evergreens beyond the farmhouse at the top of the hill. Occasionally she reared her head, snorting and seeking relief from her pain.

"Easy, girl. Easy, Penny," Dr. Dieter Harmon whispered. He softly stroked the hind leg of the cinnamon brown horse and stifled a yawn. In the early dawn, the sun hid just behind the mountains and ribbons of high clouds reflected a golden hue.

He glanced at his watch. It had been two hours since the call from the Loudermilk ranch.

Dieter tried to work his gangly legs into a more comfortable position as he squatted beside the mare. After he raised Penny's tail, wet because her water had broken, he shined his flashlight on her hindquarters to examine the distended vulva. He rubbed his hand over the horse's belly. No sign of movement; he thought the worst.

The three Loudermilk women crouched on the field grass while they anxiously monitored his every move. They wore dresses of pastel that appeared homemade but too long for working a ranch. The oldest had introduced herself as Katherine Belle. The quiet one, Marilee, kept her

6

head down most of the time. Charlene, the youngest, was frail but alert, curious. Like her sisters, she sported a tall wave of hair set back from her forehead.

Katherine Belle had told Dieter that at the first sign of trouble, she called Doc Hartwell but he wasn't around. She said that her answering service gave her the name of a veterinarian in Gardiner, of all places, but she knew better than to try convincing someone to drive all the way down to Colter in the middle of the night. Then she found Dieter's card on the fridge door although she had no idea how it got there. She'd heard that "Dr. Harmon was a nice young man." He was someone who knew how to treat ranch animals even though he was from back East. She said she thought at the time he should be able to get there quickly and probably needed the business since he was so new.

Little did they know. He would've come just to get word of mouth going. But he needed the pay, too.

He reached into his satchel for a bar of surgical soap and tube of lubricant, then rolled up his sleeve and washed his arm with steaming water from a bucket that Charlene had fetched. He slipped his greased arm into the birth canal. A tiny hoof protruded through the amniotic sac. He grabbed it, but the foal didn't yank back. He continued probing. In normal delivery, the head, neck and front legs stretched forward within the womb, as if the foal were jumping through a hoop. But now only one leg extended forward. The other hung back under the body and the muzzle faced the rear.

He withdrew his arm, reached for a towel, and took a deep breath. As he wiped at his arm he could only think that in his eleven years of practice, he'd never confronted a lateral deviation this grave. How was he going to deliver that news to the three women?

Katherine Belle hugged Penny's neck. "She's sweating like crazy, Doctor." The woman had the stern look of a mother, piercing eyes watching over her daughters and prized animals, caring for those she holds dear.

The horse wasn't the only one sweating. Dieter brushed back his hair and wiped his forehead with the back of his hand. After searching his satchel for a roll of gauze, he asked, "Can someone tie up her tail for me?"

Katherine Belle nodded toward Charlene. She caught the roll he tossed and held her smile at him for a moment, then carefully wrapped the mare's well-groomed tail.

Dieter withdrew two cc of xylazine into a syringe and held Penny's neck tightly while he injected her in the jugular and waited for the mare to relax. He lubricated his right arm again and rammed it into the birth canal up to his shoulder to get a firm grip on the foal. Gently, he shoved it farther down into the uterus and glided his hand back to grasp its neck. The mare's intestines were like bags of sand that pushed against the womb and limited the working room.

While he manipulated his arms and fingers, he sensed the rhythm of his own pulse through the throbbing in his head. He slid his hand down along the foal's neck, then slowly back again, repeating the motion several times until he gradually realigned it. Feeling Charlene's stare, he shifted his eyes toward her. As she turned her head away, the flickering lantern revealed the hint of a blush.

The drug was wearing off and Penny's contractions returned. "Push, girl, push."

A miniature snout emerged.

Caught in the excitement, Charlene squealed and clapped her hands. "Push! Push! Push!"

The exhausted mare heaved twice more and the foal plopped onto the grass. Limbs sprawled out in four directions as the lump of flesh lay crumpled like a wet gunnysack. Dieter held his stethoscope to its chest. "A normal heartbeat," he announced. "Looks like we have a healthy colt!"

The women threw their arms around each other and whooped through their tears. Katherine Belle and Marilee jumped up and hurried down the path to the farmhouse to rouse the family while Charlene stayed behind. Dieter prepared to wash the mare, which had reared her head up to sniff and lick the colt.

Charlene lay by the side of the frail creature and hummed a lullaby, as if caring for a newborn baby. "I didn't know we had such a good vet right in our own backyard, Dr. Harmon."

He smiled and passed the wet cloth along the spine of the mare.

"How long you been here?" she asked.

"Almost three months now."

"You from Billings?"

"Not quite. Pennsylvania." He put the cloth on the ground. She wanted to talk.

"That's awfully far from Montana, I think."

"I used to visit my uncle out here during the summers when I was growing up," he replied. "Always loved the West. But my wife loved Pennsylvania where she grew up."

Charlene shifted her legs to a new position and her long dress slipped an inch above one knee. He quickly averted his glance.

She twisted the braids in her hair between her thumb and forefinger then studied his face. "You got kids?"

He quickly grabbed the cloth again and began to rub the mare. "Two. Michael's ten and Megan's six."

"Your wife must have her hands full."

He paused. "She's not around anymore."

Charlene turned her attention away from the colt. "Might take you a while to get your business going here."

"I'm getting to know more—"

"Most people use our vet, Doc Hartwell. Or Homer Sellars from Butte. Some use Lester Milburn in West Yellowstone." She shook her head and snickered. "But I wouldn't trust a goldfish with *him*. Now don't you tell nobody I said that. Word gets around here as fast as roadrunners."

He put down the cloth and wiped his hands with a towel. Penny struggled to stand and allow the colt to nurse.

Charlene scooted closer and laid a hidden hand softly on his forearm. "If you need help with your kids . . ."

Startled, he leaned away.

She rose to her knees, pleading with her eyes and wrinkled forehead.

When he stood, she threw her hands on his chest and grabbed onto his jacket with her fists. "Please, Dr. Harmon."

He recoiled and knocked over the bucket of hot water with his foot.

She quickly let go and backed away as she lowered her head in shame like a child caught sneaking candy.

He turned to see a man, maybe in his sixties, with a straggly beard that covered only his chin. He glared from behind dark eyes that sunk deep into his skull below the eyebrows. "Exactly what you trying to do, Doctor?"

For crying out Jeezus! What was that supposed to mean? *Absolutely ridiculous.* Dieter quickly offered his hand to shake; he had to nip this one in the bud here and now before matters got out of control.

His hand was ignored.

"Sir, I know what this looks like," Dieter stammered.

"I thought I could trust a professional like yourself." The man spoke as if making a clinical observation.

"Oh, yes sir, you see—"

"If I was you, I'd just shut my mouth and get out of here."

Dieter scooped up his scattered supplies and quickly tossed them into his satchel. When he stood, Charlene had her back to him and her head down. He hurried back along the path off the hill. As he drew near the house he had to step carefully to avoid a clutter of toys—a fire truck with the ladder broken off, a rusted ambulance, a yellow steam shovel—and two small bicycles, one with blue ribbons that streamed from the ends of the handlebars. On the home's second story, he caught the fleeting faces of kids, tykes to teenagers, scattered between curtains and windowpanes. They stared as if looking down on an animal in a zoo.

When he reached his pickup truck, he hopped in and slammed the door, then drove along the graveled driveway to an open gate. Katherine Belle stood there, holding onto the chain and lock.

He lifted his hand and gave a sheepish wave as he passed. The anger on her face told him there was going to be trouble ahead.

THREE

"Don't eat the grass, Megan," Dieter commanded when he returned home from the Loudermilk ranch.

"It's not grass . . . it's flowers," the six-year-old replied, too occupied plucking blooms from a fistful of clover to look up. His daughter lay in the front yard dressed in jeans, a pink top with a yellow sunflower on the chest, and worn sneakers that were likely too small if he took the time to check.

The rented log cabin of western cedar that he called home stood aged and isolated among the aspen and cottonwoods. His nearest neighbor was at least a half-mile away.

"Please, I don't want you eating anything from the lawn. You could get sick."

"Amy said it's okay."

No doubt Amy was lecturing the kids again about the glory of nature and the nourishing benefits of wild flowers. "But I'm saying it's not okay," Dieter said, a little firmer this time.

"What do you know about this kinda stuff, anyway?"

"Because I'm a dad. Dads know these things."

"But Amy's a nanny. Don't nannies know something? You told me she was smart."

"Let's go inside, honey."

When Dieter walked through the front door, a golden retriever yanked at his trouser leg and growled. He reached for Rusty's muzzle and nestled his face into the dog's while rubbing its fur.

Exhausted from the Loudermilk ordeal, Dieter was glad the nanny had arrived early to take them to her parents' home on Hebgen Lake for the weekend. He needed the time to focus on his practice—in reality, to continue the tireless ritual of seeking clients. He had to take some time to get creative about the search now. It was becoming critical and no doubt the cause of his nervous stomach.

Amy stood tall at the sink rinsing breakfast dishes. Her charcoal hair, pulled behind her ears, fell straight to her narrow shoulders. High cheekbones and bronze skin gave away her Indian heritage. She opened the oven door and reached in with a large quilted mitt. "I saved a plate of eggs and sausage for you." She smiled back over her shoulder.

Dieter sat at the table and began to cut up the mystery meat to test it one small piece at a time, aware that Amy and her relatives frequently ate organs from unfamiliar critters. "Is the sausage from Bentley's?"

"Not exactly."

"You mean, it's not pork sausage?"

"Not exactly."

"Is it elk again?"

"Exactly!"

"I believe I've told you before, Amy. You can never be sure about these concoctions that local hunters make up."

"You don't need to fret. Dad made up this batch. Pretty good, huh?"

Dieter put down his knife and fork and wiped his mouth. "Megan was eating clover in the front yard again."

"I told her to be careful where she picks them."

"The way she was going after it, Amy, I don't think we're going to have a lawn left. The dog pees out there you know. And that's not all."

She flicked the side of her hair that had fallen free. "I always let Rusty out in the backyard. And I didn't tell her to eat weeds."

"Never mind. It's not that important." He had quit keeping score. She was much quicker on the draw than Fran had ever been.

She remarked that he looked bedraggled, as if he'd been up all night. While he nibbled the sausage—rather spicy and tasty, it turned out—he told her about the delivery and that it had taken place at a strange ranch.

"I've heard about Loudermilks," she replied. "I suppose everyone around here has. But I always assumed talk about them was more gossip than fact."

The colt would have died without his skilled hands, no question about it. He left out the part about the attack by the youngest woman. Her stupid reaction—was it Charlene?—wrecked it all. She was crazy. He should have seen it coming with her smiles. Old man Loudermilk would probably call the law.

"Where's Michael?" he asked.

"In his bedroom. He's looking forward to the lake this weekend. But his biggest concern right now is getting his Boy Scout uniform before the troop meeting. You didn't forget that, did you?"

"Uh . . . no." He didn't forget the uniform, it was just another item that wasn't budgeted. Those were matters Fran had always handled and now landed in his hands. He had to learn to deal with it. He was learning to deal with a lot of things he'd never bothered with in the past.

As if waiting in the wings, listening, Michael strolled into the kitchen. "Yeah, when can we get my uniform, Dad?" Built of fair skin and thin bones, the boy was small for his age.

Dieter paused for a beat. "We'll drive up to Bozeman next week."

"But I need it now." Michael sulked back to his room.

With Amy's encouragement they had visited the local Boy Scout troop leader, Leonard Farmington, at his home two weeks before. Good-natured and persuasive, Farmington radiated enthusiasm for Scouting. His zeal was topped only by his love of chatter. He had good news. Because Michael received the Arrow of Light award in Cub Scouts back in Pennsylvania, he was eligible to join the Boy Scout troop in Colter, even though he was only ten. Then and there, instead of waiting until the next year. Everything was settled . . . except for purchase of the uniform.

Dieter peeked into his son's room and found him cowering on his bed with a closed suitcase by his side. He plopped down next to him and started to place his arm around his shoulders when Michael quickly stood and walked to the dresser. Dieter recognized the stubborn streak. A characteristic no different from other Harmon family traits, like the wavy brown hair, the thick eyebrows and setback eyes. He opened the suitcase and stuffed another T-shirt into it while Dieter repeated the usual lecture on behavior.

*   *   *

Packed for the weekend trip, Amy bent her long neck slightly to keep her head away from the Datsun's roof and thrust herself behind the wheel. Dieter waved goodbye as the car pulled away, but it stopped suddenly and returned. Megan jumped out and ran to get another hug.

When the car disappeared, Dieter rushed inside to the bathroom cabinet and grabbed the bottle of aspirin. In the kitchen he splashed tap water into a glass tumbler, then sat at the table and tossed four tablets into his mouth. He squeezed his temples with his fingertips, then folded his arms on the table and rested his throbbing head.

As he closed his eyes the scenes played out again. The tiny colt sprawled on the ground, the mare preening it. The troubled face of the Loudermilk woman as she clung to his jacket. The ugly expression of the old man. The more he thought about it, the more he realized it was just a matter of time before the old man would report the incident.

The phone on the wall suddenly rang out like a fire alarm. When he answered, Molly Schoonover's voice boomed out of the earpiece. "How you doing, Doc?"

He mumbled something back.

"Didn't wake you, did I? It's the middle of the day." Molly always arose at dawn to begin her ranch chores.

"No, I mean, yes. I was awake."

"Can you come with me to the Pendleton place? You know, the llamas. Last night one was attacked. Brutally killed."

He leaned against the wall. He'd heard of the llama ranch, but what was he going to do? He didn't treat dead animals. "I really don't know what I could do for the Pendletons, Molly."

"It's Pendleton. There's only one of the old cuss. Please hurry over and I'll take you there. This is the final friggin' straw. This crazy stuff has gone on too long. It's gotta stop."

FOUR

Gus Parsons had driven due north from Tucson for one thousand and sixty-seven miles. The cost at that point was three tanks of regular gas and two nights in motels. The food was fast and the lodging cheap. Yellowstone National Park was Mecca for many who made a living his freelance photographer's way. Parsons drove up I-15 following a treeless landscape that went on forever and snow-covered mountain peaks far enough away to be only a blur on the horizon. His speedometer read eighty, but it felt like fifty. He thumbed through the Park pamphlets scattered on the front passenger seat as he drove, storing the facts a phrase at a time.

Yellowstone occupied the northwest corner of Wyoming and small portions of Montana and Idaho. The Park supported the largest concentration of free-roaming wildlife in the lower forty-eight. He flipped through pages with pictures published by his competition: bighorn sheep perched high on the Obsidian Cliffs; a wolf pack attacking elk in mid-winter in Lamar Valley; a Grizzly with her cubs feeding off the carcass of a moose calf in Hayden Valley.

A lone Amoco gas station south of Idaho Falls made for a rest stop. He needed to call home to check on Lily, his wife of forty-two years. Her health recently took a turn for the worse. When the door of the phone booth jammed, he kicked at it until it freed. After trying quarters, he banged twice on the phone box with the receiver to get a dial tone and the operator. His home phone rang eight rings before he hung up.

Parsons drove onto the highway and approached the ramp at the I-15 intersection, then swerved to the side of the road to stop. A trucker in an eighteen-wheeler behind him blared on his air horn. He could take I-15 South and head back to Arizona or continue north to Yellowstone. He took a deep breath then exhaled as he watched the cars speed by. What he was yearning to do wasn't right. He should turn around and go back home. He belonged with Lily.

If only I could get some photos to make an editor sit up and take notice.

They needed the extra income, especially if they were going to have more medical bills. Lily would understand that. He pulled back on the road and took the ramp to I-15 North. Only two hours from Yellowstone and the wilderness.

God, how he needed the solitude.

*   *   *

Dieter Harmon parked in the gravel at the front of the white wood-framed home, shaded by tall cottonwoods. A porch wrapped around it and stiff rocking chairs stood tall, eager for company. The Schoonovers owned the largest spread around Colter, thanks to Molly's inheritance he'd learned about when they first met.

Molly and the Judge's dachshunds jubilantly yapped at the prospect of a visitor. Big Mac did his best to hop up and down, but the combination of weight and miniature legs stymied him from lifting off the ground. When he reached down to scratch the perky dog behind his ears, Rusty barked in protest from the open window of the nine-year-old Chevy pickup.

Dieter rushed up the steps to the front entrance as Toby and Big Mac waddled behind on his heels, their legs shuffling twice as fast as they moved. Dieter announced himself and entered through the screen door. Molly threw aside bulky window drapes that covered her lap and jumped up from the floor. Somewhere in her forties, she was as agile as any woman he knew twenty years younger. Her dark hair curled tightly to her head atop a solid frame.

Dieter tossed a white business envelope with a check inside on the coffee table. "That's for October."

"A little early, thanks," she said.

"Where's the Judge?" he asked.

"Have you ever noticed that twenty-foot antenna sticking up from our roof? He's in the back room with his ham radio operation. I try to tell him that stupid antenna's going to attract a lightning strike and blow us up one of these days. He shrugs it off. But I can tell you that this thing I called you about has him spooked. Let's get out to the Pendleton ranch. Josh is expecting us."

Dieter and Rusty followed Molly out the door to her battered '84 Dodge Ram. When she turned on the ignition, the engine responded with a cough.

"Don't worry," she said. "Just needs the carb cleaned out. Got it on my list." She drove too fast down the dirt road that followed the fence line. He held onto the armrest, trying to avoid sliding around on the hard vinyl seat. She turned onto the highway that crossed the foothills of the Gallatin Range. Rusty sat in Dieter's lap and hung his head out the window into the wind, his ears flapping and tongue dangling like a strip of raw bacon.

A group of Holsteins had gathered in a gulch by a small pond. "So, tell me, which one of you has driven the other crazy by now?" Molly asked.

"You mean, between Amy and me?"

"No, I'm talking about you and James Fennimore Cooper. Now who do you think I mean?"

At the beginning of the summer, Dieter was uneasy about following up on Molly's suggestion to hire an Indian for a nanny. Not that he didn't trust an Indian with his children. Just an unfamiliar culture, that was all. Molly had told him that he ought to take with a grain of salt the stuff he used to see in the movies. He'd learned later that his feelings of anxiety were mutual. Amy Little Bear had told Molly "I don't care what kind of doctor he is, he's a stranger from two thousand miles away. He's single, unemployed, and wants a woman around."

When Molly arranged a meeting between Dieter and Amy, neither impressed the other. He thought her much too young. She thought him much too serious. But both had in common one thing: Molly's friendship. The deal was struck. Amy rented a bungalow in Colter but spent weekends at Hebgen Lake with her family. There, Dieter had been told, she enjoyed her favorite hobby of flying a small plane out over the big sky country of Montana.

Dieter said, "The kids love Amy. That's the important thing." He didn't want to comment any further. He swallowed a yawn and then spoke about the early morning delivery of a colt.

"I've never met the Loudermilks," Molly said. "But I've heard most people don't have much to do with them. I hope you got cash on the barrelhead from the old man."

"Not yet."

She chuckled. "Good luck with that."

While she drove, Molly chatted about Josh Pendleton, the rancher they were meeting. He'd been a good friend of hers and the Judge's for the past twelve years, ever since Pendleton moved just outside Colter and started a llama farm. A good bit older than she, he lived alone. His great-grandfather was one of a flock from Germany who followed the gold rush to the West. When he gave up on panning, he discovered real gold in peddling merchandise.

"Josh never married, never held a real job, and never intended to do anything about either," she said. A genuine Rocky Mountain roustabout, he told tales of living the life of a wildcat miner, trapper and occasional guide. "He trapped or hunted wolf, coyote, Grizzly, wild cat, and who knows what all for thirty years all over the Rockies."

They finally arrived at the ranch to the sight of a big man riding a palomino in a small corral. The over-sized cowboy, muscle-bound in his ragged denim overalls, brandished a lasso overhead as the horse cut for a calf. He threw the loop forward, but at the last moment the sprite animal dodged the snare. The rope struck it in the rump and splashed dust when the lasso slapped the ground. The cowboy cussed and pulled up the slack, coiling the rope into his free hand.

"Yep," Molly said, "that's Ol' Josh."

While Molly parked at the fence, another lasso sailed toward the calf with the same result as before. The rider dismounted with a look of disgust and tied the palomino's reins to the top rail.

Molly sauntered toward him, shaking her head. "You just ruined one fine reputation I set up for you with that pitiful performance, Joshua. I don't think your cattle have anything to worry about. Neither do those cute little calves."

Josh Pendleton flaunted red hair and a beard a few shades darker that almost hid his dewlaps. "Never pretended to be a cowhand," he mumbled.

"I want you to meet the new vet in Colter," she said.

Pendleton shook Dieter's hand with enthusiasm and a grin. "Molly told me a lot of good things about you, Doc. She don't say such things about most people. Except maybe about me and the Judge." He winked.

Dieter couldn't quite get a grip on a hand as big as a horse's hoof.

"You're married to that good-lookin' gal from the Blackfeet?" Josh asked.

Dieter jolted back his head. "Oh, no. That's Amy Little Bear. She's been taking care of my two kids this summer."

"Wish I had a fine woman like that to take care of me one or two nights a week."

"Shut your mouth, Josh," Molly said. "The Doc here's a professional." She pointed behind Josh to a llama with dingy cream wool meandering toward them. "Besides, you can always cuddle up with one of Rocko's girl friends on chilly nights." She jabbed Dieter in the side with her elbow.

The llama's banana ears pointed skyward from the top of a head that bore a half-comical expression. He studied Dieter with a haughty air, as if declaring his territory to a stranger. Josh patted the llama on the neck with one hand and held onto his back with the other. "You're one handsome brute," Josh said, as Rocko licked at his nose and cheek.

"Say hello to our professional visitor here," Josh said.

Dieter reached out to stroke the animal's neck, careful to avoid the head. The curly wool belied its look—soft, silky.

"Rocko's my master llama," Josh said. "North American breed. Pure muscle and bone. No dainty Peruvian genes in this animal, I tell you."

"One of your guards?" Dieter asked.

"You bet. Takes good care of the herd and watches over my sheep— Targhee and Suffolk mostly. Let me ask you something, Doc. What other animal do you know that could carry a baby on its back along a mountain pass but still bring down a five-point buck?"

Dieter knew that llamas were unique farm animals. He'd treated a few in Pennsylvania and never understood why more farm families didn't raise them. "How many you have?"

"Thirty-two in the field." Josh pointed toward Rocko. "No coyote or wolf is going to get within ten yards of my llamas or sheep what Rocko won't be all over it like a rat after baloney. When he puts the full force of those four hundred pounds on his raised front legs, he'll hammer any intruder to death in seconds." Josh jabbed his fists in the air. "I don't understand for the life of me how one of my prized studs was butchered by another animal, a damned wolf no doubt."

When Rocko discovered a clump of clover to munch on, Dieter thought of Megan lying on the lawn.

"Let's go take a look at the kill," Josh said. "You'll see for yourself what's keeping me up at night."

FIVE

When the clerk at the West Yellowstone Country Inn spotted Gus Parsons' Arizona address on the registration, he eagerly struck up a conversation. It turned out that the clerk had moved to Idaho from Flagstaff sixteen years before. He recommended that if Parsons wanted wildlife photos, he should take the trail along the Madison, one of the country's most celebrated fly-fishing streams. The clerk said that legions of fishermen followed that path over the years to seek wild German Brown or Rainbow. And plenty of big mammals hung out near the banks.

"The Madison comes from the mating of two easy going rivers," the clerk had said. "The Gibbon and the Firehole. When those two merge, they give the Madison one hell of a flow. And strangers to her can be easily fooled by her peaceful danger."

He spoke of how one fly-fisherman from Toledo met his death on the river the summer before. Tucked inside chest-high waders, the angler shuffled about in water above his waist. "Most likely he was battling a feisty Rainbow when he slipped on the moss-covered rocks and sank like a rock. That current is totally unforgiving, by God."

Parsons arrived mid-morning along the Madison River near Yellowstone's western border. At his first stop he snapped telephoto shots of a trumpeter swan nesting in marshes. Later, he parked his white SUV—pearl white to reflect the Tucson sun—by the roadside and collected his gear.

Taking deep breaths as he strolled, he began the hike along the trail that followed the river. The crisp mountain air smelled of meadow grass. The flowing water surged around granite boulders and rippled like a melody over rocks and gravel in the shallows. In a field by the river a pair of great blue heron stabbed their long bills into the weeds as they foraged for insects. A red-winged blackbird dive-bombed the male, targeting the bright onyx head feathers.

He quickly knelt to switch to a 400-millimeter lens when a bull moose appeared through a thicket of aspen. Planted in a pool at the river's edge the huge mammal chomped on moss that waved like a field of wheat just below the surface. The golden brown antlers spanned at least five feet.

Parsons plucked a clump of dry field grass and tossed it high. The blades fluttered down and drifted back toward him. Good.

A shadow of another creature streaked through the tall grass to his left but moved too fast to make out.

Whoosh.

A coal-black raven landed on the branch of a hemlock above. Two others landed nearby. Wings flapping, they jockeyed for space. When the moose turned his way, Parsons ducked and then slowly rose and peered through his field binoculars. A dog-like figure that was much too large for a coyote crept toward the moose from the rear. The moose resumed grazing, unaware of the impending danger.

The intruder inched forward but stayed low in the grass. Its fur was a burnished black like the feathers of the ravens surrounding him. Although much larger than he'd been led to believe, the humongous animal could only be a wolf. It stopped and twisted its head about as if surveying the area.

Parsons ducked again, now breathing faster. A wolf attacking a moose is the action shot of a lifetime. He pulled his shoulder straps with the Nikon camera and gear around to his side. Crouching low, he shuffled through the scrub oak and weeds in the direction of the expected action. More ravens swarmed overhead and cast haunting shadows dizzily around him. As if on command they flew directly down, cackling with wings swishing and settled onto tree branches.

The hullaballoo distracted from the morning peace. He stopped to stifle a sneeze, then stood tall to stretch his aching back.

Where the hell is the wolf?

Another pitfall of wildlife photography. As quickly as the midnight black wolf had arrived, it disappeared. But the bull moose stood in full view, chomping on the underwater moss. He quickly set up his tripod and pushed the canvas camo hat away from his face. His eyes itched from the ragweed pollen, and he wiped at the stinging tears with the back of his wrist. He pressed his cheek against the camera, framed an overhanging branch through the viewfinder, and held his breath. Then he squeezed the shutter release and snapped a rapid series of shots while he gave special attention to the moose's eyes. He'd learned over the years to go for that split second when a single ray of sunlight reflected off a pupil.

A commotion arose in the scrub oak some fifty yards to his right. The moose raised its head to stare in the direction of the sound then moved briskly into thicker foliage.

A raven burst from a tree and cawed. Three others surged from the cover of the tall pines and circled above. More flew in from behind and shrieked while those on nearby trees seemed to answer. One raven, with a wingspan the size of a broom, folded its wings and dived at him, landing only a few feet away with a rasping honk as if to berate him. He grabbed a stick and swatted at the damn bird then hurled the makeshift weapon at another roosting on a higher branch.

The clamoring flock flew away.

There was a sudden cemetery quiet, a stillness like he'd never known in the outdoors, as if no life of any sort existed around him. The only sounds were air rushing in and out through his nose and the ringing in his ears. When he turned to move back down the path, a rumble erupted from the brush. He jerked around.

The ebony black creature galloped straight for him.

It's not possible! Wolves don't attack people.

The wolf's lunge struck him like a sledgehammer. He threw up his arms to protect his face and gasped for breath as he tumbled into the shallow water at the river's edge. His skull smashed against the gravel and his tailbone slammed into the sharp edge of a rock. Lying on his back, he tried to move his arms to wrap them around his head, but only one arm feebly responded. When he attempted to pull in his knees, a streak of pain shot through his body as if a pitchfork had pierced his backbone.

The curl of the beast's upper lip flashed red above ivory while the animal charged again and again. He gagged as the fangs knifed deep into his throat—twisting, yanking. Ripping at flesh, powerful jaws battered his head into the mud.

After a brief eternity, it was over.

No longer feeling attached to his quivering torso he glanced down at the blood gushing like a pulsing fountain from his neck.

The wolf sat on its haunches and licked at its snout.

A raven flew down and dug its claws into the side of Parsons' face. It pecked away at the open wound in his throat, stabbing over and over and over. Another raven landed on his head and plucked the tender flesh from around his eyeballs before its beak plunged into the sockets.

The searing pain was no longer bearable. Drifting on the edge of consciousness, Gus Parsons finally worked one shaky hand up to his face and wiped at the blood that dribbled down his cheek alongside the streaming tears.

SIX

Josh Pendleton tossed aside the canvas tarp that had covered the carcass of a llama. The animal's broken body lay smashed against a twelve-foot section of the blood-splattered, split-rail fence. The beautiful animal's distended neck that had buckled over the top rail was almost severed. Flies buzzed around the gaping hole where blood had oozed out, drenching the black and white wool coat. Except for the head, the body was surprisingly intact.

"Ever seen anything like it, Doc?" Josh asked.

"Not even close."

"Damn puzzling. It wasn't only a male, but a flock leader. One of my liveliest and fastest."

"Have you spotted any tracks?" Dieter asked.

"Can't tell too much. I chased off a pack of coyotes with my shotgun twice already. They've managed to mess up the area pretty good." Josh waved his hand in dismissal. "The only scat I've found is fresh stuff from those coyotes. But no damn doubt in my mind—it's a wolf kill."

Dieter walked closer to the carcass and stooped down. He brushed back the fur with his fingertips until he found the impression of a bite just below the neck where the sharp upper cuspids must have penetrated. Making a fist, he straightened out his forefinger and little finger to form goalposts. He held it up to the bite marks and then displayed the measurement for Josh.

"That looks like three inches, Doc. Can you picture the size of the jaws?"

Rusty barked from Molly's truck bed and wagged his tail. A brown pickup with the logo of the US National Park Service wended its way toward them.

"Well, waddaya know," Josh said. "Look who finally made it."

"I can't believe the pull Josh Pendleton has," Molly whispered to Dieter.

The pickup stopped only ten yards away and two men in park ranger uniforms and Smokey Bear hats stepped out. It wasn't hard to make out who was in charge. With a royal-like stroll, the head honcho flaunted well-tanned, angular features and a chin held too high. When Josh and Molly exchanged greetings with him, there was a sudden undercurrent, as if present among feuding cousins at the annual family picnic.

Josh gestured toward him. "Chief Corey, meet the new vet in town. Dr. Peter Hammond."

Dieter held out his hand. "That's Harmon, Dieter Harmon. Pleased to meet you, Chief."

Yellowstone's chief park ranger explored Dieter's face. He didn't smile as he held out his hand to shake, a forceful grasp that lasted too long.

Jack Corey introduced his fellow ranger as Bantz Montgomery, who politely touched the brim of his hat, nodded and stepped back as if he knew his place.

"We'll take a look at what you got," Corey said. "But I'll remind you again, Joshua. We don't have any jurisdiction here. ADC should be on this. They're responsible for any wolf kills outside park boundaries."

"We haven't found the animal control folks particularly quick to respond," Josh replied. "Billings is too damn far away."

Corey adjusted his hat and looked toward the carcass, walking to it as he spoke. "I'll be happy to give you my humble opinion. We're just trying to reach out to you ranchers, like we promised."

Josh pointed but didn't move from the spot where he'd anchored. "That's another victim of your folly."

Corey stooped to look, ignoring the putrid odor. "You're not talking about my wolves now, are you?"

"You bet I am."

Corey grinned like a politician and pulled a pair of plastic gloves from his back pocket. "They're America's wolves, Joshua. They belong to everybody."

"You can tell America to come take 'em back."

Corey slipped on the gloves, carefully positioning each finger into place like a surgeon. He probed around the wound and with Montgomery's help, rolled the carcass about to examine further.

"When did this happen?" Corey asked, his eyes fixed on the fatal wound.

"A couple of days ago at most," Josh replied.

Corey reached with his right hand over to his left and yanked the glove away, then stood and removed the other. "Don't take this the wrong way, Joshua, but what you've got here is either an angry neighbor who was clumsy at wielding a dull axe or a cougar kill on your hands. This is certainly not the work of a wolf."

"How do you reach a cockeyed conclusion like that?" Josh asked.

"Straightforward. No bites on the legs or hindquarters and—"

"That don't mean nothing."

"And its belly hasn't been ripped open. The attacker went straight for the throat."

"That don't mean a damn thing."

"Your big llama males can defend themselves from a lone coyote or wolf, Joshua. But they don't have any chance with a cougar."

Josh unbuckled the sheath that hung from his belt and pulled out a hunting knife. He shuffled in Corey's direction.

Jesus! Dieter stood and quickly backed away. Corey had a side arm holstered on his hip and Dieter waited for him to draw.

The chief park ranger held his ground as Josh bent down and cut deep into the neck of the carcass, peeling away tissue to reveal bone. "Take a look at this." He pointed with the tip of the blade where he'd carved.

Corey lifted his chin and set it. The joints of his jaw twitched and he scratched the back of his neck. Dieter moved forward and crouched to get a better view.

"You see any puncture marks here?" Josh asked. "I've seen plenty of cougar kills in my day, Mr. Corey. Even watched them sneak up on their prey and attack. Cougars, just like their cousins, the lions and tigers, go for the nape of the neck—not for the throat. It just ain't their instinct."

Josh used his hands on his head to demonstrate. "They pierce the skull or spinal cord like a butcher knife. When have you ever heard or seen anything about a cougar grabbing a victim by the throat?"

"They attack with the sole purpose of killing, don't they?" Corey asked. "So what if they go for the nape of the neck or the throat or the crotch for that matter?" Corey was determined not to allow a jackass rancher get the best of an expert who'd studied wildlife throughout his career.

Josh shook his head. "They attack from the rear 'cause their inbred strategy is to blind-side their victim. These animals have a blueprint stored in their marrow. Nothing's done helter-skelter in the wild, Mr. Corey. Nothing." He shook the carcass with his fist buried deep in the fur over the backbone. "There's no teeth marks on the back of this neck or the skull." He pulled out a dirty plaid handkerchief and wiped off the blade, then looked hard at Corey. "This was no cougar kill and you damn well know it."

Dieter glanced at Molly. She returned a veiled smile, as if what they were witnessing was nothing but good entertainment.

"If it was a wolf kill," Corey said, "we'd see that llama torn to pieces by the pack." The chief park ranger wasn't going to be outdone by the likes of a trapper. "Why would we see a body with only its throat ripped open?"

Josh shrugged and threw up his hands in exasperation. "Why would a cougar attack and just take off?"

"They're easily spooked. Much more so than a pack of wolves. The big cat could've made his kill and then got scared away."

His gut curled up in knots, Dieter couldn't hold back any longer. He'd witnessed such stonewalling by law enforcement in Philadelphia. What progress had they made on finding Fran's killer? What kind of priority was the PD giving the hunt for the beast?

"Have there been other wolf kills reported outside park borders?" Dieter asked.

Corey jerked his head toward him. "Yes, Dr. Harmon, there have been. When we do get valid claims, the ranchers are compensated."

"How so?"

The look that Corey shot back at him was one of keep your mouth shut, asshole, this is none of your business. Corey paused before he answered, a pause calculated to relay that message. "Up to five hundred bucks per head. That is, if it's proved to be a wolf kill." He re-adjusted his hat and placed his thumbs back inside his belt. "And I'll tell you this—there've been a lot more reported than confirmed."

"How many wolf packs are in the Park?" Dieter asked.

"Six, last official count. We do keep track, you know."

"What about here on the western border?"

Another calculated pause, this time a lip pucker was added for effect. "None are anywhere near Colter, if that's what you're getting at. Most are radio-collared. We use telemetry and flyovers to keep track of them." He turned away and looked at Josh. "I didn't come here to get into a debate. I just volunteered to come out and give you my opinion."

"We 'preciate you driving down from Mammoth," Josh said. "Just wish you had more experience with wildlife. To understand them, you've got to live among 'em."

Without answering, Corey rolled back his shoulders and stood for a moment contemplating the scenery. He then stuck out his hand to shake with each of them as if from a sense of duty. All of the earlier feigned pleasantries had disappeared.

After the two rangers pulled away, Molly spoke first. "Helluva nice guy, huh, gentlemen?"

Dieter was stunned by the entire performance of the chief park ranger. "That's what you call a public servant?"

"It's the kind of response," Molly said, "we've grown accustomed to around here."

"How do you appeal?" Dieter asked.

"Those wolves transferred into the Park," Josh replied, "are Jack Corey's kinfolk. You don't appeal his verdicts. Least not without risking the wrath of God." He waddled with the hint of a limp as he led Dieter and Molly across the field to his living quarters.

The steel-gray trailer stood on a cinderblock foundation with yellowed Venetian blinds hanging in a large picture window, one strip bent in the middle and another missing. As Dieter walked inside the floor gave way with each step. An open counter of hunter green linoleum separated the compact kitchen from the homey living room that had the musty smell of age. A tall lamp sat on a side table, its base a woodcarving of two bears sitting back to back. A bronze post ran up between the bears and disappeared into a lampshade.

A holstered revolver hung from the wall in one corner. Josh pointed to it when he noticed Dieter's stare. "Blackhawk Colt forty-five."

"Is that thing loaded?" Molly asked.

"Safety's on," Josh answered and flung a hand in the direction of a low couch.

As Dieter and Molly sank into it she mumbled, "You'd think that steel barrel was extension of his dong,"

Dieter leaned back into an orange and black afghan, his rear end too close to the floor for comfort. Through a window at the back wall, he watched a herd of llamas cavorting and marveled at all the shades and patterns of black, white, brown, and gray. No two animals appeared to have the same mix.

Molly said, "Doc here delivered a colt early this morning over at the Loudermilk farm. Would've been breech if he hadn't straightened out the little thing before it popped out."

"Loudermilks, huh?" Josh replied. "Now that old man has something going there, don't he?"

Dieter had no idea what he was hinting at, but it didn't feel like the right time to get into a deep discussion about the Loudermilks. In fact, he'd rather avoid the subject and the family altogether. Josh walked into the open kitchen where he could work and still take part in the conversation. "I'll fix us up some seng tea while Molly fills you in on what's been going on."

She leaned back into the sofa and looked over at Dieter with a wrinkled brow. "The number of livestock kills reported around our area is frightening. I hardly know where to begin. I mean, there's the Henderson ranch down on Aspen Loop. They had two sheep killed just like Josh's llama. Then there's the heifer on the Jennings' spread, down by Cougar Creek."

"I didn't know about that one," Josh shouted from the kitchen.

"Do you want to let me talk?" she asked. "Or you gonna come in here and tell the stories?"

When there was no reply, Molly leaned over to Dieter and whispered. "Lonely son-of-a-pistol." She sat up straight and spoke louder. "The Stewarts live next to our property and they lost two calves in a way that looked darn similar to me. That's only the ones we know about. I keep getting reports of wolf kills above old Route thirty-six and even down near West Yellowstone." She shrugged as if it was all beyond mortal comprehension.

The teakettle whistled and Dieter watched Josh pull a mason jar with dried root from a cabinet. While the tea brewed, Josh commented on how much harder it had become over the years to find a good ginseng crop. Damn stuff was so popular with the herbal crowd, everybody and his brother was harvesting it. When he poked around with his stick last time out looking for seng, he ran into a diamondback coiled up right there in the underbrush. Thicker than his forearm.

"Six feet long if it was an inch," Josh added. He dribbled honey into each mug and served both before settling opposite them into his overstuffed easy chair with a coffee stain on the arm the size of a silver dollar. Josh lifted his cup and tilted it so the steaming tea rolled over the rim and down into the saucer. After swishing the puddle around, he brought the saucer to his mouth while he blew across it. He then perched his lips against the tilted saucer and slurped.

Molly turned to Dieter. "We go back a few years with Jack Corey." She said they'd become acquainted with the chief ranger when Washington started talking about bringing wolves back to Yellowstone, of all the crazy ideas.

Josh shook an index finger at Dieter. "And you know why the wolf population had dwindled to zero in the Park?" He didn't wait for an answer. "Because the feds killed every last one of 'em decades ago."

"The National Park Service in Washington was determined to return the wolves to Yellowstone," Molly said. "They couldn't have cared less what the ranchers and people who lived here thought about it. What with the terrible winters, the number of stillborn, disease, mountain lions, and now they were talking *wolves*?"

"Did they hold any public hearings?" Dieter asked.

"A slew of them," Molly said. "Josh even spoke at one." She nodded his way.

"I told 'em that I never worried about wolf packs troubling us," Josh said. He slurped the last puddle of tea from his saucer. "They'd have plenty to feed on in the Park, what with all the elk and deer. What you can't guard against is the wolf that strays. The wolf forced out of the pack and becomes a loner left to fend for itself. The history of the West is filled with the tales of renegades like that . . . and the hell they raised."

SEVEN

It was all news to Dieter, he thought as he drove back to his cabin. He had no idea what he'd stepped into with Molly's call that morning. He only knew that he was going to have to find a diplomatic way to back out of getting involved. It was all too risky for a new veterinarian in town to take sides on an issue as big as that—wolves from a National Park attacking livestock of local ranchers. Best to stay low key and just perform the service he had come there to do and do that well. That would take up enough of his time, especially with two young kids to raise by himself.

A horse trail in the distance meandered through an open meadow.

He'd grown up riding horseback on weekends at a small farm in the Amish country west of Philadelphia. And during summers in Idaho he'd learned to ride with confidence from Uncle Cleve, the same man who had taught him to love and care for animals. He could recite from long-buried memories the stories of the West that Uncle Cleve used to tell as they rode Appaloosas along stony trails beneath vast blue skies that spanned heaven and Idaho. Each summer he'd listen to the same accounts again. They would come alive with new twists, like hamburgers served up with different trimmings. He often wondered if Uncle Cleve just made up the stories as they traveled but it didn't matter diddlysquat. Even before he knew cars or girls, those brief summers of his youth with Uncle Cleve shaped his love for nature, God and creatures of the earth.

Dieter wasn't going to make it home before emptying his bladder. After crossing the bridge over the Madison, he pulled off to the roadside. Usually he'd see a fisherman or two that time of day but none was in sight, although an SUV was parked ahead. Leaving Rusty in the truck, he dashed out and hid behind a stand of aspen to relieve himself. When he headed back, his side vision caught an object bobbing downstream.

He stopped to get a better look. A glob of green camouflage had drifted into a shallow eddy where the swifter water foamed. He strolled down to the bank and hopped onto a flat boulder, stooping to pick up a canvas hat. It was green camouflage and well-worn with artificial flies hooked into the soft cloth above the brim. Any angler would appreciate getting it back. If he placed it up high near the bridge, it would be easily seen. He flipped the hat over, revealing a dark red stain.

Blood?

He began to hike upstream along the shoreline and squeezed the hat as he trampled through heavy brush and thicket, pausing every few steps to search ahead. A well-traveled footpath ran close to the opposite bank but there was no part of the wide stream he could easily cross. He turned to head back to the truck before second thoughts came on. Someone could be in trouble. Something might have happened only a short time before. He had to press on at a faster pace. Rounding a bend, he startled a flock of ravens along the shore. As they took flight, his eyes locked onto a strange feature across the river—a large object partly submerged in the water.

A body?

Ravens fluttered about it, tearing shreds of flesh from a carcass. A human body was seeping blood that the crystalline water captured in swirls. Although less than twenty yards across, the narrow stream was too deep to wade. He walked upstream where more shallow rapids riffled over rocks. Deeper pockets of water were scattered among the rapids and would make for a tricky wade. When he stepped into the river, the frigid water soaked his boots and his trousers up to his knees.

He sloshed forward, surprised by the brute force of the current against his thighs. Staring directly down into the flow, he began to sway, the river to spin. Before losing his balance, he turned quickly around and splashed back toward the bank where he fell into the field grass and scampered on all fours away from the water. He lay still with his head buried in the weeds and dug his fingernails into the dirt. When he rolled onto his back, the sun warmed his face and he placed an arm over his eyes for shade until his breathing returned to normal.

Blood stains.

Blood splattered on the sidewalk and curb and street. Fran's lifeblood in a Philadelphia gutter. But she was just another big city statistic, another thirty-second clip on the Channel Six news. Her attacker's nine millimeter brass-jacketed hollow point round had penetrated four and a half inches into her brain. If only he'd taken the time to drive her downtown that day. If only he had taken the Dodge wagon in for transmission work the day before. Or the day after. For the rest of his life he would live with a million if onlys. Francine Duval, the only woman he had sworn to have and to hold until death ripped them apart.

He jumped up and trotted for the truck, his boots squishing with each jolt on the ground. Rusty barked a welcome back through the open window and he drove up the highway until he found the phone booth he'd passed earlier. The Gallatin County Sheriff's office answered: they would send out a squad car, pronto. He should meet it back at the bridge.

EIGHT

The deputy sheriff dispatched from Big Sky stuffed the blood-stained hat into a plastic bag and tossed it into his patrol car. He had walked with Dieter to the point across the river from the scene, using the same route Dieter had traveled. After returning, the deputy asked him to explain his whereabouts since he'd left his cabin that morning.

While Dieter spoke, the deputy took meticulous notes on a small spiral tablet. He asked him to talk through every detail of locating the body, beginning with parking at the bridge. He asked Dieter to repeat twice why he didn't take the cleared trail on the other side, why he was trying to wade across the river, but then turned back.

After running out of questions, the deputy got all of Dieter's contact info and dismissed him. Dieter dashed to his truck and as he pulled away, he spotted a National Park Service truck arriving behind him. He hit the accelerator and sped away.

*   *   *

Ranger Bantz Montgomery hiked behind the Gallatin County deputy sheriff along the trail that followed the Madison River. Chief Ranger Jack Corey brought up the rear. Montgomery had received the call on the radio as he and Corey returned from the Pendleton llama ranch back to Mammoth Springs headquarters. Someone had reported a bloody body on the banks of the Madison, three miles northeast of Colter. Although the body was located inside park boundaries and technically within Yellowstone and federal jurisdiction, it was also in Gallatin County. In the case of a violent crime, the county provided assistance to the Park whenever requested and it always was. The Park had no problems letting the county take charge in these cases that could go on for months.

When the three men reached the yellow crime-scene ribbon, they stooped for a closer look at the body. Judging from the size of the crimson slurry along the shoreline, the pallid body had lost most of its blood. Where once there was a neck, there was now only a tangled mass of blazing scarlet flesh.

The deputy sheriff flipped his cigarette into the weeds and crushed it out with the toe of his boot. He spoke with the raspy voice of a chain-smoker. "Slashed up pretty bad. First murder around here in nine years. Do you recall the Skeeter Wilkins crime up in—"

"Was there a vehicle around?" Corey asked.

Interrupted in the middle of his yarn, the deputy changed his expression to one of all-business. "We found a white Suburban with an Arizona license plate."

"How about footprints?"

The senior deputy broke in. "Only the victim's were fresh. At least on the side of the river where we located him. The guy who spotted the corpse had hiked along the other bank."

"Who was that guy?" Corey asked.

"The new veterinarian in Colter. He's got an office over on Bridger Avenue. I let him go just before you got here."

Montgomery glanced at Corey, who stared down at his feet and rubbed the back of his neck.

"I'll call Bozeman," the senior deputy said. "We'll store the stiff at Winslow's until the autopsy. The ME won't likely be here before Saturday though. He's just part time. Works mainly weekends." He looked over at Montgomery. "What do you think of all this?"

Montgomery preened his mustache as he thought. "Well, it looks to me—"

"We don't have any idea," Corey said. "We'll wait and see what the pathology report says. Right now I'm afraid we have another appointment."

Corey focused on the senior deputy. "Tell me more about this guy."

"Apparently a photographer. I found his professional-looking camera and tripod."

"No, I mean that veterinarian who found the body."

"Told you what I know, Chief."

Corey scratched at his neck. "What do you suppose he was doing out here?"

"Told me that when he stopped to take a leak, he spotted a hat floating near the shoreline. When he picked it up, he saw the blood stain. He followed his curiosity upstream until he was startled by the discovery of the body on the other shore. He certainly didn't appear to be holding anything back."

"You didn't consider taking this guy in for questioning?" Corey asked.

"No real reason to."

Corey held his stare on the deputy long enough to make his point.

The deputy nodded. "I'll give the sheriff your suggestion."

"You do that. And be sure he knows where it came from."

*   *   *

Corey rode shotgun while Montgomery drove back through the Park along Yellowstone's Grand Loop. He steered with one hand resting on the wheel and the other fidgeting with his blond handlebar mustache which curled twice at the tips. In his fifteenth year as a law enforcement ranger, Bantz Montgomery was in his early fifties, ten years older than his boss. At one point in time he figured he had a good shot to be the next chief ranger. But when the job became available eight years before, the Yellowstone superintendent selected the senior ranger at Glacier National Park—Jack Corey. Within a month Corey appointed Montgomery his deputy when he'd discovered that both had served in Nam and fought in the Easter Offensive.

Montgomery knew the ropes and the local politics. But he was too close to all the aggravation the chief ranger endured. The hours he had to put in. Having attended too many of Corey's briefings, he'd memorized the numbers. The chief commanded fifty-eight rangers responsible for patrolling the highways, campgrounds, and backcountry trails scattered throughout a two million acre national park, twenty-four hours a day, every day of the year. The rangers provided all the emergency services for millions of Park visitors and investigated thousands of criminal incidents every year.

Montgomery wanted no part of the headaches that Corey took home most days, sometimes not getting to bed until after midnight, even though he was on duty every morning of the workweek by seven. When he had to work on Saturday or Sunday, which was at least twice a month, he usually slept in and arrived at seven-thirty.

He glanced over at his boss, annoyed by his lockdown attitude and never certain what his cold attitude meant. "That new veterinarian in Colter must get around."

The truck's radio blared out the classic country voice of the senior Hank Williams. Leaning back against the headrest, Corey stared straight ahead with his arms folded, bobbing his head to the beat.

Montgomery said, "Sounded as if the deputies weren't much interested in him. You think the sheriff will consider him a suspect?"

"Be a fool not to."

"Wonder if Milburn or Hartwell know they got new competition?"

"They'll find out soon enough."

"We better write up what we found," Montgomery said.

Corey let out a dreary sigh and stared out the passenger window. "Yeah. You take care of it." He cranked up the volume on the radio, sank low in his seat and jammed his knees against the dash.

Hank Williams wailed louder.

"The more I think about it," Montgomery said, "we really should brief the superintendent as soon as we get back. All this, on top of the livestock kills. Same attack scenario every time. Or pretty close anyway."

Corey shrugged.

"You know, Jack, I would hate for Gilmer to get surprised—"

"You know, Bantz," Corey mocked, "if you want my goddamn job why don't you go to the superintendent and ask for it?" He pulled his hat down over his eyes and began bobbing his head again while the godfather of country music begged for solace.

A light drizzle slowed Montgomery at Kingman Pass. The temperature had dropped enough for sleet to form until the road descended to a lower altitude. He drove with extra caution, recalling the last time a summer snowstorm at that elevation stranded them. After several miles without exchanging words, Corey shifted in his seat to get more comfortable and words crept from under his hat. "One more thing. You can forget about sneaking back to the scene and searching for animal tracks. It was a murder. Period. The sheriff's handling it."

Silence.

Montgomery's eyes stayed fixed on the road.

"Did you hear me, Montgomery?"

"Loud and clear, Boss. I heard you loud and clear."

NINE

Business was looking up. Two phone messages had come in for Dieter the next morning and he quickly got on the road to make ranch calls. The first was about treating a cow in Grayling suspected of dislocating a hip during delivery. It hadn't. The cow and calf were going to be fine. A grimmer call took him to a ranch at Cliff Lake where a lamb and ewe received severe burns in a brush fire. Both the farmer and his wife cried when he told them he'd have to put the badly burned ewe to sleep.

In the afternoon Dieter made his way back to his makeshift clinic, Colter Veterinary Services, at the end of Bridger Avenue. There were two large rooms—the reception area and a room in the rear that he used for treatment. He'd managed to fit in a stainless steel exam table and to stock some basic supplies and a few holding cages in three sizes, all with the help of an eight-thousand dollar loan from the Montana Veterinary Association.

Molly had warned Dieter that Claire Manning, the managing editor of the Gallatin County Weekly Reporter, would be his first client of distinction. Her upscale style of dress and coiffure matched Molly's description perfectly. He guessed she was in her fifties, but with the glossy face and tight skin, he couldn't be sure.

He carried her cream-white Yorkie into the exam room and closed the door. King Tut stood on the cold steel surface of the table, holding its head low and shaking. The ten-pound dog had an under-bite and was groomed in the face to give a vague resemblance to his namesake.

"Come on now . . . good doggie." Dieter stretched out his hand. King Tut lurched forward and nipped his index finger, drawing blood.

"Jeez!" He poured alcohol over the wound and placed a Band-Aid around it, then dug inside his white coat for a treat. When he gingerly held out the dog-biscuit, King Tut ignored it.

Mrs. Manning had told him that the dog whined often the last three days with spells where he shook his head uncontrollably. She suspected seizures. An exam with the otoscope confirmed Dieter's hunch. One ear was bright red with a black fungus spreading in the canal, a common ailment among small dogs with floppy ears. He swabbed and medicated them, then emerged into the waiting room.

"King Tut should recover quickly with these drops," Dieter said as he handed the pet back to Mrs. Manning and gave her a sample bottle of eardrops.

"If this works, I'll just have to tell your rival down in West Yellowstone that I may have to switch vets," Mrs. Manning beamed.

"Who's my competition?"

"Dr. Milburn. I've been driving down to him for King Tut's shots since we got him."

He walked her to the door and she said to give Molly her regards. He stuffed his hands into his white lab coat pockets, not sure whether to say anything, but she *was* the editor of the local paper. Maybe a new client. Giving her a heads up might grant him even more credibility. Or maybe he just needed to talk with somebody about it. Whatever the reason, he blurted out, "Have you heard about the body found on the Madison?"

"Nothing of a kind! When did you hear this?"

He described how he came across the victim, but didn't delve into the gruesome details. "I reported it to the sheriff's office."

"Mysterious deaths just don't occur around here," she said, shaking her head back and forth. "Do you have any idea what happened?"

"None."

They both stood quietly for a moment while King Tut panted and kicked, eager to leave. She shifted the dog to her other arm. "Must have something to do with drugs," she said. "So much of that is going around the West."

Dieter agreed with a nod.

"Or, my Lord," she continued, "it could've been an animal attack of some sort? A Grizzly maybe?"

"Difficult to tell. The body was on the bank across the stream from me."

"You never know what could happen out there in the God Almighty wilderness. You don't think it could have something to do with the wolves? It is possible, isn't it?"

"I really don't think so. I mean, I've never heard of wolves attacking people."

"I fought the Park Service bringing in wolves to Yellowstone from the start. You just never know about creatures like that. And I'll share with you something else, Dr. Harmon. The rangers running Yellowstone live and breathe those damnable wolves. Won't listen to the ranchers who've been losing livestock since they arrived. Maybe they're now going after people in the backwoods, too. I should pay the chief another visit."

"The chief?"

"Jack Corey. Yellowstone's chief ranger."

"You know him?"

She hesitated. "We're acquainted." She grabbed King Tut again to keep him from escaping her arms. On her way out, she stopped and dug into her purse. "Here's my card. If you get any more info, please give me a call?"

After waving goodbye Dieter slid the card into his trouser pocket and lingered by the door, then walked to his desk and picked up the phone. The woman at the Gallatin County sheriff's office had no information. He said who he was and why he was calling. She placed him on hold.

When she returned, she spoke fast. "I really don't have anything that I can release at this time, Dr. Harmon."

"When can I call back to—"

"I'm sorry, sir, I have an emergency on another line."

Click.

Familiar territory. Cops. Bureaucracy.

Fran's murderer was never found. His trips to the station, his calls. None of it mattered in the end. He reflected on the first time they'd met—a wedding reception at Christ's Methodist Church in Allentown. 1983. Her long, cascading hair framed a stunning face. Her carriage revealed a subtle sexiness as she pretended to ignore him, aside from one furtive smile. Her cockiness was enticing.

He was more confident in himself then, a sophomore at Penn State. But he felt guilty living off his mother's income, earned by working in the meat department at Kroger's during the day and odd jobs at night or on weekends. He was going to drop out and make it on his own, but his mother would hear nothing of a kind. "Do you want to end up like your father?" she would often ask.

He sank into one of the hard plastic chairs that had cost six dollars each at the Goodwill Store. Leaning forward, he rested his elbows on his knees. He'd come to Colter to escape, to leave all of the torment in his wake. Throughout the day, he'd thought off and on about Josh Pendleton. He had come to admire the old man, his earthy wisdom. He stood and paced, then stopped at the front door again and opened it wide. In the distance the snow-capped peaks of the Gallatin Range vaulted into the deep blue backdrop. Maybe the world hadn't been especially kind to him, but as he stared out on the scene he knew he was a lucky man. Montana wasn't so much a place to make a living as it was a place to dream. A place where you don't go chasing the outdoors, it comes running after you and caresses you like a loving uncle.

Was it a murder victim he had discovered on the banks of the Madison? Or had it been a wild animal attack? In any case, there was no doubt that a big problem had the local ranchers whipped into a fury and all of them were potential clients. He didn't know if there was a connection between the wolves and the body he'd discovered, that was too outlandish of a stretch. It certainly made no sense from everything he knew about wolves, although he had to admit he didn't know much. And what were the real reasons for the chief park ranger's inaction in the face of the obvious problem? There had to be more to the story. Maybe the ol' trapper had some answers.

He placed an "Out to Lunch" sign in the front window, quickly locked up and sped away.

TEN

Josh Pendleton stood in the middle of Teepee Creek wearing rubber waders tied to his waist with a frayed rope. Dieter guessed he could find him there when he wasn't in his trailer.

A ragged fishing vest draped around Josh's broad chest and a wide brim hat flaunted a dazzling array of trout flies. He cast the line out over the stream, waving it back with a tug of the rod and forward again without apparent effort. At the end of the line the artificial fly flew high, a little farther with each cast forward until it reached the precise spot. Then he would stop the fly in midair with a subtle wrist action. It fluttered down into the current and drifted downstream.

After a few casts, Josh gave the rod a jerk and straightened up. A twisting flash burst from the surface. The rod tip quivered while Josh held it high with his right hand and hauled line with his left. The battle lasted only a minute. He scooped the thrashing trout into his net as Dieter strolled in behind him.

"Ah, a beautiful Rainbow," Josh beamed. "Must be a good eighteen inches, hey?" He held the fish up and twisted the hook out of its lower lip. "A sprinkle of salt and pepper, some cornmeal, and butter in a hot skillet. Now that will make a fine supper."

He pulled a fillet knife out of the leather sheath on his belt and dressed the trout in the shallow water before dumping it into his creel along with a fistful of wet moss. He stooped into the grass along the bank. "Tell me, Doc, do you have any good medicine for a bum knee?"

"Have you seen a doctor?"

"Don't do doctors."

"An annual checkup is a good idea."

"Closest I ever came to a doctor was a vet down in West Yellowstone."

"A veterinarian?" Dieter asked.

"Yep."

"You went to a veterinarian for your knee?"

"Nope, he came here. Had a sick llama. I just took advantage of the opportunity."

Dieter couldn't think of a reply.

Josh said, "I mean a bum knee is a bum knee, right?"

"Well, yes, but—"

"Does it matter which kind of warm-blooded mammal we're talking about?"

"You have a point, Josh, but actually—"

"Don't try to talk me into visiting a doctor. I haven't needed one for sixty-two years and I don't plan to start now." He reached inside his vest and brought out a small flask, tossing back his head while he swallowed. He smacked his lips and offered the flask to Dieter, who waved it off.

"Looks like you've got something heavier on your mind than my troubles, Doc."

"You read me well. Yesterday I discovered a body on the Madison."

"Waddaya mean a *body*?"

"I mean a corpse. I called the sheriff's office and they sent out a deputy. I led him to it."

Josh adjusted his waders and settled onto the weeds.

Dieter told him what he'd shared with Mrs. Manning.

"Land O' Goshen!" Josh said. "I was told they just got strange body in over at Winslow Memorial. It's in cold storage waiting on autopsy."

"Quite a network you have there."

Josh took a bigger swig from his flask. "But I had no earthly idea you was involved."

"I've shaken it off," Dieter lied. "I called the sheriff's office back but wasn't able to get any info."

Josh sat staring at the ground, then looked up. "After you've lived here a while, there's one thing you'll learn. Nothing's getting in the papers what the local law don't want us to know."

"Here's what I've come out to ask you—do you think that maybe there's some connection with the attack on your llama?"

"Good question. I don't really know. Haven't seen the dead body you're talking about."

"I only saw it from a distance."

"Why didn't you get closer?"

"I . . . couldn't." He reached for the flask. When Josh handed it over, he drank the last of the liquor in a quick gulp. "Tell me something. What's really known about those lone wolves you mentioned yesterday?"

Josh gave a grunted laugh but quickly turned serious. "Plenty of stories out there, covering decades. Hardly know where to start." He paused and studied the field grass about him, seeming to collect his thoughts as he fondled his beard. "First to come to mind is the one about the Custer wolf of the Black Hills. He held a ten-year reign along the border of Wyoming and South Dakota. Just appeared, started killing livestock, then disappeared for weeks at a time. Ranchers spent six months trapping for him before they kilt him.

"Then there's Ol' Lefty of Burns Hole in Colorado. The story has it that he took out hundreds of sheep and cattle in his time. Clever scoundrel. One day he was caught in a trap. Dislocated a shoulder and lost a few teeth on the steel trying to get free. But he managed to yank his left forepaw out, a kind of self-amputation. 'Course, the paw healed in time and formed a stub. Together with his bum shoulder, it gave him a weird way of moving about. Never put that stub on the ground when he loped."

Dieter was mesmerized by the stories and Josh's recall of details. "Are renegades always loners?"

"Not necessarily. My daddy's favorite was the legend of Lobo from down in New Mexico, the King of the Currumpaw. Lobo was not exactly a loner. Had a mate, the Great White Wolf they called Blanca. One year, the story goes, the pair attacked over three hundred head of cattle. Just for the killing, you understand. Never fed on any of them."

"Were they taken out?"

"They never got to Lobo, but they finally caught up with Blanca. Shot her clean in the head. Lobo grieved for weeks. The local ranchers used to say his desperate howls were heard for ten miles on a clear night."

"What happened to him?"

"They found nary a trace of him. Everyone guessed he just crawled down into a hole somewhere and died."

Dieter considered for a moment the similarities between people and wolves. "What made these legendary loners so tough to trap?"

"They learned from watching their companions die in agony from strychnine planted in chunks of meat. That taught 'em anything smelling of man was a threat. Then they became smart as tacks. Used to detect the old number fourteen traps buried in the dirt from the human scent left on them. They'd sneak up on one and scratch all around it, exposing the trap and the chain. Then they'd take their hind feet and scatter twigs and stones onto the trap to set it off. Now that's a fact."

Josh leaned toward him. "I been thinking, Doc. How much can you learn from a autopsy anyway?"

Dieter shrugged. "Cause of death is often apparent."

"So if we could get a good look at the corpse you found out on the Madison, it might just tell us something?"

Dieter jerked his head back.

"Got a 'quaintance over at Winslow Memorial who'll likely let us sneak a view of the body if you want."

Dieter hesitated. That needed careful thought. How deeply did he really want to go? On the other hand, he'd made the trip to see Josh and find out more. Why hold back now? "I'd like to do that. How about tomorrow?"

"What's wrong with tonight?" Josh replied.

ELEVEN

Chief Park Ranger Jack Corey ordered a third drink—Glenffidich with a splash—while he waited alone and out of uniform at a corner table at Minicozzi's.

The upscale restaurant in the center of Gardiner was complete with white tablecloths and olive-skinned waiters with slicked-back hair. Good place to meet—far enough away from Colter to be a little more discreet. At least that's what he thought. A well-dressed couple two tables away had glanced at him more than once. But that happened a lot.

The reason for the third scotch was Anne. After twenty-two years, she was leaving him for another man, an asshole of an insurance agent older than he was by ten years. Anne put the blame square on Corey's shoulders.

Maybe it belonged there. He had always put his career ahead of family. A crisis somewhere ahead of anniversary or birthday celebrations. Late for dinner. Exhaustion taking the place of romance.

He caught a guy at another table staring his way. He—Jack Corey himself—had made it to the enviable position of Yellowstone's Chief Ranger. Everyone paid him respect. Whenever the annual meeting of park rangers from around the country took place, he was The Man. "Look, over there," they would whisper. "He's in charge of Yellowstone."

How about lunch, Jack? Any plans for dinner?

After she entered the restaurant, he quickly caught her eye as she drifted across the room, dressed in a sleeveless silk blouse and slim-legged jeans stuffed into leather boots.

"You look stunning as always," he said, as editor-in-chief Claire Manning approached the table with a put-on smile inside a serious expression. He called the waiter over and asked for a bottle of Torciano Merlot—her favorite.

She held up her palm. "Not for me. I'll just have a glass of iced tea."

"I'll take the bottle, please," he added.

Their chitchat began with the latest from the offices of the Gallatin County Weekly Reporter. She'd hired a recent graduate of Rexburg Technological College to run the refurbished printing press. After a few minutes the small talk shifted as usual to her husband. George's latest sporting trip—hunting on a Kenyan game farm—sounded like shooting fish in a barrel. George was the co-owner of the Manning and Weisner trucking firm that had done well and provided George all the resources he needed to travel the globe for exploration, fascinating recreation and murdering wildlife.

When the waiter brought her tea, Corey asked to give them a few minutes to look over the menu and then offered her the pretense of a toast. She tilted the bottom of her glass in his direction and the slice of lemon annoyingly rubbed against her elegant nose.

"So, what do I owe this honor of your driving all the way up here for a dinner with me?" he asked. He slid an arm forward and brushed an index finger across hers.

She pulled back her hand. "How is the Operation going, Jack?"

She'd followed Yellowstone's Operation Wolfstock from the beginning. She was even smack in the middle of the dignitaries from Washington when the first wolves transported from Canada arrived on that snowy January day two years before. But her accounts in the newspaper at the time missed the mark. She wasn't getting good info. Between phone calls with the prime news outlets on both coasts, he began giving her more time on the phone to help her get the stories straight. That led to meetings in his office for extended interviews, which led to meetings outside the office for extended cocktails, then inside her home for extended lovemaking whenever George was enjoying extended big game killing sprees somewhere around the world.

George Manning was the global sportsman, no doubt, but Jack Corey was The Man. She was the one who finally broke it off.

Lately she was probing the Operation deeper than ever. She kept on top of the spending for the program, always calling into park headquarters and asking about budget details. He finally got wind of her call to Washington when she spoke with the financial people in the Interior Department. She wanted to compare the Operation's budget figures from the superintendent's office with those from the feds. He might be spending more money on the Operation than allotted from Washington, but that was his call. Robbing Peter to subsidize Paul was standard operating procedure. Everybody did it. She struggled to uncover a story like it was Watergate and she was another Woodward or Bernstein.

"The Operation's going better than expected," Corey said. "The wolves are breeding. Spreading out and claiming territory. We had no idea it would happen this fast."

"I still have upset ranchers calling me. They want me to write about the livestock the wolves are slaughtering."

Corey shook his head. "That's just not happening, Claire, at least not anywhere close to the numbers people think. You know that the main lot of your callers are out after money. That's all. The payoff for each kill claim makes it worth their while to file. Hell, I might do the same if I was in their shoes." He brought his glass to his lips and took an extra long sip.

"Where does Superintendent Gilmer stand on all of this?" she asked.

"He's just interested in finding out what packs have moved in near Colter. Sometimes I think he believes all those cock and bull stories people come up with."

"What killed that Arizona photographer, Jack?"

He suddenly choked and spit up the wine down the front of his white dress shirt. He grabbed his napkin and wiped at the stain as he coughed. A waiter from across the room rushed in with more napkins and another brought soda water to the rescue.

After he blotted his shirt, he collected himself and scooted his chair back to the table. "You're asking about a photographer?"

"Was he killed by a wolf pack?"

"Listen to me, I know there've been reports about livestock—"

For the second time she waved off the waiter as he approached the table. "I'm not going to play guessing games with you. Why haven't we heard anything about his death?"

"The case is under investigation, Claire. The sheriff's people are on it. You should be talking with them."

"You know they're not talking. Especially with me."

He gulped his drink as he scanned the other diners. "I really don't want to talk about this here. Let's have a quiet dinner right now. I'd like to talk about other things."

The waiter showed up at the table for the third time and she glared back at him. "Okay, look . . . why don't you just bring us an appetizer? I don't know, maybe something that Venetians enjoy?"

"Some bread and Caponatina would be nice," Corey said with an uneasy smile. When the waiter left, Claire reached for Corey's wine, finished it off, and dabbed her lips with a napkin.

"Forget about the past," she said. "That's not what this is about. I asked you about the photographer."

"We don't know yet what caused his death."

"Are you even looking at the *possibility* of wolves?"

He glanced at the other tables to see if anyone was straining to listen in. The last thing he was going to do was to give even a hint about the experts they were bringing on board to tackle the very problem she was raising.

She picked up her white linen napkin and squeezed it in her fists. "You're lying to me."

"Why the hell would I lie to you?"

"Because you don't want to face the truth. Operation Wolfstock didn't make it, Jack. You've got to face it once and for all."

He reached out and touched her arm. "Claire, please. Keep your voice down."

"The wolves have got to go. They're terrorizing the entire area."

"I briefed Gilmer this morning. We're going to get on it."

"You're going to get on it? When do you plan to start?"

"Soon. It's in the works."

She flung her napkin down onto the table. "In the works?"

"I've got priorities. The busiest weekend of the year is coming up. You know that."

"Let me tell you what I know. I'm getting to the bottom of this, and I don't give a damn where the story leads."

"What is that supposed to mean?"

She got up from her seat. "Never mind. Sorry, I'm just not hungry."

Corey reached for her arm. She swatted it away like a wasp and marched off.

He slammed his fist down on the table, knocking over the bottle of Merlot. That's okay, he thought. He sat with the wine flooding the table and streaming onto the floor. She always overreacted; loved drama. She had been pushing too much of her ass into his business like she was a hotshot reporter who was going to get to the "truth."

The truth was that he was in charge. Operation Wolfstock was his priority more than anyone's. She'd been messing with him all along.

Playing him for a fool. That game was over. She would learn soon enough that you don't play that way with The Man.

TWELVE

Winslow Memorial Funeral Home stood isolated at the end of the block. Except for the town hall, it claimed the largest lot of any other building in town. Dieter learned from Josh that the Winslow family had settled Colter in the early part of the century and that the youngest of six sons had built the colonial brick structure over a three-year period in the 1950s.

More than one neighbor or friend of Josh's had been "laid out" there.

"Edna Turley promised me she'd help me out tonight," Josh said. "Edna's worked as a clerk and assistant to David Godfrey Winslow going on twenty years, if she's been there a day." He pulled into a front parking space and flipped off his headlights.

Already dark, spotlights that were distributed among holly bushes highlighted the building and the garish sign in front. Only one dim light shone inside. Dieter still didn't understand why they had to arrive so late, but left it to Josh's judgment.

Josh twisted the knob on the front door, but it was locked. He banged on the door, but no one answered. He cupped his hands to stare through the stained glass, and then stepped back and shook his head. "Just don't understand. She said she'd be here. Had plenty of bookkeeping to catch up on, she told me."

He paced along the front porch, cussing under his breath as he peeked into every window until he realized the futility of it all. Although he wasn't going to say it to Josh, Dieter felt a wave of relief. He followed his partner back to the pickup. Josh turned on the ignition and moved down the driveway to the street, mumbling to himself. Suddenly, he stopped and shoved the transmission into reverse, turned around, and pulled to the back of the building. He jumped out and gave a jerk on the doorknob of a back door. He strolled back to the truck. "Come on out, Doc. I've got an idea."

Dieter didn't like the sound of *idea*. Edna Turley wasn't there. They'd been stood up. What else was there to do? He hopped down as Josh opened the glove compartment and retrieved a flathead screwdriver and a homemade strip of shaped sheet metal with a wooden handle.

Dieter couldn't believe what he was seeing. "Wait a minute. I'm not going to—"

"Don't worry about a thing."

"This isn't the way we planned it, Josh. I'm not about to risk getting in trouble with the law."

"I'll just say that Edna asked me to come out here for emergency repairs or something like that. For all I know she fainted or had a heart attack. Could be laying in there in need of medical attention and here we are no more than thirty feet away while she's at death's door. What would they think of us just driving away into the dark as if she was some kind of nobody who we don't care about? Now how could we answer to that, Doc?"

Dieter looked away. It was a ridiculous development. He waited in the truck as Josh headed for the rear of the building. Josh must've known what they were getting into before they drove out. One hell of a trick to play on him. He had never given a waking thought to try any such shenanigans. He wanted to think long and hard about it, but there wasn't a lot to think long and hard about. The only sane decision was clear. He should walk away—either that or run. Climbing down from the truck, he searched the darkness to make certain no passerby could see them and cautiously moved toward Josh at the rear of the building.

"They have the place alarmed, you know," Dieter said. "There's a warning sign out front that I saw when we drove up—some company's Security System."

Ignoring him, Josh jiggled and pried with his tools between the lock and doorjamb. He explained as he worked that Mr. Winslow was never happy with the alarm system that he had put in three years before. It was too easy to be set off by the wind. Edna said that it didn't take too many calls in the middle of the night before Winslow lost his patience and disconnected the whole damn thing. He told her the warning signs were all they actually needed and he still kicked himself for buying all the wires and gadgets and electrical stuff that came with the stupid-ass signs.

"Look, Josh. Forgive me, but I don't want to be an accomplice to breaking and entering."

"Relax. We're not breaking anything. We're just entering."

Dieter stood watch, prepared to run at the first sound of an alarm. He hitched his trousers up a notch because he didn't want to get a cuff caught under his foot while he ran. He surveyed the vacant field behind the place as if expecting someone to leap out of the bushes.

The back door squeaked open.

Josh motioned for him to follow, but Dieter hesitated. Josh motioned again, this time waving urgently. Dieter looked around, now realizing it was too damned late. If he were going to leave, he should've left when Josh exited the truck with a set of burglar tools. He took one last deep breath and moved toward the open door.

When they entered, a dim light shone at the end of a dark corridor. He crept along behind Josh, placing each foot lightly on the carpeted floor while occasionally glancing back over his shoulder. Near the end of the hall, Josh stopped and held out his hand for Dieter to halt, then edged his head around the corner.

Dieter stood with his back and damp palms flat against the wall.

Josh continued his slow-motion walk and Dieter followed. An antique lamp on a mahogany credenza lit one wall of the foyer, casting a hue of dingy yellow over the area. A three-tiered chandelier hung from the ceiling. Heavy draperies of depressing burgundy covered the windows and thick upholstered chairs with high backs lined the walls. Two more hallways split off the foyer. Josh pointed for Dieter to take the left and he headed for the right.

Totally asinine!

Dieter inched down his hallway until out of sight of the front door. Everything around him was pitch-black. He stood and stuck his hand into his pocket, fumbling for his keys. When he pulled out the key ring, a stash of coins fell to the floor.

Slow down!

He didn't move while he switched on the penlight attached to the ring and searched the carpet around his feet, gathering the change. He continued down the hall with the narrow shaft of light leading the way. When he came to a door, he pulled it slightly open and examined the room through the crack with the penlight. Boxes and assorted supplies were piled high on shelves.

He closed the door and moved farther along, shifting the beam over the walls and floor until he found another door. He held the light up to it and read the sign: PREP ROOM. When he opened the door, the raw odor of embalming fluid drifted out. The light beam revealed white cabinets and cluttered counter tops. A long bulge under a lime green sheet appeared on a stainless steel table that tilted toward a sink.

Is that the Madison River victim? An electric chill crept over him and he stiffened.

He took a few deep breaths. Something about the scene didn't make sense. If that was the body of the victim, shouldn't it be refrigerated? On the other hand, if the medical examiner were coming early the next morning, the body could've been brought out for an overnight warming.

Someone came jogging down the corridor.

He snapped off his penlight and pressed his shoulder blades back against the wall.

Josh barged into the room. "Doc, where are you?"

Dieter turned the penlight back on and shined it toward him.

"Get that light out of my eyes!"

"Sorry."

"A patrol car just pulled up in front. We gotta get out of here."

Holy Crap!

THIRTEEN

Deputy Preston Cody was making his rounds as he drove down
South Myrtle Street when he received the call. They had never called
him from home before. His boss said he just received intel from
someone claiming two suspicious characters were hanging around the
Winslow funeral home. Preston was on top of it. He'd been working
the night shift the last two years alone. That was when he was in charge
and that was a big deal. "At night this town is mine," he'd often tell
friends.

He arrived at the front of Winslow's with his headlights off and
jumped out, careful to close the car door without slamming. The
walkway was clear in both directions. The area around the funeral
home too dark to get a good look. He walked cautiously to the pillared
front entrance. With his flashlight in one hand, he fumbled with a fat
ring of assorted keys with the other until he found the one marked
Winslow N/Alm.

Edna Turley had left a lamp on, a routine of hers. He'd been told
many times the need to have Winslow's checked during the night shift.
Edna had blabbed that plenty of weirdoes were out looking for bodies,
a fact that shocked Preston at first, but he wondered if that was on
account of too many movies that had come and gone about body
snatchers. Then he heard that Edna told the sheriff's office about what
had circulated in funeral home newsletters over the years—all about

freaks breaking in and messing with bodies, especially young women's bodies, doing things about as disgusting as you can think of with a female body. Edna damn well didn't want *that* going on at Winslow Memorial. Dirty neckro-maniac freaks was the term she used.

Those stories were more reasons that Preston never liked funeral homes. He was never comfortable being in one, what with all the smells of a corpse mingling with those of flower arrangements and the gawks of depressing people. But he especially didn't like being alone in a funeral home after dark. It just wasn't an inviting atmosphere, that was all.

After closing the massive front door behind him, he walked through the parlor with his flashlight beaming.

*   *   *

"There's no exit down the hall?" Dieter asked after Josh rushed into the room and gently closed the door.

"No, and we can't get out the back door without running through the foyer. Shine your light down here." Josh stooped to open the cabinet doors under the counter.

"What the heck are you doing?" Dieter whispered, dumbfounded.

"We gotta hide."

Hide?

This stupid game had to end. They'd both be arrested, booked and charged with breaking and entering. Mug shots would show up in the Weekly Reporter. One thing was certain, in this part of the country it would be the end of his career. He'd practiced veterinary medicine long enough to know the rules of the game. Animal docs were no different from people docs. They were expected to be upright citizens in the community.

But even worse, how would he explain it all to Michael and Megan?

Josh pushed the cabinet doors back in. "No room here."

Dieter shined the light into a corner where there was a narrow door. Josh rushed to it and discovered a broom closet.

"Only one of us can squeeze in here," Josh said.

Dieter shined the light back around the room.

"Wait a minute," Josh whispered. He tiptoed to a cold storage bin for cadavers against the wall and turned around with a determined look and a nod toward it.

"Okay, Josh. Let's walk out of here right—"

"We're not giving up that quick." Josh pulled open the long upper drawer of the bin where bodies awaiting embalming were stored. "Come on, Doc. Hurry. I sure can't fit in there."

They both heard the front door of the funeral home creak open, then quickly shut. Dieter held onto the countertop and slid his legs one at a time down the steel surface that felt like an iceberg. Josh pushed the drawer to within an inch of closing.

The door of the broom closet closed.

Footsteps were creeping down the hallway.

Dieter's teeth chattered. He didn't know which was worse, the numbing cold or the nauseating reek of embalming fluid. One arm was already asleep from being pinned against frozen steel. The finger bitten by King Tut throbbed.

What was he going to do if somebody came in the room and pulled out the slab? Play dead? Say "Sorry, sir" and trigger a heart attack?

The footsteps stopped outside the door. A voice shouted something unintelligible. The voice had strained to be a command, but there was a more tentative edge to it.

The door opened and a spasm erupted from Dieter's gut. Bile burned the back of his throat and gushed upward. *God, of all times.* He turned his head to the side and panted. It was too loud. He took deep breaths through his nose. If he began to puke, he could choke to death.

*　　*　　*

Preston Cody searched the parlor with his flashlight. He assumed the damn light switch would be near the front door. Maybe it would be better to go outside and search the perimeter. He should've done that first anyway. As he headed for the front, he wondered why he was walking so quietly. A hushed clamor arose in the back.

He stopped and turned around, not certain that he'd actually heard anything. He held his breath to sharpen his hearing while he shined his flashlight along the walls. Choosing the hallway on the left, he walked toward it as he swung his light from side to side. The doors to each room he passed were closed, but he recognized the stench coming from the next room and assumed it had recently been opened. With one hand on his flashlight and one on his holstered Glock, he yelled. "Anybody in there?"

No response.

"If anybody's in there, you'd better come out now before I blow a hole through you."

He reached for the knob, slowly twisted it, then gave a shove and stepped inside. The flashlight beam moved across the room until it reached a steel table where a sheet covered the shape of a body. He'd never seen a dead body, not one up close anyway except for his grandmother's. His Mama didn't let him linger over it though. His Grandma looked so different from his last visit at the nursing home. Caked makeup had smothered her face and the corners of her lips bore the likeness of a smile, but he'd never remembered seeing her smile before. He took his hand off his pistol and advanced to the table. Using only the tips of his index finger and thumb, he pulled the top of the sheet away.

*   *   *

Dieter held his breath as footsteps approached the prep table. He suddenly heard a roar.

Jesus Christ Almighty!

The words were so loud that he jerked his head up and bumped it against the top of his steel tomb.

Dammit.

The door to the room slammed shut and the rush of footsteps faded down the hallway.

Silence.

The closet door opened and then the refrigerated slab was finally being yanked out. "Get me out of here," Dieter growled, his words echoing as if inside a cave.

"You okay, Doc?" Josh began rubbing Dieter's shoulders.

He was too frozen to carry on polite conversation.

"Stay here and warm up," Josh said. "I'll make sure the cruiser's gone."

While Josh investigated, Dieter rolled off the steel table and paced rapidly, his arms locked across his chest massaging his shoulders. Gradually, his shivering subsided and his anger was replaced by a crazy sense of achievement, like a schoolboy who had pulled off a prank. He moved toward the prep table just as Josh returned. The green sheet was bunched around the cadaver's head. He grasped the top of the sheet and pulled it down, then cringed and turned away. Against the victim's shoulder lay a half-eaten head. The face was covered in swirls of burgundy and black surrounding dark caverns where once loomed eyes.

As Josh watched from behind, Dieter used his penlight to examine the excavated throat, a jumble of slashed arteries and veins, minced cartilage, and a shredded windpipe. The odor of decomposing flesh arose—rotting, yet a certain sweetness mingled with it. The stench of death, a haunting blend of sweet and rancid. The neck had been chewed away, gnawed down to the cervical spine. He strained to look, holding the penlight into the open wound. Teeth marks were whittled on the ivory surface of the bone.

He pulled the sheet farther down and revealed the rest of the torso covered with lacerations and dried blood. The naked chest was carved with penetrating scratches.

"Do you see anything resembling a stab wound, Doc?"

"Nothing." Dieter held the light closer and pointed to a wide abrasion about six inches long under the cadaver's left nipple. He looked at Josh, who was nodding with recognition.

"No question about it," Josh said. "Four evenly spaced claw-marks. See how they dug in beneath the skin. Must be almost an inch." He held up his curled fingers and raked at the air. "But that ain't near deep or wide enough for a bear. Only one creature scrapes and claws with a pattern like that, partner."

Dieter pointed the light to a clear bite mark with evidence of fang penetration just below the neck at the upper edge of the clavicle. He made a fist and formed the familiar goalposts with his fingers. The width looked identical to that found on the llama carcass.

"What about these pockmarks? Look at them. How can a wolf do that?"

Josh bent low to examine the tiny gouges that covered the decaying face. "My guess is that's the work of ravens. They can't rip open a carcass, so they let the wolves do the hard labor. I've always thought those birds a hell of a lot smarter than the coyotes and eagles that can only come across a kill by chance. Ravens follow wolves around like a whore after a sailor. They work as a team. The wolves do the hunting while the birds do the spotting."

They had spent too much time and were pressing their luck. Dieter placed the sheet back over the corpse, leaving it crumpled over the body with the head partly exposed, exactly the way the deputy had left it. "I think we've seen enough."

Josh nodded and they moved quickly back through the building. Dieter checked along the way to make sure nothing was out of place before they exited into the dark toward the pickup.

When they headed back to Josh's ranch, Dieter's mind raced with thoughts of how narrow their escape.

"You okay, Doc?"

"Just thinking . . . it would be a good idea if we kept in touch."

"You got my number?"

Dieter reached into his pocket to grab Mrs. Manning's business card to write on. He found his keys, a ballpoint pen and spare change. But the card was gone.

FOURTEEN

Molly Schoonover knew him as soon as he walked into the General Store that morning—the tall man with a wild patch of hair dangling like a bird's nest from his sharp boney chin. A wide-brimmed straw hat hid his eyes as he moved with elbows splayed out and hands jammed inside deep pockets. An overseer, too high and mighty to touch the merchandise.

She had talked the Judge into driving up to Colter to shop. Although September hadn't yet arrived—Labor Day was coming soon—signs of an early fall abounded. Golden aspen peppered the green forests along with the fire-red maples. The air had that distinctive chill even in the middle of a sunny day. Before long, the summer onslaught of park tourists would disappear in time with the first snows of the season.

Three women wearing dresses to their ankles accompanied old man Loudermilk. The entire family moved together as if tethered, whispering to one another and paying no heed to other customers; all tuned into themselves. She never quite determined what went on with that peculiar family. She remembered Dieter mentioning the colt delivery at their place and wished he'd learned more about them to share with her. The rumors about the family were rampant, but she made it a point to give little if any credence to gossip about families that were different. God knows she and the Judge were different in their own ways. To be fair, she'd heard favorable accounts of the

72

Loudermilk family as well, favorable accounts suggesting they were good people despite their quirks. They not only worked a ranch, but did odd jobs on the side. The women were outstanding seamstresses, she'd heard, who made wedding dresses, curtains and the like and that they worked at reasonable rates to boot. Given the miserable state of the drapes throughout her house, it crossed Molly's mind that maybe she should politely inquire about their services.

Joseph Vincent Loudermilk pointed at something on a shelf occasionally, and one of the women would pick off a box or can or bag and drop it into the basket that another pushed along the aisle. The two younger women each had their hair braided into a strand that wobbled below their waist as they strolled.

Molly leaned down to the Judge in his wheelchair and whispered. "Do you remember the story on the Loudermilks over there?"

He looked up. After a pause and a nod, he said, "Sure. He s-sued the Helena newspaper a few years back b-because of the story they did on them. Best just to avoid them, Molly."

The Judge rarely said that sort of thing about anyone and people never spoke an unkind word about the Judge. Everyone admired the Honorable Bradford Schoonover and how well he managed to get about. A judge in the Eighteenth Judicial District of Montana for sixteen years, he was best known for his fairness in the courtroom and his eloquence in putting into words the reasons for rendering his verdicts.

What a polished speaker he was. Until the day came that his John Deere tractor rolled over him. Why he wasn't crushed to death still no one could explain. Not only did he break his pelvis, collar bone, a femur, three ribs, and become paralyzed from the waist down, it did worse. Regaining consciousness three days later, he spoke with a stutter, the beginning of the end of his career.

With one eye on the Loudermilks, Molly pretended to help the Judge in selecting winter wool shirts. Then she moseyed around the corner and sidestepped down their aisle as if searching for something. The oldest of the women moved in her direction. When she was close enough, Molly turned and smartly arranged a gentle bump. "Oh, I'm so sorry. I didn't see—"

"No problem, ma'am, I'm sure."

"My goodness," Molly blurted. "Aren't you the one who did the fine drapes for Sally Pritchard last winter?"

"Well, yes. My sisters and I, that is."

"I'd love to talk with you sometime about doing up a pair for my living room picture window."

The woman caught Mr. Loudermilk glowering from a nearby aisle.

Molly tried to steal her attention. "I hope the colt that Dr. Harmon delivered for you is doing okay?"

The woman started to speak when the old man called out. "Miss Katherine?"

She lowered her head and moved away from Molly without answering.

Well, thank you very much. Next time I'll bend over and—

"What are you up to?" the Judge asked, as he wheeled up behind her.

She shrugged, put on an air of innocence, and followed him back to the men's shirt rack where he showed her three selections he was pondering. She vetoed each in turn.

On a nearby shelf, Sam Phillips adjusted stock, a ritual the store owner spent the better part of each day practicing. He greeted the Judge with a broad smile. Hard to miss, Sam hovered midway between six and seven feet. His shirtsleeves climbed high on his biceps for the likely purpose of either flaunting them or revealing tattoos of the Holy Cross on one arm and a faded likeness of Jesus on the other. "Been a while, Judge," he said.

"Just came in to browse for s-s-some hiking boots," he replied with a wink.

Sam smiled and returned to work, never looking at Molly. She once went before the Colter Town Council and complained about business owners fixing prices in the summers to take advantage of tourists—of course, punishing the locals in the process. It had been three years and he hadn't spoken to her since.

Three damn years. At least he hadn't spoken to her directly, only through the Judge. After loading up on household staples and checking out, Molly and the Judge returned to the truck. She opened the passenger door and helped him struggle into the cab, then collapsed his wheelchair and carried it to the rear of the truck, heaving it upon the tailgate. Before she climbed into the driver's seat, she grabbed a folded note between the wiper blade and windshield:

> I did not mean to be rude, my dear. Please call me at your earliest convenience: 555-7035.
>
> Katherine Belle Loudermilk

You can bet your sweet ass I'll call, Molly thought.

FIFTEEN

Bantz Montgomery pounded for the third time on the front door of
Jack Corey's home. One good thing about working at Yellowstone
headquarters was the commute between home and office. The Park
Service provided a modest house within walking distance of the offices
for each of the senior park rangers and key staff. All were built from
the same locally quarried stone as the office complex.

Already 8:15, Corey was supposed to meet him an hour earlier at the
office. Montgomery suspected a problem and had an inkling of it. He
stopped knocking and took off to find the maintenance super for the
Park homes. It was rarely better than a fifty-fifty chance to locate the
guy, but this time Montgomery lucked out. The super, a thin-framed
former cowboy had grown up in Casper and was a jack-of-all-trades.
He complained about his long arthritic fingers while he jostled the
master key around in Corey's front door lock, then gently twisted the
knob and cracked open the door.

"Thanks, Karl," Montgomery said. "I'll check on him."

"I can't keep doing this, Bantz. If the Big Wigs knew I was—"

"I'm sure Chief Corey just has a virus this time. He was coming
down with something Friday."

"It's a damn shame about his wife and all. A man needs someone to
take care of him. Don't know what I'd do without Lenora."

Montgomery shoved on the door. "Be sure and give her my regards, Karl." Inside, he called out Corey's name in a low voice at first, then louder as he walked through the living room.

No answer.

A newspaper spread out in sections on the seat of a stuffed easy chair and on the carpeted floor beside it. Three crushed Budweiser cans lay on the table next to the chair.

Corey's wife Anne had called Montgomery from her apartment in West Yellowstone late the night before. That wasn't unusual, she'd called him a dozen times since the breakup. She wanted others to understand that none of it was her fault. She had grown to hate Jack Corey's twelve-hour days. He was more than a workaholic—he didn't have a single interest outside of work. "Not a single damn thing, Bantz!" she'd yelled over the phone. Nothing other than the Park interested him. He didn't know how to live or love anymore. Montgomery never told his boss about the calls. He gradually came to understand Corey's mood swings, but didn't totally sympathize with his plight.

The bedroom door was ajar. Corey lay sprawled out on the bed on top of the covers, snoring and smelling of hard liquor. When Montgomery picked up a glass tumbler from the bedside table and sniffed, his hunch was confirmed. He grabbed Corey's shoulder and shoved, but he might as well have been a sack of flour. Calling out his name, he shook him harder and the bed began to rock. He placed his mouth down to Corey's ear and shouted again. "Jack!"

Corey jerked up from the pillow as if someone had yanked him by the hair. "What the hell," he groaned.

"I've been waiting for you at headquarters. You're late. Remember our job this morning?"

After sitting up on the edge of his bed, Corey squeezed the sides of his head.

"The superintendent wants you to report to him by noon, Jack. He wants to know what we find out about the poacher."

Corey rolled back onto the bed and over onto his stomach. "I don't give a shit what Gilmer wants or when he wants it. I'm resigning."

Montgomery walked into the bathroom and picked a damp towel off the tiled floor.

Corey called after him. "Did you *hear* me?"

Montgomery turned on the cold-water spigot and soaked the towel.

"I said I was resigning. Answer me, dammit!"

Montgomery returned to the bedroom and tossed the wet mass at his boss' head. "Come on, Jack, get up. We've got this scum nailed. We can't let him get away from us again."

Corey rose up slowly while wiping his face on the towel. With Montgomery supporting him on one side, he staggered into the bathroom. Montgomery reached in and turned on the shower.

"You've done your job, asshole," Corey muttered. "Now get out of here."

"I'll wait for you in the kitchen and make a pot of coffee. We've got to move on this, Jack. It's already—"

Montgomery ducked in time to miss the shampoo bottle flying at his head.

*   *   *

Montgomery sat in silence as his boss sped down the highway toward the town of Red Lodge.

"Tell me the name of this guy again," Corey demanded.

"Dietz. Nathan Dietz."

"Sounds like a kraut."

"I really don't know."

"You're sure he's at home?"

"Can't be absolutely sure. But we've—"

"You got me outta bed and you're not *sure* he's home?"

"Look, Jack. We've determined that weekends are the best times to hit. That's all we can do under the circumstances."

Corey shook his head with a mock-grin.

"You might want to slow down a little here," Montgomery said. "The local cops pay their bills with their radar gun."

Corey was doing 65 in a 35 zone and didn't let up. Down one of the gravel roads was the home of the suspect, Montgomery's best guess as to the poacher of wolf labeled 10F, which had strayed from the Rose Creek pack. Its radio-collar had given off a signal indicating total absence of motion for twenty-four hours. Whenever Montgomery brought such warning signs to Corey's attention, Corey directed the rangers to drop everything—*everything*—locate the wolf's body, and give him a full account.

They had found the radio-collar near Highway 212, west of Cooke City. Those investigating the incident told Montgomery that the collar had been slashed with a knife and the body missing. Dried blood splattered the ground along with casings from .30/.30 shells. The missing mom—10F—left a den of pups. Only half survived. The others were found rotting. But it was not just a den of pups they'd found. She also left behind a grieving male, the same wolf often seen at the site where the slashed collar was found.

Evidently Nathan Dietz didn't have many friends in that part of Montana. Park Service investigators said they had no trouble in locating informants who pointed fingers at him. His reputation for fishing over the limit, hunting out of season, and bagging more illegal game than anyone in four counties had caught up with him. The investigators said that Dietz complained to too many people about the government wolves. He carped about them breeding, then leaving the Park and killing his goats and sheep. He boasted often if he ever saw one "that would be one less goddamn wolf to worry about."

Montgomery pointed to a mailbox at the head of a dirt road winding back into the trees. DIETZ was painted in black on the side of the steel box atop a wooden post.

"Loaded?" Corey asked.

Montgomery patted his holstered revolver and nodded.

SIXTEEN

Corey stomped on the accelerator and spun down the dirt driveway, trying to give the SOB who lived there a reason to confront them with a weapon. Even better, to shoot at them.

People who fired on park rangers were the lowest of criminals. Having a chance to fire back at a poacher was, to Corey's mind, a great chance to take revenge on those bastards who always received the lightest of fines and rarely a sentence.

The truck spun to a stop in front of a shack with a sagging tin roof. The windows were either too grimy to see through or boarded up. On one side of the dilapidated structure a half re-painted Ford with tail fins rested lamely on blocks. A propane gas tank nestled among the tall weeds that surrounded the sorry excuse for a dwelling.

Montgomery rushed for the trees to make his way toward the back. Corey stepped onto the porch as a granddaddy beagle with visible ribs slinked from underneath the shack and labored to give off a threatening bark. A man wearing a red plaid and soiled shirt with the sleeves torn off opened the front door. Sporting week-old whiskers, he appeared to be in either his late fifties or his mid-seventies, depending on which angle you studied him from. He glared at Corey, then flipped onto the ground a cigarette that was smoked down to the grime on his long scraggy fingers.

"Are you Mr. Dietz? Corey asked. "Nathan Dietz?"

"S'ppose I am," the man replied with a hoarse voice and matching attitude. He turned his head to cough before ambling over to the side of the porch and spitting into the breeze in a way designed to amaze the uninvited guests with his range. "And who the hell might you be on my property?" He coughed again.

"I'm Chief Jack Corey with the National Park Service."

"Am I supposed to be impressed?"

"You're under suspicion for killing one of the Park wolves."

Dietz tried to laugh but was stymied by another coughing fit. "And what if I did?"

"These wolves are a species protected by the US government. Killing one is a felony."

Montgomery walked out from behind a tree onto the porch. Dietz whipped a pack of Lucky Strikes from his shirt pocket, hammered out a cigarette, and speared it between his lips. He squeezed a pack of matches from the same pocket and lit up, blowing the smoke directly downwind toward the trespassers.

Corey said, "I would appreciate it, Mr. Dietz, if you didn't blow smoke in our faces."

"To tell you the truth, I would appreciate it if you got the hell off my porch and went home." He found it tough to complete a sentence without coughing. "Then my smoke wouldn't get anywheres near you now, would it?"

"Do you own a thirty-thirty?" Montgomery asked.

Dietz took a slow draw on the cigarette and turned his head to the side this time to exhale. "I ain't saying I do and I ain't saying I don't."

Purple streaks sprouted across Corey's neck. "I take it you won't mind if we look around." He yanked a piece of folded paper from his front pocket and held it up to Dietz's face. "We have a search warrant, Mr. Dietz. I'd be happy to call in the sheriff to help me enforce it. His office is standing by."

Montgomery smiled to himself. The local sheriff didn't have a clue they were in his county. If he did, he'd have jumped at the chance to order them out of his jurisdiction pronto. Corey hadn't followed or even considered protocol.

"You want to show us your gun collection, Mr. Dietz?" Montgomery asked.

"What makes you think I collect guns?"

"Just a hunch, sir."

Dietz hesitated, then led them into his living room where a pride of cats scattered away. Along one wall a polished oak gun rack held four rifles and three shotguns—the only organized place in the house. Two of the rifles were .30/.30 caliber, one a Winchester and the other a Smith & Wesson. After a quick survey of other rooms, Corey asked to see the shed behind the house.

"Nothing out there but tools," Dietz replied. "Besides, I got a doctor appointment in town." He snatched a cheap watch out of his pocket and checked the time. "I'm gonna be late."

Cough.

"Now I don't mind if you gentlemen want to come back later. You can do all the questioning you want then. For now, I'm right sorry—"

"I don't give a damn about your doctor appointment," Corey snapped. "We're going to search your shed. Understand me?"

He glowered back at Corey, uncertain how to react, then moseyed to the kitchen sink and spat into it. Wiping at his chin, he led the way out of the house while lighting up another cigarette.

Montgomery struggled with the knob on the shed door.

"It's locked," Dietz said between puffs. "Don't know where the key might be."

"Not a problem," Corey replied. "Got an axe in the back of my pickup. Comes in handy at times like this."

"Hold on." While the cigarette clung to the side of his mouth, Dietz dug out a ring of assorted keys from his pocket. As if by magic, he found the right key and managed to open the door. "I hope this don't take long. Hate to keep the doctor waitin'."

The odor of mold and grease spewed from the dark interior of the shed. Rusted hand tools, decades old, hung from the walls. Some lay on the workbenches among used cans of paint and solvents.

"You got any light in this place?" Corey asked.

"Nope. Don't come 'round here much."

Montgomery discovered it first. He nudged Corey and pointed to the animal hide nailed to the far wall.

Corey strolled to it, scratching at his neck as he walked. "Where did this come from?"

"Oh, that piece of rubbish? Bought it at a flea market down at Cooke City. Long time ago. Don't remember exactly when it was."

Corey leaned over the workbench to inspect the head of what was once a beautiful wolf. He stroked the soft fur as if petting a newborn puppy and caressed the snout as he fingered the sharp incisors, gently pressing his forehead against the hide.

Dietz coughed. "Didn't pay that much for it, I think it was—"

"Why did you have to shoot it?" Corey asked, almost a whisper.

Montgomery stepped toward Corey.

"I didn't shoot nothing. Hell—"

Before Montgomery could get between them, Corey grabbed Dietz's ragged shirt collar with both hands and rolled his fingers into tight fists. "Don't try to tell me you didn't shoot my wolf, you Godforsaken son-of-a-bitch!"

Montgomery reached out for Corey's arm, but too late. Corey rammed the lower back of the startled man against the jagged edge of the workbench.

Montgomery struggled to get both arms around Corey's shoulders.

Corey snatched Dietz around the neck and squeezed until Montgomery jerked him away.

Turning scarlet and then purple, Dietz bent over and coughed. "My back!" he squealed.

"Okay, Mr. Dietz," Montgomery said. "We're taking in this hide and two of your rifles. Even just having a wolf hide in your possession is a crime. You should know that."

"My back is broken!" Dietz rubbed his tailbone with the palm of one hand, groaning.

Corey picked up a hammer with a narrow claw and slammed it down on the workbench. "Tell it to the judge." He continued to pound the hammer as if playing a drum, a funeral tempo. "On the other hand, I can explain to him how difficult it is to wrestle with a suspect who's swinging one of these at me."

Dietz took deep rhythmic breaths and glared back at him.

Corey continued to hammer. Dietz stood erect and stumbled for the door, shaking his head, no doubt with a newfound respect for the law.

After packing up the wolf hide and rifles, Corey and Montgomery backed out of the driveway with the evidence under a tarp in the truck bed. Nathan Dietz watched the departure, crouching on the ground by the porch and puffing on a cigarette with one hand while the other crept down the rear of his trousers massaging his lower back.

As they drove back to headquarters, Montgomery couldn't help but notice the sassy grin his boss flashed from time to time.

"You don't think he'll try to file a complaint on us, do you?" Montgomery asked.

"Complaint for what?"

"I don't know, maybe about getting a little roughed up?"

"If I had wanted to rough him up, he'd be out cold right now. But I don't really care if he does try to complain. His word against ours. Who's going to believe a word that crosses that bastard's lips?"

Montgomery nodded and pretended to smile. "By the way, has the superintendent been around lately?"

"Thank God, no. McFarland neither."

That wasn't a good sign, Montgomery thought. Having neither the Park's superintendent or his deputy Greta McFarland checking in with Corey was a bad omen. One or both of them should be keeping up with the progress on Operation Wolfstock. They should be finding out directly from the Chief Park Ranger's mouth what he's hearing from the locals, what he's finding out on the road. With them not staying in contact on a regular basis with Corey suggested that there could be plenty going on that Corey wasn't aware of. It was likely they were intentionally leaving Corey out of the loop. Isolating him because they had other ways of getting info, other plans. Montgomery could get trapped in the middle. He wasn't about to put up with that along with the constant agony of keeping Corey out of trouble, a thankless task. It was all beginning to weigh on him. More and more he was wondering whether it was worth it.

"It seems our problems around the western border are growing," Montgomery said.

Corey sighed and stared at the passing scenery. "You mean Colter?"

"Especially there. Just wondering if the superintendent's doing anything about it."

"Gilmer's been on top of it from the day the body on the Madison was found."

What? "But I thought you weren't going to brief him."

"He got wind of it quick enough. That same day he called the forensics lab in Ashland. They flew in that evening."

"He called the wildlife lab in Oregon? The fed investigators?"

Corey stared back at him. "That's what I said."

Montgomery couldn't believe what he was hearing. The Superintendent had suspected wolves in the death of the photographer from the get-go?

"They've had a team snooping around for days," Corey added. "We're going to meet with them tomorrow. Behind closed doors at Lamar Valley."

"Shouldn't I be there?"

"Thought I told you about it."

Corey had never breathed a word to him about such a meeting.

"In any case," Corey said, "you'd better be there—just keep quiet about it."

"What about that dead photographer?" Montgomery asked. "Have you heard anything from the autopsy?"

"Nobody's filled me in yet."

"What will we do when word gets out?"

Corey twisted his head around to face him. "Who said word's going to get out?"

"For one, that new vet in town . . . Harmon," Montgomery said. "I'm sure he's asking questions."

"Don't worry about Dr. Harmon. He's being dealt with."

SEVENTEEN

Dieter picked up his pace. He'd never told Amy to keep his children out of the water, but he assumed she had enough common sense to ask him before taking them swimming anywhere. He jogged away from his parked truck along the path toward the Little Bears' home, an elaborate hand-hewn log house that overlooked Hebgen Lake.

When Michael and Megan saw their dad, they waved with an enthusiasm that he hadn't seen in them for a very long time. Amy stood waist high in the clear lake water. From her puzzled stare, he knew she sensed his mood.

Rusty was running into and out of the shallow water, splashing and chasing a stick Michael threw. When Megan ran toward her dad, Dieter grabbed a beach towel from the grass. He wiped the water from her back as she laughed and shook her head to spray the water from her hair into his face. Michael remained planted in the water alongside Amy.

"Come here, Michael," Dieter called out without smiling.

Michael meandered toward him with his arms wrapped around his chest and shuddering from the breeze. Amy followed and picked up a towel to dry her long hair while ignoring Dieter.

He spoke without looking at her as he toweled off Michael. "You really should have asked me about taking them into the lake."

She tied a knot in the towel wrapped around her waist. "May I ask why?"

"I suppose I should've told you that they haven't had swimming lessons. We didn't have any opportunity for that in our old neighborhood in Pennsylvania."

"That's why I was giving them lessons."

"You want to see me go underwater, Dad?" Megan shouted, aiming for the lake and ready to run back into the water.

"No, honey. You and Michael go on up to the house and change into dry clothes."

Both scrambled away as Rusty barked but stayed by Dieter's side. As soon as they were out of earshot, Amy spoke. "Let's face it, I haven't worked out very well for you this summer, have I?"

"Of course, you have . . . don't be silly. You're taking this way too seriously."

"But you want me take it seriously, don't you? That's why you made a scene. Once again, I've stepped out of bounds. This time I've even placed your kids in danger. Correct?"

I'm not going to get into that right now. "My children are all I have in this world, Amy. They're everything to me."

She stared back at him, a hard expression he'd never seen from her.

"Look," he said. "Maybe I'm a little edgy today. I didn't mean to be so abrupt."

He held out an open palm and she gave it a half-hearted slap and matching smile. "Okay, let's forget about it, Dieter. Dad's preparing a feast for all of us this afternoon." She turned and started for the house.

"Wait."

She stopped and looked back.

"I haven't had a chance to tell you what happened to me."

"What happened when?"

"After you brought the kids up here, I was out running around and stopped at the Madison. Hiked upstream and found a body."

"A *body*?"

"A dead hiker. I called the sheriff's office and they sent out a deputy."

She sat down in the grass and folded her legs in front of her. "My God, Dieter. You're not talking a murder, are you?"

"I don't really know. They're going to do an autopsy."

"A murder's unheard of around here. Please tell me you weren't waiting for me to find out about it on TV?"

"I should have called you, Amy. I'm sorry again. But there's one more thing you should know."

She cocked her head to one side.

"I'm considered a suspect."

"A *suspect*?" Her lower jaw hung on the word.

He quickly explained that since he'd discovered the body and there was no other obvious evidence, anyone who found it would be a suspect—standard operating procedure. He'd get it all straightened out with the sheriff's office. But the longer he talked the more he realized she wasn't listening to his words. Her eyes were bouncing around trying to grapple with the crazy thought that she was providing nanny services to a killer. The more he talked the more defensive he sounded to himself. He was babbling, trying to sound innocent. Hell, he was innocent.

"You do believe me, don't you?" he finally asked.

She shot him that look of *come on now!* "That's a silly question and you know it. Of course I believe you. I just can't imagine how they even considered—"

"Please, Amy. Forget about this, too, for now. Forget about *all* of this. Maybe I just wanted you to understand why I'm a little rattled today."

She agreed to keep his plight to herself. After reminding him of the planned visit to the powwow that evening, she stood and walked back toward the house while Dieter stayed behind. Rusty rushed to Dieter's side with a wagging tail and a stick between his teeth. He stooped to put his arms around the dog's neck and rub his fur.

Amy was right; he shouldn't have been so angry about the kids in the lake. He had botched that miserably. Everything was moving too damn fast.

EIGHTEEN

Molly rested her arms on top of the split-rail fence and hitched her foot up onto the bottom log. It wasn't the welcome she'd expected. A padlocked chain snaked through the rusted gate at the Loudermilk ranch.

A sign nailed to a post seemed to shout:

Absolutely NO Trespassing

NO Soliciting

Katherine Belle Loudermilk had been apologetic again when she spoke on the phone the evening before. Her husband was never one for social grace, she'd said while Molly listened politely. Katherine Belle sounded genuine in the invitation for her to stop over at their ranch with measurements to discuss new window treatments and to look at fabrics. From everything Molly had heard, these women not only did good work, they were cheap. A winning combination.

After the Judge had reminded her, she did recall the hubbub when a reporter for Helena's *Independent Record* portrayed the Loudermilks as some kind of religious cult. That's the family's own business, the Judge said at the time, and the newspaper deserved to be sued.

"Now, you pay no never mind to those posted signs, my dear," Katherine Belle had said on the phone. "Joseph Vincent put them up just to keep busybodies away. I'll have the gate unlocked for you."

The only problem Molly faced at that moment was she'd forgotten whether Katherine Belle mentioned the morning or the afternoon. She was going to have to start taking notes whenever she made plans. Must be age, she thought, as she gripped the top of the fence and threw her rear end up on the rail to rest.

Buzzing grasshoppers soared among the tall weeds and overhead a red-tailed hawk circled against the clouds, searching for a meal. Maybe Katherine Belle meant for her to come in the afternoon. Or maybe she forgot to unlock the gate. Plenty of possibilities loomed. Maybe it was best just to walk up to the house and knock.

Brakes from a vehicle squealed behind her. A postman stuffed what looked like a catalog into the mailbox.

"Is this gate always chained?" she called out.

"I've never seen it open, lady," he replied before pulling away.

Katherine Belle wouldn't know what time she might arrive and probably wouldn't want to keep the gate open all day. Molly hopped down onto the private property. Under a glaring noonday sun and with her underarms feeling clammy like molasses, she ambled down the graveled road toward a distant farmhouse. More doubt seeped in as she walked, an uneasy feeling, one of sneaking up on the family. She might be pushing the situation a little too far. No damned doubt what the Judge would say if he was there.

A gabled roof rose above the trees. She stopped, uncertain what to do next. Twisting her head about, she spotted the pillars of the front porch. She meandered toward it and waved her arm high, hoping to see the door open and someone wave back.

A muffled noise arose from a clump of trees on the other side of the road. She turned to her left to locate the source. There was no sign of life from the house and a strange noise had erupted from among the trees. What else did she need to tell her that she wasn't supposed to be there? It was time to turn back. She had to keep her wits about her, had to use her better judgment at times like this.

Her old cousin curiosity shoved her into moving closer toward the source of the noise. She moved off the gravel and into the field grass so that her steps would be softer. A small shed appeared among the trees. The sound became more distinct.

An animal in distress?

She stopped to listen. Someone was weeping. She moseyed toward the weathered structure when there came the voices of a woman whimpering and a man grunting with labored breathing. Every few seconds there was the sound of a . . . *whip*? Something thrashing against a wall?

Creeping closer, she sneaked up to the shed and stooped to squeeze between two scrub bushes, wiggling into a twisted position to press her ear against the wooden siding.

A woman was humming a lullaby beneath the slashing sound of a whip, delivered in a haunting rhythm. The crack of a whip, the muffled cry of a girl, the grunt of a man, a woman chanting a lullaby.

What in the name of . . . ?

She cautiously rose up to the window. Through a thin layer of dirt and haze, a girl stripped of every stitch of clothing was bent over, clutching the back of a wooden chair. Her frail legs were spread-eagled, and her head and hair sagged down between her arms.

Straddling her from behind, with his coveralls and underwear dropped down to his ankles, was a tall man with a straw hat. He was shoving his member into the girl with a throbbing cadence, his eyes closed and his head tossed back in a trance, groaning with clenched teeth and saliva dribbling from a corner of his lips.

None other than Joseph Vincent Loudermilk grappled with one hand under the naked girl's belly, jerking her into his crotch as he pumped. In the other hand he brandished a willow branch that he used to strike the girl across her cream white back, now covered with welts and crimson streaks of blood that trickled down her rib cage. The girl cried out only meekly, sobbing between thrashes.

Katherine Belle sat on a chair beside her, humming a sweet lullaby that Molly vaguely remembered from her youth. A shallow ceramic bowl of rust-colored water rested in Katherine Belle's lap. She rubbed a coarse sponge over the young girl's back to soak up blood between pauses in the whacking of the willow branch.

The repulsive contradiction of humming and grunting and weeping and whacking were more than Molly could bear. She turned from the window and braced herself against the shed. Sliding down the side of it, she ignored the rotting planks scraping against her neck and the sting of a splinter embedded in the back of her scalp. Not until she looked up did she see the barrel of a shotgun aimed at her face.

Trying hard to make out the person behind the weapon, Molly shifted her head and squinted through the shrubbery. Whoever it was had every right to shoot an intruder.

"What you doing here, lady?" an angry voice shouted.

The shotgun that reached out for Molly's face didn't budge. Neither did Molly. She crouched, staring into the rays of sun reflecting off the steel barrel and desperately wanting to rub the back of her head where the splinter had lodged.

"Hey, lady! I'm talkin' to you."

Molly recognized one of Katherine Belle's daughters from the encounter in the general store. "I . . . I had an appointment with your mother."

"My mother?"

"With Katherine Belle. I assumed—"

"She don't make appointments, and she ain't my mother."

Molly dropped her hands and placed them on the ground, carefully pushing her weight upward. The long barrel of the shotgun tracked her like a coiled rattler. She rolled up onto her knees. "I was confused. I—"

"Why, Miss Schoonover! I didn't expect you this early." Carrying a towel and drying her hands, Katherine Belle rounded the corner. "Now put that gun away, Marilee!"

"Sorry, ma'am," Marilee said, her voice trailing off. She gingerly lowered the weapon to her side.

Katherine Belle turned to Molly. "Please come with me to the house." We can look at a fine batch of fabric samples I've collected for you. I was planning to spend some time with you this afternoon."

Molly wrapped her arms around her chest. "I apologize for coming over early. It was rude of me. I'll just go back home now."

Katherine Belle reached out to take her by the arm. "Don't be silly."

Molly recoiled. "No!"

Her shout startled the women.

"I should be going," Molly said.

Peering from around the corner, Joseph Vincent Loudermilk leaned against the shed. "I'd advise you, Miss, to pay closer mind to trespassing signs." He straightened up and walked toward Marilee, grabbed the shotgun and nestled it across his midriff.

Molly backed away without taking her eyes off the weapon.

"Be careful!" Katherine Belle yelled.

Molly tripped over a tree branch and fell hard to the ground. Unnerved, she jumped up and turned, then jogged down the graveled driveway without looking back.

NINETEEN

Dieter palmed a cold beer while he chatted about the miserably hot weather. He stood on the deck of the sprawling lake home as Mr. Little Bear prepared a barbeque of pork and glazed duck on the grill. Each side of the log home offered a grand view of either the water or the forest.

Amy often spoke of her Dad and family, who moved off the Blackfeet Reservation from upstate not long after she was born. Her dad was a guide and outfitter in the wilderness surrounding the lake, a lucrative job. An increasing number of outdoor sportsmen were coming to Montana from around the world to fish for wild trout or hunt for trophy elk, bear, bighorn sheep, and deer.

Mr. Little Bear's bronzed face had features chiseled by the harsh Montana seasons. While he tended the grill, a single-engine prop flew out over the lake and gave him reason to talk about the Cessna he proudly owned. Dieter was surprised when he mentioned Amy's talent as a pilot. She not only had a license to fly—Mr. Little Bear had given her lessons at age fifteen—even before she had a learner's permit for driving.

"So, it was you who found the body down on the Madison?" Mr. Little Bear casually asked.

Dieter walked to the corner of the deck to toss his empty bottle into the trash. Had Amy gotten to her dad so damned quickly? After promising him she'd keep it to herself? "You heard about it?"

"It's a small town. Entertainment is limited," Little Bear said. He brushed more sauce onto the meat. "Lots of crazies out in the wilderness. I can tell you that from my years of guiding. But I don't worry about those things too much whenever I'm out there." He leaned down and tugged on a trouser leg above his boot, revealing a pearl-handled pistol no bigger than a pack of cigarettes.

A steady afternoon breeze triggered a light chop on the lake's surface. Dieter's glance followed Michael and Megan as they scampered down to the edge of the water with Amy. The tails of her blouse dangled outside her jeans and her long sleeves rose above her elbows. She radiated youth and vitality. It was the first time he saw his kids laughing together since he and Fran played with them in their Bucks County backyard.

When he noticed Dieter's stare, Little Bear asked, "You know that Amy won't be with you much longer, don't you?"

"Our agreement was until the kids got settled in school," Dieter replied.

"Her heart is set on California. The Pacific coast has always enticed her, for some reason I can't figure out. That's where she's headed." He paused to turn the meat over with his spatula. "Unless of course she ends up marrying."

Dieter had to scramble. "She hasn't told me much about her interests."

"You have to give her a chance to talk. Lead into it gradually. Like her mother, she doesn't do much talking about herself. Prefers to listen and learn. She's a teacher when you come right down to it. Loves kids." His eyes beamed as he spoke. "I've tried to talk her into returning upstate to Browning where our people are. Living on land provided so . . . generously. The reservation needs teachers as skilled as she is."

Michael and Megan ran up the steps of the deck. Rusty followed on their heels and Amy tagged behind.

"I had a *great* time yesterday," Megan announced, trying to catch her breath as she spoke. "We gotta ride a lot. I got to gallop once!"

"Gallop?" Dieter asked, surprised.

"Now, I don't think you were galloping on Belzer," Mr. Little Bear said.

"Daddy, did you know that Indians can ride horses without a saddle?"

"I suppose Amy showed you how that's done?"

"Amy's not a real Indian, you know. But her daddy is!" She shoved a peppermint into her mouth and then spoke out of the side of her teeth. "I think her mom is, too." She ran down the steps and back into the yard, chasing Rusty.

Dieter grinned and turned to Mr. Little Bear. "That's a beautiful herd of horses you've collected out back."

"We love those animals. The Blackfeet early on took up horses as a way of life. It all began the day the Shoshone surprised them by riding on horseback into battle. Shooting as they rode!"

"I remember a few movies along those lines," Dieter quipped.

"Ahhh, those were the days," he said with a smile. "Everyone feared the Blackfeet—the Shoshone, the Sioux, the Nez Perce."

"I would guess that the government eventually put a stop to all of the rivalries?"

"Luckily, they didn't take away our horses, but they did put an end to our culture. Our real problems started with the Baker massacre on Two Medicine River. The government's never even acknowledged that happened, if you can believe that."

Dieter quickly sensed an extended story coming on, one that could wait for another time but one he felt he'd better learn about. He switched the subject to the powwow taking place on the outskirts of town. Thanks to Amy, both kids had been looking forward to it for days.

*　　*　　*

While Dieter strolled that evening amid the hubbub of the powwow he picked up the sweet scent of fry bread. The thumping of drums intensified above a background of singing that seemed like a chant. The annual powwow brought in Indians from the nations and tribes in the tri-state region. Everywhere signs of the original inhabitants of the land popped up—teepees painted with images of bison, bear, wolf, deer, lightning bolts, and symbols depicting the circle of life and death.

Amy placed an arm on Michael's shoulder. "Listen carefully to the rhythm of the drum. That beating comes from the heart of the people. It has magical powers."

Michael's eyes opened wide with the thrill of youth encountering the bizarre. When they reached the drummers sitting in a tight circle, other Indians in full regalia were dancing about as they pounded the earth and spun about in their beaded buckskin moccasins, singing as if in a trance. Bustles and breastplates flashed in the sunlight, each dancing warrior wearing a headdress of feathers that distinguished him apart from the others.

Amy led the way as they weaved through the crowd. Vendors were scattered about selling buckskin jackets with a rainbow of loom beadwork or funnel cakes sprinkled with powdered sugar. Michael's eyes flitted among the curious sites, then stopped and pointed. "Dad, look!" A group of Boy Scouts surrounded one of the long tables. Michael tugged on Dieter's hand and pulled him toward it.

Boys and adults stood chatting in khaki uniforms. Golden scarves decorated their necks and shoulders and patches and badges adorned their chests. The babbling paused as their collective eyes caught sight of Amy.

Dieter recognized the scoutmaster from Colter. In his fifties, Leonard Farmington sported a salt and pepper beard on a round plump face. "Hello there, Michael!" Farmington cheered. "Fancy running into you all the way out here. Will we see you next Monday at our troop meeting?" He shot a big grin toward Dieter and Amy.

"Yes, sir," Michael replied.

"And you haven't forgotten about the tri-state Camporee next weekend, have you? It's in Yellowstone, you know."

Michael glanced up at his dad.

"We have more information packets," Farmington said. "They're here on the table if you need one." He reached over and grabbed a large manila envelope, then turned around and handed it to Amy as he looked at Michael. "Here's some info for your mother."

"Oh, no, I'm not his mother, Mr. Farmington. Just his nanny."

"Sorry, my mistake, Miss."

"Will there be archery and hiking?" Michael asked.

"You bet. We're having an overnight hike and a canoeing adventure, too. Permission slips for both are in the packet. Your timing was perfect in moving to Colter, young man!"

No doubt that was coming, but Dieter knew better than to allow a boy of ten to go canoeing on high country lakes or hiking the wilderness no matter how well chaperoned. When they left the booth, he bent down to Michael. "You'll have to wait at least until next year before taking part in big events like those."

Michael's head immediately drooped.

"You know, Dad," Amy tossed in, "there'll be boys around Michael's age attending. The Yellowstone Camporee every year is a rite of passage for all the boys in Colter."

Thanks a lot, Dieter thought. Once again Amy had butted in where she should've stayed away. He understood what she was saying. He also wanted his son to meet other boys and learn about the outdoors. He was a boy once, for God's sake. There would be plenty of opportunities for all of that when Michael started school on Monday and attended his first Scout meeting after school. He'd meet boys his own age with a slew of interests.

Fran had wanted Michael to go to science camp that summer. She'd already put down a deposit to hold a place for him at Cold Springs Harbor. They couldn't afford it, but Fran thought it a terrific investment for the boy's future. She hauled around both kids to movies, children's concerts, museums; Megan to ballet and tap-dance lessons; Michael to karate and gymnastic classes. On the other hand, what Dieter wanted for his children wasn't found indoors but in the open air, the fields and mountains and streams. What he wanted for them surrounded him outside the walls of the school at the moment. That was the main reason for the decision to move to Big Sky country. But he wasn't about to have his kids dive head-on into the vast opportunities available. At least not yet.

Doing his best to smile, Dieter looked down at his son. "Let's get this straight now, Michael. Overnight hiking and canoeing will have to wait until you're a little older. But of course you can go to the Camporee." The thought popped out in words before Dieter had a chance to weigh them, the words saying one thing, his gut screaming another.

TWENTY

The following morning Dieter parked his pickup at the curb in front of Campanula Creek Elementary, twenty minutes before school was scheduled to start. When he strolled with Michael and Megan up the concrete steps to the entrance, he glanced over his shoulder. A patrol car had pulled in behind his truck. A lone lawman sat behind the wheel with his engine off. It was good to know that the guy was there to keep a watchful eye, especially the first day. After entering, they began the long walk down the hallway lined with army-green lockers on either side. Dieter felt inadequate and out of place. Fran had always taken Michael to school on the first day.

The principal made her way through the shuffling throng of kids and greeted them with an obligatory smile but displayed an extra dose of warmth on learning they hailed all the way from Pennsylvania. By Michael's request, Dieter didn't follow him to his class. It was humiliation enough to be seen in the hallway with Dad and little sister. Fran had often confided in him her fears that shy Michael might be bullied by older boys.

As Dieter led Megan by the hand to her classroom he realized that neither he nor Fran had ever worried about Megan. He smiled thinking of his daughter's enthusiasm for this long-awaited day. She always managed to take charge of any situation, charming everyone around her. He kissed her goodbye at the classroom door and she gave him an anguished hug.

Mrs. Stevenson spoke above all the clatter and bawling inside the room to reassure Megan that she was going to have a great time in first grade.

"But why are so many crying?" Megan asked. The young teacher took her hand and led her quickly inside.

*   *   *

Gallatin County Office of the Sheriff.

Dieter spotted those words on the side of the patrol car when he exited the school. It was still parked behind his truck, the lawman still sitting behind the steering wheel. His nervous system kicked into high gear. He could only think worst case—the incident at the Loudermilk ranch. If there were anything that could destroy his career, it was that. The whole affair had lurked in the back of his mind and the pit of his stomach from the minute he pulled out of the gate at the ranch and saw the threat on the oldest woman's face. Old man Loudermilk had called the law. The hit on him by the youngest woman when he delivered the colt at the ranch would be impossible to defend, just his word against that of the whole family. Everyone in town would assume that where there's smoke, there's fire and all that crap.

He kept his head down and focused on the door of his truck as he unlocked it. When he switched on the ignition there was a tap on the passenger window and he lowered it. The uniformed officer asked if they could talk.

The lawman, who looked surprisingly young, took off his hat and slid in. He introduced himself as Deputy Preston Cody. His voice had a familiar ring, but Dieter couldn't quite put a finger on it.

"I wonder if I might ask you a few questions, Dr. Harmon?"

Dieter swallowed hard. "Of course. Not a problem."

"Did you by chance visit the Winslow Memorial Funeral Home recently?"

Jesus! Not that. No one could have seen them. Although he and Josh might have *technically* broken in, they didn't harm anyone, didn't steal or destroy anything. He had to keep his cool with the questions. This wasn't the worst thing that could've come up and he should count himself lucky.

"No, I didn't, sir." He wondered how much training the young deputy had in lie-spotting.

"Were you in town on Friday evening?"

Dieter pretended to think about the question for a moment. "As a matter of fact, yes."

"Were you alone?"

He could feel the stress in his neck and knew he couldn't hide the tension in the muscles of his face. "Yes, I was."

"What if I told you, sir, that someone saw a person matching your description in the vicinity of the funeral home? After hours on Friday night."

That's a hypothetical. The deputy wasn't saying someone *did* see him, he was just testing him and he didn't have to answer that. On the other hand, if he hesitated too long, that would arouse suspicion, the last thing he needed right now. "I suppose I did stop in the parking lot."

"You *suppose* you stopped in the parking lot?"

Dieter looked out the window and back at the deputy. He was screwing up fast. "I mean, yes. I stopped at the parking lot." If he were wired to a lie detector, it would all be over. He'd be locked up.

"You stopped there, but you didn't go inside?" the deputy asked.

"It was closed. Why would I go in?"

"If you don't mind, I'll ask the questions. Is that all right with you?"

"Yes sir, it is." He wondered if the deputy could see his heart pumping through his checkered shirt.

"Why would you stop at a funeral home after closing hours? Long after closing hours, as a matter of fact?"

"I was driving through town when I heard a noise from the engine. I decided to check it out."

The deputy didn't respond, but mulled over his answer. That was good—it was an outstanding answer.

"Did something happen at the funeral home?" Dieter asked.

The deputy raised his eyebrows. "Do you think something happened?"

Dieter had fallen for it. He saw the setup coming from a mile away and still fell for it. "I have no idea, sir."

The deputy reached into his shirt pocket and pulled out a business card.

"Have you seen this before, Dr. Harmon?"

The card had an unrecognizable logo, but beneath it were the words *Gallatin County Weekly*. He read in the center of the card: *Claire F. Manning, Editor-in-Chief.*

The deputy grabbed the card from Dieter's grip. "Unfortunately, that particular card was smudged up so much that we couldn't get any good fingerprints from it." He gave him a look of *you're lucky on that one* and then continued. "I talked with Mrs. Manning. She said she hasn't been in the funeral home for a year. I forget who she told me died, but he was a close friend of the newspaper's."

"I'm sorry, but I'm not following you."

"I figure most people are like me," the deputy replied. "If someone gives me a business card, I generally carry it around for a day or two and then either toss it away or store it in my wallet. She said the last card she remembered giving out was to you on Friday morning."

"That may be true, but—"

"Would you happen to have that card on you, Dr. Harmon?"

He pulled out his wallet and flipped through the bills and cards and junk pieces of paper. Then he shoved a hand into each pocket, fishing for anything that felt like a card. "I must have thrown it away. I didn't have a reason to hang onto it. But I don't understand what this has to do with me."

"Well, here's how I figure it. If you were the only one she gave it out to recently, you would be the only one to have it on him—like in a convenient pocket. Mr. Winslow found the card laying smack in the middle of a hallway on Saturday. That was after I told him I checked out his place the night before. Someone said they saw very suspicious activity around the funeral home and called the sheriff's office. Could be drug activity or something like that, they thought."

"You don't think I was there and somehow just dropped the card on the floor?"

"I'm just trying to put it all together, Dr. Harmon. Don't know how else it would get there."

Didn't you search the place? You didn't find me, did you? "I don't understand why you thought I would have any reason to be there?"

"You were the one who discovered the body on the Madison. Do I have that right?"

Dieter nodded.

"Although the county sheriff doesn't consider you a suspect, we have been alerted that you are a person of interest." He paused and shifted to a more serious level of concern. "You do understand that, don't you, Dr. Harmon?"

"I wasn't told that specifically."

"I'm telling you now. It turns out that the body was at Winslow's funeral home on Friday night, waiting on the county medical examiner to come down from Bozeman on Saturday. We know someone was there. The sheet over the body was messed with."

You did that before you ran out of the room!

"You can see that for you to be the only one to locate the body from a crime that we don't yet have a suspect for, and then, lo and behold, to find evidence you *somehow* made your way into the very place where the body was stored . . . well, you see where I'm coming from."

The deputy didn't have any evidence. He was trying to mark time, to get him to admit to the crime, to throw up his hands and say *I did it. Lock me up!*

The deputy continued. "And you made your way there on the only night the body happened to be there. It all smacks of too much coincidence."

Dieter's head was spinning. By now, the medical examiner must have concluded exactly what he and Josh had found. When was he going to report to the sheriff and get him off the hook?

The deputy reached for the handle on the passenger door. "I take it you'll be staying in town for the next few weeks?"

"I really don't have any other plans."

"Good. I was told to ask you to make certain of that. Now you have a good day, Dr. Harmon."

TWENTY-ONE

Molly slept past seven for the first time in years. The Judge thought she was sick from something she'd eaten because of her trips to the bathroom during the night. She hadn't yet shared with him the trauma she'd witnessed at the Loudermilk place, much less even mention the shotgun held to her head. He would have hitched a ride there and waited with a pistol for the old man to drive out of the gate.

What disturbed her most was her guilt. She saw what had happened in the shed and hadn't said or done anything about it. Not yet anyway.

Toby and Big Mac barked from the yard. Molly walked to the front door, holding her ribcage, still sore from the heaving during the night. She gasped. The sight that met her blood-shot eyes had to be a mirage.

Katherine Belle and Marilee Loudermilk stood in the doorway. The two women who'd taken part in the most violent act of crime she'd ever witnessed stood before her looking as innocent as Sunday School teachers. How could such despicable women now show up at her door? They should've left town by now. She should call the local police or the Gallatin County Sheriff and do it quickly.

But what would the law do? Where was her evidence? She was the one who had trespassed on someone else's property. She knew what a jury of her peers in the Gallatin County would say to that.

The yapping of Toby and Big Mac brought the Judge wheeling into the room.

"Just visitors," she said softly. "I'll handle it." She flicked her wrist for him to scat. He didn't need to hear what they would be talking about and especially what she had to say.

When she opened the door, Katherine Belle looked her straight in the eye and spoke. "I know what you must think of us, Miss Schoonover."

No, you don't. Otherwise you'd both be running for your friggin' lives back down the steps. "I take it you don't have visitors at your ranch very often?" Molly asked. Without waiting on an answer she invited the two women in, motioned for them to take a seat in the living room, and quickly excused herself to prepare fresh coffee over their mild protest. She didn't give a damn what they thought or what they wanted or didn't want. Maybe they were nervous that she might be going after her shotgun. They were on her property now and she would make up the rules as she went along. In truth, she needed time to cogitate how to best deal with the sudden turn of events.

After a few minutes she returned and poured steaming coffee for each into fine china cups on a silver tray etched around the border with a soft floral design. She sipped her beverage slowly. They left theirs untouched and sat stiffly, avoiding placing their backs against the chairs as if needles might be poking through the fabric. Both wore dresses of pastel blue reaching to their ankles and wrists; their look, a plain vanilla quality, a disturbing cardboard veneer.

Molly spoke first. "Could you give me one good reason why I shouldn't call the sheriff on the both of you right now?"

The Loudermilks remained as rigid as the log fence at their ranch and glanced at each other. Katherine Belle then leaned forward. "We were afraid you may call on the law. So, we thought it best to call on you." Her voice had a pleasant timbre, close to a southern drawl. "We were hoping that maybe we could chat and explain some things about us."

"We know people talk," Marilee said with a voice that grated like rusty hinges on a gate. "We try to be good neighbors by offering our services from time to time." *Fingernails on a chalkboard.*

"What the Judge and I have heard about you and your family is rather hard to believe," Molly said. "Some people say that . . . I'm not exactly sure how to best put it."

"That we're a polygamist clan?" Katherine Belle blurted. "Miss Schoonover, may I speak in confidence?"

Molly's fingers played with her flushed neckline as Katherine Belle told her story. She spoke in an evangelical cadence, as if reading from a script. Her chin high and her back arched, she spoke of growing up in southern Utah, the oldest daughter among fourteen children. A domineering father had taken five "sister wives." She left public school at age twelve. By age thirteen, she cooked for her entire family and became a midwife for the deliveries of the rest of her siblings.

When she was fifteen, her father arranged her marriage to Joseph Vincent Loudermilk. His grandmother was Elizabeth Jennings Owen, a member of the well-known and respected Owen clan of polygamists from Utah. She knew Joseph Vincent, who was a bishop in the local Fundamentalist Church. But she didn't know he would be her husband until her wedding day. All she remembered about that day and night was the time she spent crying. Everyone thought her tears were tears of joy.

Molly sat spellbound. "Are you Mormons?"

"Heavens, no! The Mormons are the Latter Day Saints," Katherine Belle replied. "But we belong to the Fundamentalist LDS Church. The Mormon Church was founded by Joseph Smith. He surrendered his beliefs to man."

She called their lifestyle the Celestial Principle, a divine tenet handed down from God. "We believe plural marriage is a protected freedom. The laws of man can't prohibit that. It would violate our constitutional right and our freedom of religion. Our lives are dictated by a higher authority, Miss Schoonover."

Interesting term, Molly thought. Plural marriage. Sounded innocent, like a plural noun. "So how did you and your family get here?"

Katherine Belle said they lived in Colorado, in a town called Short Creek. After a year of their marriage, Joseph Vincent fell out with the church elders and decided to leave the church and move away. Far away. Montana was their first and only stop.

After a month they met Marilee. At first, she just wanted to make extra money by helping out with the farm chores and their six children. "But it wasn't long," Katherine Belle said, "before God chose Marilee to be Joseph Vincent's second wife." She placed her hand on Marilee's arm.

"And you didn't have a problem with that?" Molly asked.

"I certainly did not. The Lord visited Joseph Vincent in a dream and revealed His desire."

"But . . . it's against the law," Molly said, realizing immediately how silly the comment was.

"Against the law only in the eyes of man," Katherine Belle replied. "I am Joseph Vincent's wife of record in the court of law. Marilee is his wife also but only in the eyes of the Lord. That's what matters, isn't it?"

Molly shifted her weight. She wanted to be careful how to select her words. "And what about your other sister-wife?"

"Joseph Vincent found Charlene hitchhiking on the highway two years ago," said Katherine Belle. "She was running away from her family in Rigby with a newborn son in her arms. She needed a caring family so desperately. After a few months, we realized God sent Charlene to us."

"Joseph Vincent had another dream?"

"No," Katherine Belle said. She looked perturbed by the sassy nature of the question. "The Lord spoke to me one evening and He—"

"It was *your* idea that your husband take another wife?"

"I would give full credit to the Lord. Joseph Vincent hesitated at first to accept the notion."

I bet he did, Molly thought. His pecker was probably so hard he could've driven it through sheetrock. "But why in the world would Marilee or Charlene marry a man who already had a wife?"

"I had no other prospects!" Marilee said. "What's a woman to do? Stay single all her life?" She spat out *single* with a hiss.

"What would be so terribly wrong if you're a single woman?"

"Cause a single woman cain't enter the Kingdom of God. When Jesus returns to earth the man introduces his wives to Him."

"We are sisters in the Lord," Katherine Belle interrupted. "All of us belong to Joseph Vincent Loudermilk."

Molly took a gulp of coffee then positioned the cup and saucer on the edge of the side table. While the women waited on her to respond, she smoothed out the doily beneath the saucer. "Don't you really mean the three of you share one penis?"

Marilee brought her hands to her cheeks and Katherine Belle raised her eyebrows.

"I presume," Molly continued, "that Charlene is taking care of all the children today?"

"Charlene is gone," Katherine Belle replied, after collecting herself. "We are concerned, of course, but she has done this before."

"What about her son?"

"You mean her children."

"She had another child by your husband?"

"A beautiful daughter," Katherine Belle said. "Only five months old now."

Marilee spoke up. "And that's not—"

She tried to hide the hand she pressed against Marilee's knee. "You should know something," Katherine Belle said. "It angers us that Charlene leaves her very own children behind on these excursions of hers."

"But we take care of them," Marilee chimed in again, "like they was our own."

"We take care of all Joseph Vincent's children," Katherine Belle added. "From whatever womb they may have emerged."

Molly gritted her teeth with each rehearsed word that spewed from Katherine Belle's mouth. This woman, her black hair with streaks of gray piled high in such a perfect pompadour, was nothing but a flimsy shell surrounding a rotten yolk. So decayed, so foul with brainwashing by her parents, her husband, and her church. She speaks with such eloquence, so confident in herself, her credo, her lifestyle. This woman actually believes all the bullshit she tries to force-feed others with a silver fork from a bone china platter.

One step at a time. "Why do you think Charlene runs away?" Molly asked.

"She's different," Katherine Belle replied. "The dear girl struggles with her inner soul. Joseph Vincent often counsels her in private. Reads to her from the scriptures. At times he has to punish her, severely I am afraid." She looked up sharply at Molly. "And in ways others may think harsh."

"Satan tries hard to win our souls, Miss Schoonover," Marilee added. "If Charlene doesn't return this time, Joseph Vincent says we must pray for her—"

The hand grabbed Marilee's knee again.

"Pray for her blood atonement?" Molly asked.

"Joseph Vincent warned her before this," Katherine Belle said.

Molly leaned back in her chair. "Do you think being raped had anything to do with her leaving?"

Katherine Belle reared her head back as she slowly drew in air. Marilee's pale frightened face darted back and forth between her sister-wife and Molly, as if wondering who was going to throw the first punch.

Helluva time to be without your shotgun, isn't it, Marilee?

After Katherine Belle gathered herself again, she spoke. "I'm sorry, I don't understand your question, Miss Schoonover."

Molly didn't flinch. "Yesterday, when Marilee caught me snooping through the shed window, I witnessed a beating and rape. I assume the victim was Charlene who was being raped by a man old enough to be her grandfather."

Katherine Belle's face flushed.

"And it sure looked a lot like you," Molly said, "helping the scoundrel and humming as if this was just another sorry day at the ranch."

The women jumped up from their chairs and grabbed their purses.

"And you think that condoning the rape of an innocent girl who couldn't be a day older than fifteen is supposed to be blessed by God?"

They charged for the door. Marilee wrestled with the doorknob before rushing out past the Judge sitting on the front porch. Both women tried to avoid Toby and Big Mac, but the dogs chased the women, licking at their ankles.

Molly leaned into the threshold with her arms folded and a sneer across her face.

The Judge held steady as he watched them speed away in their truck. "Does this have anything to do," he asked, "with why you've been on another p-planet today?"

"It's a long story. But I'm planning to change the ending to this one."

TWENTY-TWO

"They're onto us, Josh." Dieter held the phone close to his ear and spoke softly.

"What do you mean?" Josh asked.

"When I took the kids to school this morning I was surprised by a Gallatin County deputy. He said that they got a phone call Friday night about suspicious activity around the funeral home. He asked me questions. Lots of questions. It was the same guy who almost caught us red-handed."

"How you know that?"

"The way he talked about what he saw. I made a stupid mistake, Josh. I dropped Claire Manning's business card on the floor when we were there. He tracked her down and learned that we had recently met. That along with knowing I found the body on the Madison. He was trying to put it all together."

"What did he want from you?"

"He told me to stay around home and said I was a person of interest. I would've stopped by your place, but truthfully, somebody may be following me. I didn't want to give any impression that we're in cahoots."

"Lay low, partner. I'll be in touch if and when any of 'em stops by here."

* * *

Thank God, Molly thought, that she didn't have to drive all the way to Bozeman. The Gallatin County Sheriff's Office was headquartered there, eighty miles to the north. But there were deputies' offices spread throughout the county and fortunately one was located in Colter. Although close to sundown, she knew Deputy Sheriff Harlan Ward worked late most days and hoped that he wasn't out and about somewhere around town, struttin' with his badge and combed Stetson hat.

Harlan Ward had a visitor when she arrived. Preston Cody, the only patrolman who worked for Ward, invited her to sit while she waited. She'd known Preston since Margie and Allen Cody brought him home from Deaconess Hospital two days after his birth. She remembered it because Margie always talked about how they had to use instruments to take Little Preston out of the womb. Left him with ugly scars over his right eyebrow and under his left cheekbone. Whenever she saw Preston she always paid careful attention to his face, looking for any sign of a remaining scar.

She tried to hide her surprise when Deputy Ward's office door opened and Ranger Jack Corey walked out. She didn't know what to say, but it didn't matter. He tipped his hat and strolled away without speaking.

Harlan Ward greeted her with a polite but reserved smile. "Come right on in, Molly." As he closed the door behind her, he asked, "You see that Bucky Lambert died?"

Bucky Lambert was a popular kid who played football at Lakeview High where she and Harlan went to school. Harlan and Bucky had graduated in 1976, but she never finished her senior year. Taking care of her dad after his stroke was a full-time job.

She took a seat in front of his desk and they proceeded to discuss the status of former classmates, like those who had died an untimely death, moved out-of-state, attained a parcel of land that equaled a kind of rancher's wealth, or performed some deed, good or bad, that got one of them in the newspapers.

"Does the chief park ranger visit you often?" she asked.

"Jack stops by occasionally. Sometimes we have to coordinate our duties with the Park. How's the Judge doing these days?"

"He sends his regards."

"We could use him back in the courtroom, you know."

"An awful lot of people would go along with that."

They both sat for a moment and nodded agreement with each other. "I don't have a lot of time, Molly. What's on your mind?"

"There's a girl missing, Harlan."

"Missing from where?"

"Colter."

"Nothing's turned up here," Harlan said.

"That's because I'm just reporting it now. Do you know the Loudermilks from down on Duck Creek?"

She told him everything that happened—witnessing the rape and the strange follow-up conversation with the two Loudermilk women in her living room.

"How come old man Loudermilk hasn't reported her missing?" he asked.

"That girl is just another piece of . . . property for the SOB."

He pushed back his chair and leaned on his desk. "Look, Molly. What a family chooses to do in the privacy of their own home is none of my business. And, frankly, yours neither."

"It's against the law, Harlan."

"Beating your wife is against the law, too, Molly. But there's nothing I can do if it's not reported by one of the victims. I need evidence. Or at least a court order to go after lawbreakers. Now you can check that out with the Judge."

"But the Loudermilks live and breathe among us. They're our neighbors. That poor girl could be—" She slumped back in her chair and closed her eyes.

Harlan was right. It was the damn world that was wrong.

"Remember the missing Sweet Grass County girl?" he asked.

She vaguely recalled the strange case. Harlan said that it began four years ago. The missing girl's face was posted everywhere in the tri-state region. In time, a local handy man reported to him that he caught a glimpse of the girl. Or at least someone who looked like her. It happened on the Loudermilk farm, right after he was hired to help the old man repair the roof of his barn.

At first, Harlan blew off the account and forgot about it. But an off-duty deputy from Madison County reported seeing a girl who resembled the one in the picture wandering near the highway. When he stopped to question her, she became suspicious and ran. He turned his truck around to follow as she disappeared across a field in the direction of the Loudermilk ranch. The deputy reported it to him, and the next day Harlan showed up at the Loudermilks with a search warrant that the Judge had signed.

He searched every square foot of the ranch for two hours. When he questioned old man Loudermilk, he claimed he knew nothing about the missing girl. The way the other family members responded to his questions, it was as if they had all rehearsed their stories before he arrived.

Except for one of the women.

He remembered asking if she ever saw anyone who looked like the girl in the picture he showed her. "She took one look at it and shouted back at me. *Stop!* Yelled at me like I was attacking her. Then she started doing the weirdest thing."

He paused and shook his head, as if he couldn't believe it himself. "She started pulling her hair out. Damnedest thing I ever saw."

"In heaven's name, what for?"

"Who the hell knows. Kept yanking her hair out one clump at a time."

"What eventually happened?"

"Nothing. The missing girl was never found. But I'll always remember the sight of that woman standing there, shaking and plucking her hair out by the roots."

"I hope for the love of God, Harlan, you'll look out for this other Loudermilk kid. Would hate to see her end up missing . . . or worse."

When Molly returned to her truck, she sat with her head mashed against the steering wheel and her arms clutching her stomach. She jerked up when someone walked up to the open window.

Deputy Preston Cody leaned down and said he really wasn't eavesdropping, but what with the thin walls in the old building and his boss' deep voice—"

"Are you trying to tell me something, Preston?"

"Does the woman you're looking for have long braided hair? Is she kind of on the skinny side?"

Molly nodded. "Yes. Both."

"It might interest you to know, Mrs. Schoonover, that I believe I saw the young lady around noon. She was eating lunch down at the Bar and Grille."

Molly switched on the ignition. "Thank you, Preston. Thank you very, very much. And you remind your mama that I told her you'd grow up to be a fine-looking man. Yes, siree. A fine looking man."

She gunned the engine and raced away.

TWENTY-THREE

Bantz Montgomery gawked at Dr. Matthew Wallace—rumored to be the country's foremost wildlife detective—as he opened a thin burgundy briefcase. His reputation as an investigator of animal attacks around the country was just shy of legendary.

Dr. Wallace's long bushy sideburns revealed a tinge of gray. He wore Wrangler jeans held up by a tattered leather belt with an oversized silver buckle with an engraving of an Aztec eagle. A veterinary pathologist, he served as Chief of Special Investigations with the National Fish and Wildlife Forensic Laboratory in Ashland, Oregon. For years the Lab had provided analytical services and crime scene investigations in support of wildlife-related crime. The lab's forensic specialists identify species from animal parts and make every possible attempt to match illegal wildlife activity with a victim, suspect and crime scene. Their goal: conviction in a court of law.

Montgomery had learned that what Corey told him earlier was spot on—Park Superintendent Gilmer had called Dr. Wallace on the day the photographer's body was found on the Madison. At that time the superintendent charged Wallace with flying to headquarters and going out into the field to determine what was going on. Not with just the photographer's death, but with the livestock kills as well.

The meeting convened that morning at the Park's Lamar Valley Conference Center, thirty miles from headquarters and near where the first wolves were released in Operation Wolfstock. Corey began the session by reminding everyone it was officially "Confidential Restricted" and would follow federal guidelines for classified discussions and reports.

Montgomery was stupefied. In all of his years at Yellowstone, he'd never been in a meeting like this. *Classified*? Some kind of *Top Secret* government meeting about wildlife? He'd received earlier a two-page memo about the other visitor at the table, Professor Ian Hornsby. It was evidently the superintendent's idea to bring in Hornsby and the professor's job was to advise on wildlife behavior. Hornsby was on the faculty at Cambridge University in England, and wolves were his specialty. Wearing an open-neck dress shirt under a navy-blue blazer, his commanding frame and British accent gave him a highbrow air that announced *expert*. According to the memo Montgomery read, the professor had just finished a project at Colorado State in Fort Collins. He agreed to postpone his return to England to be there for the meeting. The memo made it clear that the wildlife world knew Ian Hornsby for his pioneering research on the wolf in Wood Buffalo National Park of northern Alaska.

At the far end of the table sat Greta McFarland, the deputy park superintendent and the only African American working on headquarters staff. A petite woman with penetrating eyes that advertised a studious demeanor, she was also the only one who didn't wear a uniform. That was a habit that added to her aloofness, along with her preference for always taking her place at the far end of tables during meetings. She told the group that Superintendent Gilmer sent his apologies that he couldn't be there to hear from them directly. Montgomery knew that to be nothing but bullshit.

After the introductions, Dr. Matthew Wallace tossed a stack of eight-by-ten color photos onto the conference room table and began his spiel. The top photo showed the scene of the Arizona photographer's death with the body sprawled on the bank, half in the water and half on shore in a pool of blood. Wallace said that the Gallatin County Medical Examiner ruled that spine had been severed and that death was due to blood loss from the carotid artery. The fatal throat injury was the result of shredding and tearing . . . definitely not from a knife or sharp object.

The remaining photos in Dr. Wallace's cache were close-ups of livestock kills from farms and ranches along the western border of the Park. All of the pictures showed abrasions and lacerations about the head and neck. For three, blunt force injuries had apparently occurred because of severe shaking and twisting following the initial bite. The slain animals had a common characteristic—throats ripped open with no evidence of any victim serving as a meal for the attacker. Strange, Montgomery thought.

With a felt-tip pen Dr. Wallace highlighted areas on the photos where hide or fur showed bite marks. "We can get a decent idea of the attacking animal's identity from the shape of the bites," he said. "The arc of front teeth for all members of the dog family is deeply curved. Just like the obvious imprint on the carcass in this picture."

On one photograph with a dead calf he pointed to a spot near the open neck wound. "We saw this bite pattern on several victims. In five cases, we took caliper measurements of the distance between the tips of the long cuspids . . . the fangs, if you will. They were all approaching three inches."

"And if you're dealing with a member of the dog family," Professor Hornsby broke in, "it had to be one of unbelievable size."

Greta McFarland spoke up. "I wonder if we could cut to the chase. We're talking about Yellowstone wilderness. So isn't this a no-brainer? The park's known for its Grizzly population. Now we have wolves. It seems an open-and-shut case of one or the other."

"The Grizzly leaves unmistakable tracks and scat," Dr. Wallace replied. "And I've been told that only four grizzly killings occurred in Yellowstone the last twenty years."

"So that leaves wolves, right?" McFarland said. "I would guess they're attacking—for whatever reasons—anything that's easy picking, like sheep and cattle on ranches around the boundary. Maybe even someone who drifted alone into their territory. So, you capture the wolves and take them back to Canada. It seems our experiment with wolf restoration in Yellowstone didn't work out."

"Wait a minute, Greta," Corey broke in. His face was flushed. "Don't jump ahead so fast. We haven't determined yet that wolves are responsible for any of this."

Montgomery knew what his boss was thinking. *She couldn't recognize a wolf if it came up and bit her on the ass.* Corey was searching for the right words to respond to someone he considered an idiot.

"Miss McFarland," Wallace said, "in my twenty-six years in this business, I've never known an animal attacking with the kind of ferocity we see here."

"If I might make a point," Professor Hornsby said. "The wild dogs of the Serengeti can even be more ferocious than wolves. They've been known to disembowel prey on the run."

Corey glanced at Montgomery and rolled his eyes.

Dr. Wallace peered over the top of his rimless glasses and slid another photo across the table. "Here's a forepaw print. It was found fresh near the body of the photographer. For perspective, note the flashlight next to the track."

Professor Hornsby reached for the photograph and held it close to his nose, squinting. "My God," he muttered.

"That," Wallace said, "is a classic print for the North American gray wolf. But look closely at the paw print."

Corey sat slouched in his chair, both feet stretched out under the table. He tapped the fingertips of each hand together in front of his face. "How can you be sure those aren't cougar tracks?" he asked.

"Good question," Dr. Wallace replied. "The primary difference between cougar and wolf tracks are the claw marks. The cougar's print rarely shows any claws. Like all cats, they retract. But what strikes us about this track is that the paw is actually larger than my hand."

"I'm puzzled," interrupted Professor Hornsby. "The largest wolves in North America have paws half that size and they're males in the one hundred thirty pound range."

"No doubt about it," Wallace said, "these paw prints are the largest I've ever encountered by a long shot."

"But they suggest a wolf of perhaps—"

"More than two hundred pounds."

"I'm sorry," Hornsby said. "That's not possible." He sat back confidently in his chair.

"But that's not all we have, Professor," Wallace replied. "To back up our observations, we examined further the tracks near the photographer's body. The animal was on the run—attacking. We set white markers square in the middle of each track and measured the distances between them."

Dr. Wallace focused on those around the table, one by one, as he spoke. "We compared the stride measurements of this animal—we're confident now it's a wolf—with others in the data base. The wolf has to be at least six feet nine inches long, not counting the tail." He stopped, allowing the weight of his words to sink in.

Professor Hornsby wrinkled his brow. "I suppose if you have a wolf tipping the scales at two hundred pounds, approaching seven feet from head to flank makes sense. But the question I would ask is, how on God's green earth could a wolf get *that* big?"

"I believe the greater question," McFarland said, "is why would a lone wolf attack and kill a human. Everything I've learned tells me they don't do that. I can understand the livestock deaths, but even then, don't those attacks come from a pack?"

"Livestock kills usually take place in packs," Hornsby replied. "But not always. A stray sometimes leaves the pack on its own. Because the loner can't get meat from pack hunts, he has to provide for himself."

He bathed in the rapt attention. "To your second point, wolf attacks on people are rare, but they do happen. About a half a dozen have been confirmed in North America this century." He placed his eyeglasses and then his elbows on the table. "But most troublesome are the unofficial reports from India. In some of the rural areas, wolves have devoured children. They're three- to six-year-olds for the most part. Last year, reports listed over fifty kids attacked and killed in the Uttar-Pradesh region alone."

It was Wallace's turn to look skeptical. "We've seen no reports on that."

"The stories are anecdotal of course," Hornsby said. "But from what I can gather, the victims are considered feeble, either physically or mentally. Rejects by their parents, you might call them. The poor kids are taken out to the edge of the woods and abandoned. By the time wolves find them, identifiable body parts or clothing are all that remain."

McFarland shook her head. "Hard to believe a parent anywhere in the world would resort to that."

"There's another important point," Hornsby said. "The state soon provided subsidies to families with proof a wolf killed their child. They are handsome payments, eight hundred rupee per child. As you might imagine, the money has made the situation worse."

Silence.

"I wonder if we may return to my presentation?" Dr. Wallace asked.

"I have to admit," Hornsby said, "the evidence here does suggest a wolf attack. But it's too bad that no traces of tissue or body fluids were recovered from the attacking animal.

"As a matter of fact," Dr. Wallace replied, "We swabbed the skin around the photographer's throat wound for DNA analysis. We also had swabs available from six of the livestock kills. What we've learned so far has taken us by complete surprise. Shocking, really." He reached into his briefcase and pulled out a notebook and more photos.

TWENTY-FOUR

"You mean the wind can blow those big trees down?" Charlene Loudermilk said, teasing her new companion.

"Well, that's what it says in this guidebook. You can read about it right here." When the driver reached behind his seat to the floor, he steered off the shoulder of the road.

"I believe you!" Charlene cried out. She grabbed hold of the door handle and the Volkswagen jumped back onto the highway. She'd met him earlier at the Colter Bar and Grille while he sat alone at the table next to hers, eating breakfast and reading a paperback. Every now and then he stopped his chewing when he came to something interesting, it seemed. A passing comment led to chitchat—the weather, the town, the food. He was the bookish type with little round glasses and long straw-colored hair that stayed planted behind his ears except when he laughed. Then the bushy strands would shake loose and he'd rake them back again.

After he joined her at her table, she found out he was a student from Boston and on his first trip to the West. He said he always wanted to explore the Great American West. That's the words he used, like he was on a romantic journey in some faraway country. She reminded him it was only Montana.

He planned to take a trail that wasn't too tough of a hike according to the guidebook. He said it gave a warning about hiking, the dangers of the scorched trees from the fires of 1988. "Snags" the book called them. They could fall at any time, especially on windy days.

Like today.

She loved all that book-learning stuff. All her education came from home- schooling in Idaho, until she got pregnant the first time. She didn't learn much from her mother except how to wash, iron and read. She loved reading and used to slip into the Westminster College library in Rigby where she'd grab books and magazines off the shelves and sit and read like she belonged there. She'd watch for hours the rich kids study and talk and flirt like they didn't have a care in the world. No doubt they didn't.

Overnight hike in the Park? She'd love to. He was cute and smelled nice, not like regular men. She acted natural, didn't have to put on airs. She just let him talk about himself. Men liked doing that. They drove along Highway 191 looking for a trailhead at the western border of Yellowstone. She pointed ahead. "Can we stop right up there for a minute?"

The words didn't sound right. She wondered what he thought she wanted to do. He pulled into a small graveled parking area and she led the way to a ramshackle log fence surrounded by heavy thicket.

A sign on a post read: FIR RIDGE CEMETERY

They stood under an ancient pine that was wider at the trunk than she was tall. Weather-beaten headstones reared up from among the weeds. In one corner, cut and trimmed, were two graves. Instead of tombstones, perfectly placed rocks and baskets of wildflowers lined the plots.

He slipped an arm around her waist. She stiffened and stared straight ahead.

"Someone here you knew?" he asked.

"Just someone I never got a chance to." She brushed the hair from her face. "Let's go for a hike, slugger."

*   *   *

When the pair arrived at the Fawn Pass trailhead, he loaded the camping gear onto a metal frame to carry on his back. The freeze-dried meals and fruit were sealed tight in plastic bags, which he stuffed into his backpack. While he worked, he chatted on about bears and their keen sense of smell.

"Yeah, I know," she said. After thinking about it for a moment, she decided it best to leave it at that. Wouldn't be lady-like to make him think she knew more than he did about wild animals. Men don't like that.

He shifted the camping gear higher on his back and they set out toward the trail. She wore jeans and sneakers, a long-sleeved plaid shirt buttoned at the wrists and a gray cotton jersey tied at her waist. She could walk five miles without a hitch and told him she did so many times with her sisters. Her small backpack was stocked with snack food, a can of Mountain Dew, and some girl stuff purchased when they stopped at the Colter General Store. Out of the corner of his eye, he'd examined what she bought. Kind of sneaky of him.

They paused at the trailhead to read a yellow warning sign nailed to a post:

ATTENTION
Horn Hunters and Hikers
Grizzly Bears Are Active In This Area
MONTANA FISH, WILDLIFE AND PARKS

"You want to go on?" he asked.

"Sure. You're not 'fraid of Grizzlies, are you?"

"I wish I'd bought that pepper spray now."

"Oh, I don't think you need that. The last thing you'd wanna do is make a Grizzly mad at you." She winked. He didn't particularly get it, at least he didn't smile.

She wasn't good at reading minds, except of course for Joseph Vincent's wicked mind, but her new friend seemed to have something on his mind as they chatted. It was kind of weird, really, but kind of cute at the same time. Whenever he had a point to make, he'd furrow his brow and fix his glasses back on the bridge of his nose with his index finger, then clear his throat. It was some sort of automatic ritual, like stroking your chin while you think.

"Now I hope you don't mind, Charlene, but I need to ask you a personal question."

What was that supposed to mean?

"Are you having your period?"

She glared back at him, ready to snap off his head. Asking a lady a thing like that.

"I don't mean to be—"

"I know what you *mean*, mister."

"Bears have this real sharp sense . . ."

She turned and scurried away. All men were alike. She knew men. She knew men better than men knew men. He caught up with her eventually along the trail, but by then her anger had dwindled. Really wasn't anger, more like a little outburst to keep him on his toes. She let him get ahead of her, even though he was slow. A pup tent and sleeping bag were rolled up on top of his backpack. The sleeping bag made her a piddling nervous, but the thrill of it all was enough to keep her wet.

She finally passed him on the path as she strolled with a sense of freedom—the wilderness air, the summer colors. She pointed out the different flowers as they shuffled through the meadows, the yellow golden eye, monkey flower, violet aster, patches of the pink fireweed. Occasionally she turned around to see if he was still with her. He didn't have the energy that he'd claimed. Not surprising, of course.

When they stopped to rest in a field he admitted he never hiked much. But he thought there'd be no better way to learn than in Yellowstone. All this outdoors was "beyond my imagination," he said. An only child, he was raised by two college professors, which probably explained his sorry imagination. He learned to play the violin at age eight. As a boy he spent all his free time in the City Library. His used-to-be girlfriend told him wild stories about the West often when they laid together after making love. That's the way he put it—after "making love." He was hinting, of course, dropping that little line out there like she was a catfish going after a dough ball.

She squirmed and looked away when he asked about her own life. She had to remember to keep quiet about the kids. "My family lives just south of Colter, only a few miles from here. Can't say how big our ranch is, but we sure have some beautiful horses. Cattle, too. Must be, I don't know, maybe five hundred head. But the ranch hands take care of 'em. You know, you gotta have ranch hands."

He nodded as he listened, staring off into the distance. She pulled up blades of grass, tossed them into the air, and watched them flutter back down. She didn't let him see her smiling. The lower the sun dropped on the horizon, the more exciting it was all becoming.

TWENTY-FIVE

Montgomery studied Corey's face as his boss rested his hands on the table and tapped the tips of his thumbs together. One eye twitched as he waited for Dr. Matthew Wallace to continue.

"When the coroner examined the photographer's clothing," Dr. Wallace said, "he found animal hairs. We searched for foreign hair and saliva around the open wounds of the photographer and slaughtered animals. All the samples were analyzed for DNA in our lab. It was those results that nailed it."

When Wallace said *nailed it*, Corey flinched.

"Hair shafts and saliva hold plenty of DNA that make up the genes," Dr. Wallace said. "Combinations of genes determine coat color, body size, leg length, skull shape, even tail characteristics. Whether the tail should curl, hang down, or stick up. From the genetic patterns we could verify the specific animal. Unquestionably, the attacker for each victim was a North American gray wolf, at least in part. But what surprised us, all the DNA samples matched. The killer was the same wolf in every case."

Corey quickly sat up and spoke. "I'm afraid I'm not following you here. You said a wolf in *part*?"

"The wolf we're talking about is clearly a mix with something else. It has to be an offspring of a wolf with another member of the dog family. A breed that's been tough to pin down. Unfortunately, our database for all the variety of dog breeds is limited, but we picked up telltale DNA sequences. They suggested bulldog terrier and bull mastiff. Even Great Dane. Not surprised at that, given the apparent size of this hybrid animal. I asked myself what kind of dog breed would show such a mix. I kept searching our archives and running iterative software designed for those kinds of matches."

He stopped to make sure everyone was paying close attention. "We now have an ID with better than eighty percent chance we're correct. In this business, that's as good as it gets."

Everyone around the table was glued to Wallace's face. "Tosa Inu," he said. "This . . . creature is best described as half wolf and half Tosa Inu."

"Tosa Inu?" Professor Hornsby asked, that now permanently puzzled look still contorting his face.

"It's a rare Japanese breed," Wallace replied. "From what I've learned, it was bred solely for organized fighting in nineteenth century Japan. Once this strain was perfected, it made all other fighting dogs obsolete."

"So, there's a hybrid wolf roaming around, killing?" Professor Hornsby asked.

Wallace leaned back. "This hybrid is no doubt responsible for every attack we've investigated."

McFarland sat spellbound, as if not knowing what to ask next.

"There's even more supporting evidence," Wallace said. "I called one of the country's top breeders of wolf-dog hybrids, a gentleman from Fort Worth. We all know that a wolf has an innate fear of man and tries to avoid any human contact. But as the breeder explained, a hybrid wolf doesn't fear people, no matter what breed of dog is in the mix."

"It's more hostile?" McFarland asked.

"It's far more aggressive than any wolf in the wild. Will attack anything that moves. Think about that. Imagine the offspring of a wolf that's mated with the most vicious fighting dog in existence."

Professor Hornsby couldn't hold back. "With that conclusion, Dr. Wallace, I can only think of one question. How could a wolf in the Canadian Rockies have any chance in hell to mate with a prized Japanese fighting dog?"

"I did plenty of head scratching over that one, too," Wallace replied. "Then I called a colleague from the Wildlife Service in Ottawa. He told me that dog fighting for sport happens all over rural Canada. No different from small town America, from coast to coast. I bet England even has its share of dog fights in the Cumbria region."

"But you said," McFarland responded, "that you're continuing to analyze DNA samples from the victims. Why?"

"I believe we can determine exactly which Yellowstone wolf we're talking about."

"How is that possible?"

"I met with the wildlife biologists who were part of the team that captured the wolves in Alberta at the start of Operation Wolfstock. Before the animals were transported to Yellowstone, they were given complete physicals. Blood was drawn and samples frozen and stored. So, if any disease outbreaks occurred, they could test the stored blood to help track down the problem."

"Luckily," Wallace continued, "I've had access to five cc of blood from every wolf brought in from Canada. My lab techs back in Oregon are analyzing DNA from each blood sample to look for a match. If we get one, we'll know the hybrid wolf is among the Yellowstone wolves."

McFarland looked over at Corey. "What's your take on all this, Jack?"

Taken by surprise, Corey sat up and cleared his throat. "It all sounds interesting. I'm just not sure that—"

"I'm asking what if Dr. Wallace's lab can pin down a specific wolf among those in the Park?"

"As you know, every wolf we've brought in was fitted with a radio-collar."

"So, once a wolf is identified, what can you do?" she asked, clearly perturbed that she was having to drag information out of him like she was drawing blood.

Corey scratched his neck and took a deep breath. "Well, then we can go to the charts and check its exact transmission frequency. Then we can locate it with our electronics in a flyover."

"Whichever way it goes," McFarland said, "the superintendent wants this taken care of . . . now."

"When do you plan to post warnings to the public?" Professor Hornsby asked.

McFarland squirmed in her chair. It was her turn to get uncomfortable. "Our policy, Professor, was carefully developed with the Department of the Interior in Washington. We have to eliminate the danger before making announcements to the press."

"But you could give out an alert to visitors at the gates," Hornsby replied.

"If we released anything right now," McFarland said, "we'd alarm the throng of visitors coming in over the weekend. We wouldn't be in a position to provide any guidance or reassurance to anybody."

What she meant, Montgomery thought, was that closing Yellowstone on a Labor Day weekend would lead to a public relations disaster. Forest fires, they could fight. Earthquakes, they could deal with. But no disaster was like a PR disaster.

"Fortunately," Corey said, "with the last long weekend of the summer starting this week, we're almost out of the woods. After the weekend, the number of visitors will fall off dramatically." He faintly smiled.

McFarland buried her head in her hands.

Wallace scooted back his chair and straightened up. "My techs are working twelve-hour shifts to finish the job. We should have results on the exact identity of this hybrid by next week."

McFarland kept her elbows on the table supporting her head as she looked up. "That's not soon enough, Dr. Wallace."

"I beg your pardon?" he asked.

"The superintendent needs to take action quickly," she responded calmly. "Not only do we expect at least ten thousand visitors spread over the Park, but we have a regional Boy Scout event all weekend at Indian Creek campground. We need to know what's going on with this so-called hybrid by Thursday."

"But it's Monday already, Miss McFarland. Getting the data you need in only three days will require working around the clock."

"Yes, I know."

*   *   *

After the meeting broke up, Montgomery followed Corey into his office. Corey threw himself down into his chair and sat with his feet on the windowsill, staring outside and ignoring him. Montgomery wanted only to walk away at that point. He knew what was coming; had seen it too damn many times before, although lately it was getting worse. Nowadays you could never be sure what topic to stay away from. He especially saw the erosion of Corey's nerves day-by-day after his separation from his wife of twenty-two years. He tried to talk with Corey about it, but he would always change the subject and focus on the crisis of the day. It was as if he felt that ramming his head into the sands of a job would somehow make his other problems run away and hide.

"You okay, Jack?" Montgomery finally asked.

Corey swiveled around to face him. "They're after my wolves, Bantz."

"There's no way in hell that we or anybody else could've known this might happen."

"After all these years of fighting to bring wolves back to the Park, to—"

"I found out we got another call from Washington today," Montgomery interrupted.

"What about?"

"They gave Claire Manning the budget figures she's been looking for. They didn't have a choice. She threatened to make a ruckus."

"She's trying to second guess me, the sonofabitch. McFarland's been doing the same thing since day one. All over my ass. Just like my wife."

Corey rambled on. Maybe a stray wolf was on the loose, a killer hybrid. So what? The wilderness was a dangerous place. What can you do about it? Better to keep people away and leave to nature the wildlife and the woods and lakes and the streams. Removing the wolves was not going to happen. Not on his watch. He paused as if to wait for moral support.

"It's not the end of the world, Jack. If the superintendent does decide the Operation failed—"

"What kind of talk is *that*?"

"I mean, worst case, if the superintendent decided to move the wolves out of—"

Corey slammed his fist on the desk. "I don't want to listen to that shit! Do you hear me? The only way this project will come to an end is over my dead body, goddammit." He turned to stare out the window again, breathing hard. Then he twisted back around. "And don't look so smug, ranger. There could be more casualties than me around here."

TWENTY-SIX

Molly arrived close to dusk at the Colter Bar and Grille on the south end of Main Street, across from the Mountain View Chevron Station. Next door was Conover's Laundromat, a place that made it convenient to drop a load of dirty clothes into a front-load washer, deposit four quarters, and stroll over for a cold brew.

Peanut shells crunched under her boots as Molly sauntered across the floor through a haze of cigarette smoke and the reek of barbeque and beer. On one wall a bison head glared out over a country-western house band gearing up for the evening's entertainment.

"Nothing to drink," Molly announced. "The Judge has the nose of a bloodhound."

"I can sneak you one to go for him, too," Leeanne replied from behind the bar. She'd been a good friend of Molly's for the past nine years. Molly told her she needed help and would tell her more when she didn't have to talk over the damn band. She described Charlene's features.

"We were busier than usual at lunch," Leeanne said. "But I might have seen her eating with a stranger. Jodi served them. 'Course she's off tonight."

Molly wrinkled her nose and mouth into a plea. "Could you do me a real big favor?"

"Exactly how big a favor you talking, honey?"

"Would you give Jodi a call for me?"

Leeanne bit down hard on her back teeth and glanced up at the ceiling. Shrugging, she grabbed a pen and scribbled on a bar napkin, then handed it to Molly and glared back at her from the tops of her eyes. "Some of us gotta work for a living, girl. Tell Jodi I said 'Hey.'"

Molly rushed to the hallway. The pay phone, by some brilliant feat of architectural design, was located within easy earshot of the bandstand. Jodi answered on the fifth ring. Molly raised her voice to compete with the battering from the drummer in explaining her predicament.

Yes, Jodi remembered the girl. On the skinny side. Had three glasses of lemonade and added heaping teaspoons of sugar to each glass, if you can believe that.

"What about the guy?" Molly asked.

"Sorry, did you ask about a guide?"

Molly held the receiver down to her chest and stared at the frigging band, as if the nastiness of her glower would somehow stop the music, if that's what they called it. She took a breath and shouted into the phone again. "The *guy*, Jodi. The man that joined her."

"Oh, they got together all right. He was a tall drink of water. Wore tattered jeans and gold wire-rimmed glasses. I overheard something about hiking. He appeared to be a tourist. Maybe a student. But he was a nice-looking kid, Molly. I mean, I'd let him eat crackers in my bed."

"You said hiking?"

"I said *what*?"

"Hiking, Jodi. You said something about hiking."

"That's right. And I heard him say Yellowstone a few times, too."

"Did either mention where they were headed. Or the name of a trail or a place?"

"Name of what?"

"Name of a *trail* or a *place*."

"Can't help you on that one."

"No problem, Jodi. Sorry I called so late." Molly slipped the receiver back on the hook and leaned against the wall just as the singer in the world's only one thousand decibel band announced a break.

Good timing, asshole.

She jabbed her hands into her sweater pockets and walked back down the hallway.

The phone on the wall rang out.

She turned and hustled back. When she shoved the receiver into her ear, Jodi answered. "I have that phone number there memorized, you know."

"Did you forget something?" Molly asked, crossing her fingers.

"I can hear you a helluva lot better now."

"The band stopped playing. What did you forget?"

"It's probably nothing . . ."

"Right now I don't have a clue to work with, Jodi."

"The kid was talking about peppers."

"Which kid?" Molly asked.

"The guy. The one I'd let—"

"Peppers?"

"He was concerned about stopping to get some kind of peppers. I thought it was ridiculous. But remember, he looked like a college kid. Can't expect them to know that much."

Molly couldn't make any sense of what Jodi had overheard and it was late. The Judge would be worried. She had to get home before he called the sheriff's office and reported her missing.

As she drove, she played back the conversation in her head over and over.

Student . . . Yellowstone . . . hiking.

Anyone new to Yellowstone would want to do the Grand Loop. But how many miles was that?

Peppers?

Maybe they wouldn't go to the Park. He probably wanted to get to a motel. They could always hike tomorrow.

Halfway home, it hit her. She pulled off to the side of the road.

Bears.

The guy who picked up Charlene was afraid of coming across a bear when they went hiking. He wanted one of those canisters of pepper spray to bring along on the hike. They were supposed to thwart off a bear attack.

Marketing!

She'd rather put her trust in kicking the shit out of the bear. Only one place in town would carry pepper spray.

* * *

When Molly arrived at the General Store, the door was locked but lights glowed from the back. She pushed her face against the window and waited. Someone inside moved and she rapped on the glass with her knuckles. When no one responded, she walked to the door again and jiggled the handle, then hammered on the door with her fist.

Lights came on up front and Sam Phillips shuffled to the entrance.

"When the door don't open," he barked, "you can usually take that as a sign we're closed." A frown permanently adorned his long, trail-blazed face.

"Sorry to disturb you, Sam."

He motioned for her to come in. Without speaking, he led her into the back room where he was opening boxes from a shipment.

She scampered to keep up. "Of course I wouldn't have knocked this late unless it was important."

He stopped to grab a box and give it a swift karate-chop. She knew he still held that grudge over the price-fixing charges she'd brought to the town council against Main Street businesses. "Could I ask a question, Sam?"

Another chop. "You can ask, I suppose."

"About a customer from this afternoon."

Sam reached inside the opened box and held up a transparent package of fish hooks. He examined it from every angle. She wondered if he was counting every damned hook.

"Tall guy," she continued. "Small, wire-rimmed glasses—"

He threw the package into a pile with the others. "Lots of customers come through here. Tall, short, bald, fat."

"Maybe in his twenties."

Sam pushed his glasses to the top of his head. "What the hell is this all about?"

"Don't mean to grill you, but there's a girl from down on Duck Creek who's in trouble. Big trouble."

He raised his eyebrows and shrugged.

"She's missing, Sam. Ran away. I think this guy picked her up and he's probably up to no good."

Sam reached for another box and ripped it open. "So you're some kind of sex cop now?"

"I'm talking about the Loudermilk family, Sam. She's one of their girls."

"You mean the Mormons? They've always been regular customers. Good people."

"They're polygamists, Sam. The girl was being abused by the old man."

He stopped and stared back at her. "That's one helluva charge to bring against someone."

"I know what's going on with that family," she said.

"Then let the law handle it."

"Old man Loudermilk isn't about to report her missing. I was thinking maybe you talked to this guy today. Tall? Glasses?"

"Look, I'm busy right now."

"The girl was raped and beaten, Sam. By a customer of yours and a neighbor of mine. We can't stand back and do nothing."

"Don't raise your voice at me. I don't care who your husband is. I told you I'm busy."

She didn't have to put up with his stubborn asinine ignorance. When she turned to walk out, she stumbled over a box.

Dammit.

Molly bent over to rub her knee as blood trickled down her shin. Could've ruptured a vein. Would serve him right if she sued.

Limping back toward him, she asked, "Would you have anything I could wipe this blood off with?"

He looked down at her leg and walked over to a table and found a rag. He tossed it to her. "Did he look like the brainy type?" he asked.

"Probably," she said, not looking up as she dabbed at the blood.

"Maybe I remember the guy," he said. "He was going hiking. He read somewhere that he should carry a can of pepper spray for Grizzlies. I told him I wouldn't have the guts to get close enough to use it."

As he spoke, Molly examined the rag and then flipped it over on top of a box. "By chance did he say—"

"I told him that I always tie some bells on my knapsack. Like to give bears plenty of warning. That scares 'em away. He laughed it off."

"Did he mention what trail he was planning on taking?"

Sam pulled on his giant earlobe. "As best I recall, might've been Deer Pass. It was miles north of here anyway, by the way he was talking ."

Molly smiled and nodded. "Thanks, Sam. I'll check it out."

They looked at each other for a moment, then he said, "We're just trying to make a living around here, Molly. It's not like we're getting rich doing this day in and day out."

As she drove home she rehashed her earlier meeting with the Loudermilk women, still trying to gain a glimpse into what might be going on deep inside their brain-washed heads. For now, she had to get home to take care of the dogs and the Judge, in that order. She could do nothing more for Charlene Loudermilk at the moment, but she'd sure as hell be ready to take off at dawn.

TWENTY-SEVEN

"Can we drive up to Bozeman after school tomorrow to buy my scout uniform?" Michael asked his dad. "The Camporee is Saturday."

"I was planning on Bozeman later in the week," Dieter replied. They sat at the kitchen table where Michael was gobbling a hot dog with spicy mustard dripping onto his T-shirt. Dieter watched Megan counting the cooked carrot slices on her plate. She'd exhausted stories by now of her first day at school and was quickly winding down.

Rusty scratched at the back door and barked. When Dieter opened it, Rusty flew inside. Dieter walked out onto the deck where a light breeze stirred treetops. As he scanned the yard and the thick forest backing on the property, a pair of ravens cawed from the upper limb of a cottonwood. Again he thought how lucky he was to call Colter home. When he returned inside, Megan had dropped a carrot slice on the floor for the dog.

"Please take Rusty out on the deck, Megan, and play with him a little while. Your brother and I need to talk."

"I wanna stay here," she whined.

"Mind your daddy please." He patted her behind and gently shoved her toward the back door. "And stay on the deck like I told you."

She reached up to the door for the slippery brass knob, careful to keep her other hand out of the jamb. He remembered the time she made

145

the mistake of closing the sharp edge on her tiny fingers and her anguished crying.

When Dieter sat back down at the table, he turned to his son. "Bozeman's an hour away. I'll see if I have any calls later in the week. If not, we can drive up there." Maybe he'd been too harsh. He wasn't sure how to deal with his son at times like this. Since his mother's death, Michael was drifting away. He could sense it in so many little gestures. The way he looked away from him at times, ignored his questions, or shrugged off his touch.

"Have you decided if I can go on the overnight hike?" Michael asked.

"We've talked about that a dozen times. I'm not changing my mind."

Michael took another bite of his hotdog and chewed, appearing to think about his next move.

"You do know," Dieter said, "that mountain hikes can be pretty rough going. Especially for guys your age. Sometimes even a little dangerous."

"How come dangerous?"

"Lots of reasons."

"There's no snakes . . . like in Pennsylvania."

"How do you know that?" Dieter asked.

"My friend told me."

"You made a new friend?"

"Randy Cunningham. He's eleven and he's going on the Camporee."

"Do you want more milk?" Dieter scooted his chair back to get up, but Michael didn't answer him. He sat back down. "What's the matter, son?"

Michael dropped the hot dog onto his plate and grabbed the bottom of his chair with both hands and squirmed. "Are you going to find somebody else to be our mother?"

Dieter reached out to place a hand on Michael's shoulder. "Who knows what life might bring, son. But I'm certainly not looking for anyone, if that's what you mean."

"I've watched you stare at Amy."

Low blow. "My main concerns are you and Megan. I want you both to be happy."

Michael took a gulp of milk, then picked up his napkin and wiped at his mouth. "Mom was my den mother in the Cub Scouts."

"I remember that."

"I bet she would let me go on an overnight hike."

"I don't think so. You're too young. Next year, maybe. Please don't badger me about that anymore."

Michael sipped more milk and looked up. "Dad, do you know what a 'pisskaan' is?"

"That's a strange word."

"It's a buffalo jump. Kinduva cliff out in the middle of the plains." Michael looked proud that he knew something his dad didn't. With a burst of confidence, he spoke about how Indians used to round up herds of buffalo and chase them into a stampede toward the cliff. The flustered animals would run right over the edge without knowing where they were going. "They would *crash* down below and *smash* their skulls and die."

Dieter knew exactly the source of that history lesson. "Did Amy explain why the Indians did that?"

Michael folded his hands into his lap. "How did you know she told me about it?"

"Just a wild guess."

"They tried to kill them to get their hides and meat and stuff."

"Did she also tell you that the Indians did that so often that the buffalo almost disappeared?"

"Amy said the white man caused that."

Dieter thought it better to read a little more background before getting any deeper into the discussion. "That's interesting."

"I had a dream last night," Michael said. "It was kind of scary."

"You mean a nightmare?"

"I was running. Running very fast down a dirt trail with lots of other people and—"

Rusty barked loudly from the back deck. Dieter rushed to the door as the dog kept barking. Megan was nowhere in sight. He shouted for her as he charged down the steps and into the yard. He should never have done it. He should never have let her go outside in the yard alone. It was a stupid mistake, but Michael had taken his mind off of—

"Surprise!" Megan popped out from under the deck behind him, laughing.

He turned to catch her as she ran into his arms, then stooped to his knee and looked directly into her eyes, breathing rapidly. He held her chin up with his thumb and finger, trying his damnedest not to lose his temper. "When I tell you to stay on the deck, Megan, I mean it. Do you understand me?"

She nodded and frowned, then twisted away from him and scampered up the steps.

Michael stood on the porch. "She was only playing a game, Dad." He followed his sister in and slammed the door behind him.

*   *   *

Dieter drifted into the kitchen with aspirin tablets in his fist. He reached for the bottle of Early Times nestled under the sink, then walked out onto the back deck and sank into the weathered rocker. The kids had gone to bed early that evening, both still upset with their dad's unusual bout of anger. He couldn't blame them—he was upset with himself.

He hitched up his boots on the log banister and stared out on the trees and fields as the crickets and tree frogs sang out too damn loud.

Fumbling with the aspirin in the palm of one hand, he clutched the whiskey bottle with the other. He'd overreacted with Megan. Inexcusable. Why was he so much on edge?

One thing was for certain—the summer with Amy hadn't worked out. Even her tribal stories—once filled with harmless moral lessons— were now scaring hell out of his son and causing him nightmares. The fact she was soon leaving turned out to be well-timed. No matter what she thought, Michael was too young to get deep into scouting at his age. What did she know about things like that?

A spotlight lit up the corner of the yard. It was a good idea to keep it on every night. When he leaned back and closed his eyes, the image arose of the nearly decapitated body in the funeral home. No report had yet come through on what the coroner had found on the autopsy. Why? Meanwhile, everyone kowtowed to Yellowstone's chief ranger, a jackass who dismissed *any* claims of wolf attacks with a wave of a hand. End of discussion.

He stood, uncapped the whiskey bottle and dropped the aspirin into the neck of it one tablet at a time, then twisted the top back on, moved to the far edge of the deck and heaved the bottle into the pine trees. He was tired, angry with himself. Angry with everybody.

He had put it off too long. It was time to go over Chief Jack Corey's head.

TWENTY-EIGHT

The sun drifted below the snow-capped mountain tops as Charlene and her friend from the East reached a grove of tall willow trees dangling like green ghosts over a slow-running stream that gurgled over smooth river rocks. She sat on a log to pull off her shoes and socks. Her ragged pair of sneakers didn't quite fit right—size and a half too big.

Marilee wouldn't mind that she had borrowed them, she was certain of that. No doubt at all because they were good to each other and didn't have many other friends. Actually, didn't have any other friends, but they had each other.

Charlene slid down from the log and leaned back against it. In the afterglow of the sunset, steam from a distant geyser climbed high and vanished in spirit-like wisps. While she munched on trail mix excavated from the corners of her pockets, she cogitated on the sight of her companion gathering firewood. How clean and handsome he looked as he squatted there, trying to coax the kindling to burn. He had to be smart, he was going to college, so he'd catch on eventually that it don't do no good to use green twigs.

Wasn't her place to say anything. He'd figure out on his own that the smaller dead limbs that snapped instead of bending would make for proper tinder. She dug up another M&M and two peanuts from a wrinkle deep within one pocket and quickly popped them into her mouth before he caught her.

Soon, smoke drifted upward and a tiny yellow flame glittered. He finally got the water boiling over his sorry excuse for a fire and he dumped in freeze-dried packages of peas and carrots and some fancy chicken. The meal tasted like cardboard with salt and spice, but she scarfed down what she was offered. He saved a little more for himself.

By the time the high country's evening chill arrived, they were snuggling close to the rosy embers, holding hands. They sipped hot tea and waved the stinging smoke away from their eyes. She massaged the back of his hand with the tips of her fingers and gently stroked his knuckles. A man's hand softer than hers seemed strange. Weird, really. She didn't know if he liked having her around because she wasn't smart and would never lie to herself about being pretty either. She thought long and hard about it all, but it didn't matter.

He sprung to his feet. "How about dessert, Charlene?"

Her eyes opened wide with delight. "You gotta Baby Ruth, slugger?"

She watched as he jogged through the weeds down to a willow tree by the stream and cut off two small branches with a pocketknife while the tree thrashed about him in the wind. He then shaved off the leaves and sharpened both pieces into a fine point. When he returned, she jumped up, wrapped her arms around her shoulders, and slowly backed away. He strolled to his backpack and fumbled around inside it until he found a package of marshmallows that he waved above his head. "Have you ever roasted these?"

She paid no attention to the question but pointed to the willow branches. "What you plan to do with them switches?"

"Watch me!" He tore open the package, plunged a stick into the center of a marshmallow, and held it out over the fire. A sweet caramel smell soon drifted her way. He slipped the brown melting lump from the stick and blew on it. Instead of puckering his lips out like you would when you blow out candles on a birthday cake, he stretched his lips back and pulled the upper one down over his big front teeth. They formed a slit instead of an "O." Ever so gently he blew through the slot like a girl.

She wrapped her thumb and forefinger around his wrist and chomped down on the gooey treat. Squishing it with her tongue, she swallowed hard, and then mumbled through puffed cheeks. "My word, slugger, you sure know how to cook." She licked each finger, pausing to suck on a sticky thumb and grin.

He quickly placed more kindling on the fire and flames flared inside the circle of stones. They roasted marshmallows until the bag was half-empty, all the while giggling and feeding each other like real lovers. Staring into the night sky, he said that he'd never seen so many stars. It didn't make sense. Why would there be more stars in Montana than back East?

"Look," she shouted and pointed her stick at a brilliant light streaking low across the sky. "A shooting star."

"Did you know that it's not really a shooting star, Charlene?"

"Is too. I seen lots of them on dark nights."

"It's actually a meteor."

"I read that once," she replied. "But have you noticed when you say 'me-te-or' you sound hard and serious-like. You have to keep your mouth wound up all tight. But when you say 'shooting star,' you have to speak softer and pucker up your lips." She slowly repeated the phrase. He seized on her invite and lowered his head to her face. She cuddled closer to him and burrowed into his bulky sweater that felt like the belly of a lamb against her face, but reeked of burned pine. They lay holding onto each other and staring down into the smoldering logs when the howl of a solitary wolf rolled in on a gust of wind.

She caught his startled eyes darting about. Playfully, she dug the tips of her fingers into his sweater and began making tiny circles. He bent his head lower and nibbled on her earlobe. Gently exploring her face with his soft lips, he allowed one hand to slip under her jersey and sneak to the top button of her woolen shirt. Then he slid the hand across her warm chest until he reached what all men go for first. Caressing her small breast, he gently freed it and brought his lips down to it.

She tossed back her head and held her breath. His fingers crept to her jeans, but stopped when the cold steel rammed against his stomach. The tip of a four-inch blade had snapped out of a brown and ivory scrimshaw handle. "Caught you, didn't I, slugger?"

He suddenly straightened up. "I . . . I'm sorry, Charlene. Please . . . put that away."

"You can kiss me all you want, but I'll decide when it's time to fuck. I'm not particularly ready right now."

He nodded more than necessary. She flicked the blade back into the handle and shoved the knife into her pocket. She wished she could find better ways to express herself. "Besides," she said, "I'm having my period."

Son-of-a-bitch, he mumbled.

She heard him anyway. Why was he so befuddled? Nice girls aren't easy. She buttoned up and gathered herself.

For the umpteenth time, he fixed his glasses up on the bridge of his nose with his index finger. "Do you want to—"

"Beg your pardon?" She couldn't tell if he was talking to himself like he was before or to her.

"Do . . . do you want to use the sleeping bag?"

"Well now, that is so kind of you! I don't mind if I do."

She crawled into the tent and took off Marilee's shoes. He followed her inside and crouched against the canvas wall, facing her. She thought better of taking off any clothes and slipped into the nylon bag, then zipped it up to her chin. "You gonna be warm enough, slugger?"

"I'm fine, just fine."

Light from the campfire's dwindling flames cast a tangerine glow on the canvas walls as they fluttered with the wind. He yanked the collar up around his skinny throat and wedged his knees together against his chest. Occasionally she opened one eye. Each time she caught both of his fixed on her. He probably didn't trust her anymore. Men were like that.

The howl of that lone wolf arose again. She shuddered and buried her head deep into the sleeping bag.

TWENTY-NINE

It was early morning when Dieter drove into the Park to Madison Junction and joined the Grand Loop Highway toward the Roosevelt Gate at the northwest entrance. Getting an appointment with Superintendent George Gilmer at his headquarters office was easier than he thought. He assumed his DVM credentials helped make it happen.

When he arrived, the secretary he'd talked with on the phone asked him to wait in the reception area, then excused herself and entered the superintendent's office. Dieter picked up a copy of National Parks Magazine from a side table and rifled through it as he rehearsed his spiel. Discussing the delicate matter of the chief park ranger's idiotic behavior required political savvy, a trait he'd never even come close to mastering.

It didn't take long before the secretary returned. "I'm sorry, Dr. Harmon. The superintendent is on an unscheduled conference call with Washington."

"That's not a problem at all. I can—"

"I'm afraid the call will take him into his next appointment, but he doesn't want you to have made a wasted trip.

"Oh, no—I have no problem waiting until—"

155

"Now you just follow me, and I'll take you to the chief ranger's office."

Dieter froze, trying to think of a quick reply.

The secretary headed for the hallway and Dieter followed. "Mr. Gilmer is very apologetic. You know how—"

"Pardon me, Miss, but what I'm trying to say is that I expected to see the superintendent himself."

She stopped and looked back at him with a raised eyebrow. "Now, don't you be at all concerned. Chief Corey has many years of experience here in the Park."

"I came to speak with Mr. Gilmer. It's frankly about a private matter."

"Thank you, Barbara," a voice from behind blurted out. When he turned around, Jack Corey approached. The sharp creases in the trousers of his immaculate uniform could cut down a small sapling. The chief ranger held out his hand to shake. He was all smiles.

"I would be more than happy to see you, Dr. Harmon. Please, come on down to my office."

Corey led him into his lair and closed the door behind them. He motioned for him to take a seat. "We really regret that Mr. Gilmer's too busy for you today. How can I help you?"

"As I told the receptionist, I came here to see the superintendent."

"I'm sure you can appreciate that a National Park superintendent has a lot on his plate every day of the week?" He wouldn't wipe the fake smile off his face. "These sudden calls from Washington happen often."

"I understand, but I'm here to file a complaint."

The smile finally dissolved. Dieter leaned forward. "There've been too many wolf kills reported outside the Park. Some kind of action needs to be taken."

"But I explained all this to you at Joshua Pendleton's ranch."

"That explanation didn't fly," Dieter replied. "Pendleton knows what he's talking about. He's been around the Western wilderness more than anybody. When he speaks about wolves—"

"He's speaking for the ranchers who live around here? Is that what you want to say?"

Dieter struggled to avoid raising his voice. "Don't you think the Park Service should at the very least be more willing to hear them out?"

"Both of us need to calm down." Corey turned toward the large picture window across the room. Lush green ferns, trimmed by a meticulous hand, decorated the window sill. Dieter stared out the window and began to recover normal breathing. Outside was a grand view of the open meadows of Mammoth Springs and distant mountain peaks, but what immediately caught his eye was a large vertical antenna on an adjacent building in the headquarters complex. An idea popped into his head, the same thought he'd had during his last visit to Molly's home.

Corey walked to a file cabinet and opened a drawer. After pulling out a bulging folder, he spread a stack of photos on the desktop. "Let me give you a history lesson," he said. "At the beginning of the century, wolves were the equivalent of rats, so they were eradicated from the Park. So, Operation Wolfstock's been underway for two years now." The new goal of the National Park Service, he explained, was to establish wolves in Yellowstone permanently and allow them to breed in numbers large enough to be removed from the endangered species list. He slid a black and white photo across his desk. It showed a motorcade of park rangers and politicians passing through the Roosevelt Gate on a cold January day two years before. Another photo showed a pickup truck hauling a steel cage and carrying eight wolves.

"These wolves," Corey said, "along with six more two weeks later, made up the three original packs—Rose Creek, Crystal Bench, and Soda Butte. They were named after the landmarks where we released them. All of them were captured in Alberta and transported here. Their survival and breeding have passed all our predictions. Restoring that good ol' balance of nature, just the way God and Bruce Babbitt intended."

Dieter knew the lore of Bruce Babbitt—the Secretary of the Interior and the champion of environmental activists everywhere.

Corey squinted. "Did anyone ever tell you what happened to the wolves released up in the Park's northeast corner?"

"I really came here to—"

"Unfortunately, those wolves didn't know about Yellowstone boundaries, so they denned on a ranch just outside the Park. Everybody around got all worked up. Mad as hell. Their cattle were going to become feedstock for the wolves and their pups. Can you guess what happened?"

Dieter didn't answer.

"Nothing. Absolutely nothing. Cattle and sheep even grazed within sight of the den. We monitored the situation every week. Not a *single* livestock death was ever linked to a wolf. But of course, we eventually had to come in and capture and move the entire pack."

"Because?"

"Too damn many complaints, Dr. Harmon. You see, we do care about those who live here, despite the propaganda you hear. Like the eloquent tales I heard from your friend Joshua Pendleton."

"People in Colter aren't the ones who asked for the wolves," Dieter replied. "That was a political decision. Made two thousand miles away in Washington."

Corey clasped his hands behind his back and looked out the window again. "How long have you been a veterinarian, Dr. Harmon?"

"I really don't think we have anything more to discuss." He gripped the arms of his chair to stand.

"I would think," Corey said, "that a professional who takes care of animals would have a better understanding of wildlife and the issues we face in the Park." He strolled over to a credenza beside the window and mechanically poured a mug of coffee without offering anything to his guest.

Dieter scooted to the edge of his chair. "So, why are you so opposed to even considering the idea of wolves killing livestock outside the Park?"

"There's no reason to get upset."

"Who's upset? I came here to ask the superintendent why there's been no action."

"Do you have any idea," Corey asked, "how many bear attacks we have each year in the Park?" He took a sip of coffee. "The average number the last two decades has been nine a year. We had thirteen last year alone. And I've just been talking about attacks on people. Would you like to take a guess at the number of bear kills on sheep and cattle and horses on farms and ranches *near* the Park?"

Corey paused as if to give Dieter time to digest his point. "Okay, look. We've called in a team of experts. They're investigating all the attacks we know about. Give us a little time. We'll get to the bottom of this. I can promise you that."

"Time is what we don't have."

Corey shrugged. "So, what would you like me to do, Dr. Harmon?"

"Josh Pendleton and I are working together on this. We've done some probing on our own. We think a renegade wolf is responsible for most of these kills. Maybe all of them."

Corey cocked his head to one side, as if listening to nothing but balderdash. "One lone wolf?"

"A solitary wolf. One far bigger than any of the others."

"So, tell me . . . what kind of probing have the two of you done?"

"We've looked at tracks and examined corpses," Dieter replied.

"What types of corpses?"

"Just hear me out. We're willing to help search. I can get ten or more volunteers with a few phone calls right now. I could ask Claire Manning from the *Weekly* to put out the word."

"You can ask who?"

"Claire Manning. The editor-in-chief at—"

"I know who she is. How do you know her?"

Corey's face shouted that Manning was the wrong name to bring up. "She stopped by the cabin to ask me about the body on the Madison."

"A reporter for a newspaper just happened to stop by and ask you about a murder? You ushered her right in, offered her a glass of wine, and gave her all the gory details, I suppose. Did you smile for her camera or just give a somber look, maybe one more befitting a professional in the community?"

Dieter rose from his chair.

"What would you propose to do with this army of volunteers?" Corey asked.

"Look for tracks . . . search the Park perimeter."

"Were you aware, Dr. Harmon, that hunting down one of our wolves is a federal offense? You could get six months in the pen."

"I know it's illegal inside the Park, but if we can take care of the problem outside park boundaries."

"You mean, *shoot* the wolf?" Corey asked.

"If it's threatening our livestock and families, yes."

"Shoot an endangered species? Let me ask you a question. Let's suppose for a moment you and Joshua are correct. A renegade wolf has drifted off from one of the packs. Gone on a killing rampage and is on the loose right now. You would propose we track it down? Destroy it?"

"It could be captured," Dieter said, "and moved to another wilderness area."

"Captured? Because the animal is killing some domestic livestock that ranchers are making no small profit from?" A sudden calm came over Corey. "You know, Dr. Harmon, in nature there's no such thing as right or wrong. Agreed?"

"I don't see where you're going."

"You've made a career of treating pets and farm animals. Does a wild animal have rights in this world?"

"To some degree . . . of course."

"I'm not talking about dogs and cats in comfy homes. What about creatures without a highfalutin lobby to protect their rights." He rose out of his chair and walked to the corner of his desk where he sat and pressed his hands against one knee. "Do you think, Dr. Harmon, that an animal has a soul?"

"I certainly believe animals have feelings and emotions."

"That's not what I'm asking. Does a wolf have a soul? A soul like you and me. An immortal spirit? An afterlife?"

"I'm just a vet, Mr. Corey, not a theologian."

"I take it you're not a philosopher either. Aristotle believed animals have souls. Have you studied Aristotle by chance? Or do you just read the sports pages?"

Dieter turned for the door. "I'm sorry, but we're just not getting anywhere on this. Have a good day."

Corey banged a fist on his desktop. "Another thing before you go." His chest heaved rapidly as he spoke. "If a ranger of mine catches anyone within the boundaries of the goddamn park, even looking like he's hunting wolves, you understand how the full force of the law will come slamming down on him like a sledge hammer?"

The door creaked open and the secretary stuck her head in. "Sorry to interrupt, Mr. Corey. The gentleman from the Oregon Lab is on the line for you."

Corey nodded and with a flip of his hand motioned Dieter toward the door. "Remember, Dr. Harmon, this is wild country. You need to be careful out there."

THIRTY

A wolf has a soul? As he drove to Molly and the Judge's place, Dieter thought about the conversation with Jack Corey—more a sermon to a congregation of one. And the more he thought about it, the less sense it made. The threat bounced around inside his head like a verse from an old song that wouldn't go away.

If a ranger of mine catches anyone even looking like he's hunting wolves . . . .

It wasn't just what Corey said that grated on him, it was the determined rage in his eyes while he preached. Dieter wasn't up to threats, especially when coming from the likes of an asinine bureaucrat on a mission.

He made his way to Molly and the Judge's while the idea was still hot on his mind. The notion had come to him twice: first, when Molly told him about the towering antenna on their roof and the Judge's hobby. The next time was the day before, as he stared out the office picture window in Jack Corey's office.

Dieter had called ahead of time to see if the Judge would give him a tour of his amateur radio setup and talk about his idea. He followed the Judge as he wheeled into a small back corner room, explaining over his shoulder that Molly had gone out on one of her excursions. A rack of electronics surrounded a cluttered desk. Wires dangled from the back of the hardware that displayed dials like on an aircraft console.

162

The Judge beamed as he explained his ham radio hobby. He handed Dieter a stack of post cards. "These are from all over the world. They acknowledge contact with Station WUZ8." He pointed to the one Dieter was examining. "That's one from Bishkek. Did you know that's the capital of K-Kyrgyzstan?"

Dieter shook his head, smiling.

"I took up this pastime soon after my accident," the Judge continued. "I've learned more about the world than I ever learned in school. Easy to do, if you have the right equipment. You can catch good sky waves at night and get reception for thousands of m-miles. Are you planning to get into ham radio?"

"No, not really. But I was told that many of the Yellowstone wolves have been radio-collared. I assume those are signals that can be picked up somehow."

"Those s-s-signals almost always transmit near the amateur radio frequency band. But the type of transmitter a wolf would have around its neck has a range of only a couple of miles at most."

"Where could I get my hands on a receiver for that?"

"You mean to pick up the wolf transmissions? Locate their whereabouts?"

"That's the idea."

The Judge nodded with a smile and thought for a moment. "You just need something thrown together from a few parts. It's close enough to the upper TV frequencies that you could hook up a small antenna to an S meter."

"You're getting over my head, Judge."

"My point is that I've got enough junk between here and the garage to jerry-rig you up a system you could c-carry around like a lunch box."

"How can I help?"

"I don't need help. With Molly out and about, I've got some time on my hands. Just give me a few hours and stop back."

*   *   *

Molly latched the trailer carrying her all-terrain vehicle onto the hitch of her truck. She'd worked past midnight tuning up the three-wheeled Honda that could take her anywhere. She had been up and at it before the Judge awoke to get ahead of traffic and the chance of suspicious onlookers. Although the Park banned ATVs, there had to be a way to finagle it. Unlike the Judge, she wasn't into analyzing the hell out of situations. The only way to find out was to try.

She'd searched a Yellowstone map the day before for what Sam Phillips at the General Store thought was the Deer Pass trail. He was close. The Fawn Pass trailhead was only eleven miles up Highway 191. As she drove she kept watch on the overcast sky and trees fluttering in the gusting winds. The temperature had dropped ten degrees from the morning before. When she arrived at the parking lot for the trail, one lone vehicle sat in a far corner. Frost covered its windshield. A yellow and black folder in the console between the front seats looked a lot like a rental car agreement.

She unchained the ATV from the open trailer and coasted it down the ramp. After unhitching the trailer, she pushed it into a cluster of trees to hide it from passing motorists. She then hopped onto the ATV and prayed her tune-up would do the trick.

On the second crank, the engine purred.

THIRTY-ONE

Charlene woke up to the aroma of bacon sputtering over a fire. She unzipped her sleeping bag and scuttled out of the tent to stretch in the brisk morning air. He was hunched over a campfire with his back to the tent.

After she squatted behind a pair of birch trees to pee, she hurried to the stream for the can of Mountain Dew that she'd wedged between rocks while he was struggling the night before to build the fire. She sauntered back to the campsite, waving the cold beverage high and smiling. When she got close enough, she leaned down and kissed him on the lips, but he didn't put any real desire into it.

"No longer interested in some nooky, slugger?"

He let her comment pass.

She sat on a boulder and yanked at the tab on the Mountain Dew. While he cooked there wasn't much in the way of conversation. She took big swallows and belched. She'd thought about it most of the night and had decided that she might've overreacted last night. As soon as he made his next move, she'd be more accommodating, that was for sure.

When they got back on the trail she strolled at an easy pace, free of the worry and tension. She wondered what Duncan and little Sara were up to. Katherine Belle and Marilee would take good care of them, no doubt about that. Taking good care of them like they did for all the others. She would go back for her precious ones in due time.

The morning sun peeked through the dark, racing clouds as they hiked. The air smelled nice. The leaves on the silver maples flapped about in the wind and turned over so you could see their undersides. Rain was coming. Thousands of spider webs clung to the meadow grass and sparkled in the heavy dew.

"Don't those webs look like giant snowflakes?" she asked.

He nodded.

She didn't ask any more questions. He wasn't in the mood for small talk, but small talk was what she knew the most about. When he stopped to rest and take the load off his back, she sprawled on the ground beside him. She wasn't tired by a long shot. A flock of ravens burst from the trees. Shading her eyes, she followed them when something moved about in the bushes on the other side of the stream. Wasn't the wind, because it had died down.

Could be a foraging bear.

If one of those took off across the stream, it'd be on them in no time. She stood and ambled toward the water, placing each foot softly down so not to make any more noise than necessary as she studied the bushes across the way. She couldn't make anything out. Then flashed a frightening thought—Joseph Vincent. But it wouldn't be him over there hiding, because he'd already be on them like a wildcat if he'd spotted her. He was probably out searching for her though, driving up and down the highway, not stopping to ask nobody questions of course, just making plans to teach her a God-fearing lesson. Him and his cave.

Joseph Vincent would be rubbernecking at everybody out there on the highway, gawking with those eyes, those sickening eyes, those magical eyes that could see into her soul. They were the eyes of the Devil, that's what they were.

The ravens flew in, low and circling, cawing at each other, squawking at her for nosing around in their territory.

She despised her Uncle Withrow, too. He used to tease her real bad and tell her how ugly she was, but that didn't stop him. He wasn't going to hurt nobody no more. She made damned sure of that seventeen times. Her mother used to tell people that he likely upped and walked away, but she would just smile every time his name was brought up.

The bushes across the stream quivered again and she froze. An enormous wolf crept into the open, a wilderness beast that looked like a wolf anyway, but it was actually too big. Her companion rushed to her side and tossed an arm around her shoulders. Too shocked to speak, she clutched him around the waist. The wolf darted toward the shallow stream where boulders jutted above the surface.

"Looks like it's trying to come across," he whispered. "I think it's rabid." When he let go of her shoulder, she ran for her backpack.

"No!" he shouted. "Leave it. That might be what it's after."

"My backpack?"

"The food. It smells the food."

He grabbed her hand and they took off as a dark cloud of ravens joined in the chase. When she glanced over her shoulder, the wolf was climbing up the bank on their side of the stream.

"Come on, Charlene." He tugged on her arm. "*Run*, for God's sake!"

The path led them out of the open field and into a grove of pines. In the thicker cover they ran straight for a pile of fallen trees blocking the path. Panting, he boosted her over the logs and she flopped to the other side and slammed hard onto the ground. She screamed as pain shot through her ankle.

He dropped down beside her and pressed a finger to her lips. "Shut up!"

She tried to stand but couldn't put weight on the injured foot. She scanned the trees. A pair of golden eyes buried in wet, black fur hid in the tall grass and stared back. She yanked on his arm and pointed. He reached for a dead branch on a log and wrenched it off, then jabbed the air above his head with his weapon and shouted.

The wolf exploded from the weeds.

Like some kind of fool, he stood and heaved the limb at the charging animal and struck it in the head with a blow that toppled the beast into the dirt. It quickly recovered and stood with an arched back, bracing for another attack.

Then her dream was shattered in a blink. Her boyfriend from back East, so handsome and caring, raced away like that bat from hell she had always heard about. She curled into a ball and covered her face while she prayed to God Almighty and sobbed. The cawing ravens gathered on the ground about her. Through the fingers covering her eyes she watched as the wolf jumped high over her head and chased after her friend. She could've told him you can't outrun a creature from the wild. Running away was nothing more than a tease. He probably didn't learn things like that in college.

The wolf broke into a gallop, tail curled above its backbone, snout held high as it sniffed fear in its prey. It circled about him while he ran, nipping at his heels as if taking down a frightened lamb. The wolf leaped high and slammed its paws against his victim's back, smashing him into the weeds. He kicked wildly as his screams pierced the air.

As the wolf buried its open jaws into his neck, both of his fists hammered away at the attacker. The wolf chomped deeper into his throat. Twisting and wrenching, it battered his head into the stone-hard ground causing his pretty hair to flap about like a flag in a storm.

Finally, his body lay still. Then it twitched. Madly at first, but soon only in clumsy jerks.

The wolf unlocked its jaws and turned in her direction. She tried again to stand but grimaced and dropped back down. Her injured ankle had begun to swell. She snaked on her belly through the weeds toward the dead branch he'd used as a weapon. Gripping it firmly, she used it as a crutch to heave herself up to her feet.

The wolf loped toward her. She hobbled with all of the speed she could muster to a fir tree and lifted her good foot up onto a lower limb. After dropping the crutch, she reached up to a branch with both hands, yanked upward, and stepped onto the limb. It snapped. She fell to the ground with a jolt and tumbled backwards. Her ankle throbbed while she crawled to the tree trunk again and stretched high for a larger branch. Squeezing her thigh muscles, she grunted up the tree, hand over hand, one limb at a time as the scorched bark scraped like sandpaper against her face. She shimmied higher until she could cram her body into the thick green branches. Comforted by the sweet smell of pinesap, she spread apart the limbs to peek through the fog bank that was now closing in.

His body and her fantasy of what might have been, lay in a pool of blood. A swarm of cackling ravens battled over pieces of his shredded flesh. If only she could remember his name.

She wrapped her arms around the tree and hugged it passionately as if there was no one else to hold. Mashing her cheek tightly against the bark, she could sense the feeble tremor of claws grating on the trunk below.

THIRTY-TWO

Molly's ATV skidded over the rocks as a chilling rain fell. According to the odometer she'd gone four miles over the narrow trail blazed only for hiking. She was forced to steer around fallen trees and over the tops of smaller ones lying charred and scattered like pickup sticks. Stopping often, she called out for Charlene.

When the wind died, the rain settled into a drizzle through a hazy curtain of fog. She picked up speed until the mist grew heavier and reduced visibility to only a few yards. The vague image of a boulder appeared on her path. Maneuvering closer, she braked too hard and killed the engine.

Mother of Mary!

Blinded by the blowing rain and fog, she had driven into the middle of a herd of bison. If she'd glanced away from the trail for even a split-second, she would've rammed one of them anchored on the path. Shivering, she sat motionless and thanked the Lord that her blustering arrival hadn't invited a stampede. She zipped up her jacket to the neckline and pulled the hood over her head.

As she sat and patiently waited for the herd to move on, she thought about the Judge's advice. The night before he'd argued that, for once, Deputy Harlan Ward might be right. *What can you do, Molly?* How often did abuse go on in families around America? The way to approach the problem, the Judge had said, was to call the Loudermilks.

"Tell 'em we'd both like to stop over. Begin by offering our friendship and trust."

"Bullshit," she'd responded. Not quite a retort to persuade a judge or jury, but she wouldn't stand for a young woman—just a girl, really—being treated as if she was a piece of meat. Beaten and raped within the sacred shrine of her own family. How were you supposed to begin by "offering your hand in friendship"? In no way would she tolerate that kind of violence going on anywhere near the place she called home. If the Judge chose to stay out of it, fine. Let him try to sleep on it. She'd read once—and long remembered how the passage struck her—that the only thing needed for evil to win out was for good people to do nothing.

When the fog finally began to lift, the herd meandered. Among the last to budge, one young bull lay in a patch of dirt thirty yards away. When she started the engine, the frightened animal jerked around and stared at the intruder that had come to life. Streams of vapor gushed from his mammoth nostrils in pulses. He lumbered toward the ATV and gradually gathered speed.

With no desire to discover what he had in mind, Molly reached behind and opened a storage compartment where she kept a twelve-gauge Remington loaded for action. She held the weapon high and fired one barrel followed by the other. Startled, the confused creature turned and jogged back to the herd. Molly sped away and didn't slow down until the last bison was out of sight.

The rain stopped and the skies cleared. The late afternoon sun drifted in and out through the low clouds. Arriving in a field by a stream, she cut the engine and repeated the calls for Charlene while opening and closing her fists to relieve her aching hands.

The wilderness swallowed her hopeless shouts. The whole damned venture was a waste. She wanted to kick herself for thinking it might be otherwise. Her thoughts began to overwhelm her when a flash of sunlight bounced off an object in the grass. She climbed off the ATV and walked toward it. A backpack on a metal frame lay on the ground with a small tent rolled up on top. A smaller pack was nearby and she yanked it up and unzipped it. There were panties, packages of snacks, a Bible with a red cover the size of her palm, and a couple of tampons.

A flock of black birds were feeding among the weeds. When she headed in their direction, they scattered away from a mixture of mud and what appeared to be dried blood. The scratched up and furrowed dirt quickly suggested a vicious fight among animals had taken place.

*   *   *

Charlene jolted upright when gunshots rang out across the valley. Then came the roar of an engine.

They were coming after her. She knew they would, in time. Joseph Vincent—him and his sister wives. She'd wrapped her legs around the trunk of a fir tree at the junction of two limbs and sat anchored ten feet above ground. She pulled the knife with the scrimshaw handle from her pocket and snapped out the blade. Clinging to the tree with her thighs, she dragged clumps of her wet hair down to her shoulders and grabbed one fistful at a time. She sliced the steel blade across the strands and let them fly into the wind.

The sound of an engine arrived nearby and shut off. A voice shouted her name, a voice she didn't recognize. She slipped the knife back into her pocket and reached higher into the tree. When she hauled herself up, she suddenly lost her grip and plunged through the branches.

"Help!" she yelled as she slammed into the ground like a bale of hay.

A crazy woman ran for her. She cried out and flailed her legs, holding onto one aching arm. "I'm not going back! Get away from me!"

She sat up, wrenched out her knife, and thrust the blade toward the stranger while her other arm hung limp.

The woman dropped to her knees and spoke softly. "Charlene . . ."

She hissed like a wildcat. "You come any closer and I'll stick you."

"Listen to me, dear. I'm Molly. I've tried to find you the last two days. Please, let me help you."

Charlene wrinkled her forehead. She couldn't tell if the woman was lying. "Did Joseph Vincent send you?"

"No, no. I saw what he did to you."

"Are you one of Uncle Withrow's people? He got what he deserved, you know."

"Please . . . just let me help."

Charlene brought down her hand and shoved the knife into a hip pocket as a wide smile crossed her face. The woman who she remembered rescuing her from the shed rushed toward her with outstretched arms. She was not going to cry. She was strong, and she would get stronger by the day. There had been plenty of time during the haunting night in the tree to plan her long overdue mission.

THIRTY-THREE

Dieter arrived at the Little Bears' home, eager to fly out over the Park with Amy's dad. The day before the two men had met for a beer at the Colter Bar and Grille and discussed in detail the location of each wolf pack. Thanks to his popularity as a guide, Little Bear had the good fortune earlier in the summer to spend time with a Yellowstone wildlife biologist. That experience provided him regular updates on Operation Wolfstock.

Mr. Little Bear lacked a formal education, but he was a man of obvious wisdom who spoke confidently and passionately about wildlife in the region. To his amazement, Dieter learned from their conversation that Mr. Little Bear had been deeply involved in the plans to bring back wolves to Yellowstone. Molly and Josh hadn't mentioned it before, but Little Bear had played a major role in the government hearings that were held in Colter two years earlier. A crowd of over one hundred had mobbed inside the walls of the town hall, a mix of people like Little Bear had never seen, from farmers and ranchers to politicians and developers. "On the one side were tree-huggers who fought to restore Yellowstone to its prehistoric origins," Mr. Little Bear said. "On the other were those who made a living with livestock."

He spoke about homemade signs that some waved about, like *Bring back the wolf: I need the Target Practice* or *Save a Wolf: Shoot a*

Rancher. "Every soul present had an opinion. And to beat all, Yellowstone's chief ranger—Jack Corey himself—gave the welcome."

Little Bear represented the Blackfeet because he was the former chieftain from the reservation. He arrived in full Indian headdress and when he was invited to speak, he said a prayer to the Creator and gave thanks to the Earth Person for the beauty of all creation. "It gave a near supernatural mood to the evening," he said.

"I voiced how the we natives from the beginning of time lived and hunted the area now called Yellowstone. The wolf is our elder brother, I told them. The Blackfeet learned to live in peace with the wolf before the White Man arrived. Then I delivered my punch line. We support the return of the wolf to Yellowstone."

He then shook his head and smiled, as if it had just happened yesterday.

Dieter asked, "So, why did you change your mind?"

"Simple. My neighbors," Little Bear replied. "I've heard enough stories from ranchers about livestock that have been mauled. The wolves aren't worth that kind of price."

Dieter had told Mr. Little Bear about the electronic rig that the Judge was putting together for him, how it would pick up signals from those that were radio-collared. The plan was that the two of them would do the recon under the ploy of a guide service flying over the Park—a risky game to play behind the Park Service's back.

In spite of all the planning, what Mr. Little Bear hadn't expected was the visit from Eliot Culpepper. The California land developer was on his way back home from signing a deal in Boston for a new shopping mall. Culpepper thought he might stop in Montana, maybe spend a couple of days fly-fishing for some monster trout on the upper reaches of the Snake. Mr. Little Bear had guided him on occasional fishing and hunting trips over the past eight years. Eliot Culpepper was not the kind of guy you dismissed. He had more money than Little Bear had time to explain how booked-up he was.

Little Bear pointed out over the lake at a single-engine plane flying much too low. When it buzzed over, the pilot waved.

"I didn't want to disappoint you today," Little Bear said. "So, I talked to my backup."

"Do I know him?"

Little Bear smiled. "Oh, you've met her indeed. Remember, I told you Amy has her license. Excellent pilot. Knows the Cessna inside and out."

"But—"

"You couldn't have someone more qualified to fly you. The only thing she knows better than that Cessna is Yellowstone. That's a promise. I've got to get moving now. Can't keep my client waiting." As he rushed away, he motioned toward the strip on the backside of the property where Amy was landing.

The whole idea began to look stupid. Flying a small plane around ten thousand-foot peaks and at treetop levels while he held a make-shift antenna looking for wolves. And Corey had made no bones about the outcome if they got caught.

Amy hopped down from the plane and strolled toward him. "Dad told me you were looking for a bird's eye view of the Park. If only you'd told me you were interested."

"But we just planned it out over a beer yesterday. He knows *everything*. I mean, everything there is to know about the wolf restoration and Operation Wolfstock, Amy. I was totally taken aback about how much—"

"You're afraid of flying with me, aren't you?"

"Of course not!" His reply may have been a little too energetic, he thought. "That's the furthest thing from my mind, Amy."

"No it isn't. You think I can't handle a plane." She shook out her long black hair and pulled it back over her shoulders.

"It's not that at all. It's just that—"

"Let's face it," she said. "I've brought this up before. It seems nothing I've tried meets with your approval, does it?"

"That's unfair and you know it."

"I've taken care of your kids the best way I know how this summer, Dieter. But you've complained all along about the food I've cooked for them, how I let them play in the woods, telling them the legends of my people. I could go on."

"Did you know Michael had nightmares after you told him about your people running buffalo over cliffs? Smashing them to smithereens on the prairie floor?"

"What? I shouldn't tell your son about Native American history? I suppose you want me to give him the bastardized version you grew up with in your pasty white Pennsylvania classrooms?"

"I'm only saying," he spoke slowly, softly "that your tales can sometimes be too much."

"Okay, forget the stories. How about when I try to teach them water survival? How to swim? This is the God Almighty West, Dieter. Not some concrete suburbia with make-believe playgrounds made up of plastic slides and padded jungle gyms with cedar chips covering the ground so that, God forbid, the little ones don't scrape their knees when they fall."

"Fran and I had plans on how we'd raise them."

"I can't believe what I'm hearing. Are you listening to yourself?" she asked.

"No, I can't hear anything. My blood's pumping too loudly." All she was saying was crap. Why was she unloading on him?

"Fran's gone, Dieter."

"Excuse me?"

"Fran's gone," she repeated gently.

"You think I don't know? That a day doesn't go by without my seeing her face?"

"What I'm trying to say —"

"A day that I don't see her smile, the scent of her hair after a shower? The trail of her powdered feet across the red carpet of the bedroom?"

"Okay, stop! Look, I'm sorry. I know how you've gotta feel."

No, she didn't. She was too young. She was too damned new to the game called life to understand the loss of someone whom you loved more than any treasure on earth. To feel the loss of someone you held and kissed every night before you slept and now you wake up every morning and forget for a second or two that she's not there. Then the pain returns.

No more sharing of your dreams and knowing that no one else will ever love you as she had loved you. One night you ram your fist into a pillow, the next night you cry. Everyday you are torn among your worst emotions competing for your attention. Amy had pricked a sensitive nerve and he wasn't about to forget it.

"I'm only asking," she said, tearing, "if you've ever thought that . . . maybe it's time to let go?"

"Let *go*?"

"To let go of Fran. Let go of trying to guess what you believe she would want or do for Michael and Megan. It's all up to you now, Dieter. You, alone."

If there was anything or anyone he needed to let go, it was Amy. It was time to tell her straight to her face. A barbed hook yanking at his gut, the timing was perfect.

She grabbed for his arm before he could speak. "We shouldn't be talking like this. We come from two different worlds. But the fact is we both love Megan and Michael and we want the best for them." She clutched his arm and tugged. "Come on, let's take off. You won't believe what the Park looks like from ten thousand feet above!"

THIRTY-FOUR

The ER staff at the one-story West Yellowstone Hospital had performed a host of x-rays and physical exams on Charlene while Molly sat in the waiting area flipping through magazines without reading a word. She prayed that she didn't cause any more injury when she struggled with Charlene to help her onto the back of the ATV or in driving her over the rugged terrain.

Molly stood to greet the young doctor on duty when he approached. With a somber look he spoke in a cold, matter-of-fact manner, saying that Charlene had hit the ground on her right side, tearing her rotator cuff and sustaining a hairline fracture in her wrist.

"Is she going to be okay?" Molly asked.

He placed his hands into the pockets of his green garb. "Do you mind coming with me, Mrs. Schoonover? I'd like to ask you a few questions in private."

Bewildered, she followed him into a small room off the ER, bare except for a table of sparse supplies against one wall and the two chairs where they sat.

Another wonderful example of the myriad of topics you weave into your story line, educating without preaching .

"How are you related to Miss Loudermilk?" he asked. He appeared detached as he spoke. Maybe that's the way it had to be at an ER.

179

Maybe he'd been without sleep for too long. Or maybe he was too damned young to have learned beside manners yet.

"Not at all," Molly said.

"A neighbor?"

"No, just a friend of the family."

The doctor listened while leaning back with his legs crossed, holding a notepad and intensely focused on her face. His words were slow in climbing out. "How long have you known her?"

"Less than a week."

"But you said you're a friend of the family."

She looked away and back again. "I lied, Doc." She confessed her interest in having draperies made by the Loudermilk women and what she'd learned about the family and their oddball ways in the one surprise meeting at her home. She avoided the incident at the shed because it was none of his business. His job was to treat Charlene's injuries. The traumatized girl needed medical attention. As far as everything else about her despicable family, Molly and the Judge would deal with them down the road. That was a case for downhome justice, not for the medical profession.

"I'm sorry to probe so much," the doctor said, "but I have to tell you that Miss Loudermilk has—" he interrupted himself and paused to contemplate his words. "She has serious issues. We're quite concerned about her right now."

Does she have some kind of fatal disease?

"There's more than her injuries from her fall," he added. "Have you noticed the older bruises on her arms and neck?"

"I've seen a small bruise or two."

"I was shocked when I examined her, Mrs. Schoonover. She has old scars. Signs of welts and contusions all over her body. Even evidence of an instrument or object used forcefully in places I won't mention."

Molly could believe it, every word he was saying. In time she would see to it that Joseph Vincent Loudermilk would get everything that was coming to him. If there was any redeeming justice on earth, he would arrive in Hell with a pitchfork up his ass and signed by Molly Schoonover. She brushed her eyes with the back of her hand.

The doctor shoved a box of tissues toward her and continued. "She also appears anorexic. That condition is common among women who've been chronically abused."

It was time to tell him everything, beginning with her unplanned visit to the Loudermilk farm. She described her creepy walk down the graveled road, the strange sounds coming from the shed and the horrible scene in the window.

"Are you certain Charlene was the victim?"

She wiped her nose and sniffled. "As sure as I sit here."

He moved closer to her. "I'm required, Mrs. Schoonover, to report this incident to the police."

"I know," she said, relieved Charlene would finally get some protection. "My husband's a former judge. You're just beating us to the punch, Doc."

Molly stayed by Charlene's bed, holding her hand and keeping close watch on her pale swollen face covered with bruises and tincture of iodine. As she brushed Charlene's hair back from the scrapes on her forehead Molly realized that her fondness for animals—from the horses and sheep on their ranch to those barking dachshunds—was nothing more than a substitute love for the child she never had. Her one regret in life was her inability to provide the Judge with a child they both always wanted. She promised herself that she and the Judge would confront the Loudermilk clan after the ordeal was over. He would take care of the legal work to regain Charlene's children. She'd take care of the rest.

When Charlene awoke, Molly wet her chapped lips with the corner of a washcloth dipped in ice water. Charlene murmured and Molly lowered her head. "I can't hear you, honey."

"Don't tell Joseph Vincent I'm here. Okay?"

Charlene spoke about her adventure as if still struggling to understand it. When the wolf came for her, it scraped at the base of the tree, growling and waiting below on its haunches for her to grow weak and fall.

"In your dreams, pooch!" she kept screaming at it.

She told how the wolf dashed away like a bolt of lightning when a humongous brown bear trudged out of the woods. Might have been a Grizzly; she was too frightened to tell if it had a hump. The bear crunched and chewed on her friend's body before dragging him away like a sack of feed.

"I was scared that his head was gonna come off on a snag."

Molly wiped tears from Charlene's cheeks and stroked her hair, assuring her that she wouldn't let Joseph Vincent or anyone else take her away.

A young nurse at the door motioned for Molly. She hurried into the hallway and stopped. Staring back at her with a grim look plastered on his face was Deputy Harlan Ward. "I'm sorry, Molly."

She gave him a warm hug and they walked down the hall to a seating area. Harlan wanted to get involved. After Molly repeated to him everything she'd told the doctor, Harlan promised the Loudermilk family would be investigated straight away. But the first priority was Charlene. "I'm going to try to talk her into staying with the Judge and me for a while, Harlan."

"You'd better be careful on this one. Could be getting into something too big to deal with."

"She's a sweetheart. An absolute darling of a woman. Would you like to meet her?"

They stood and he followed Molly down the hall and into the room. Charlene wasn't in the bed. Molly tapped on the bathroom door. "Are you okay, dear?"

When she didn't answer, Molly twisted the knob and cracked open the door. No one was there.

She peeked into the small closet and discovered Charlene's bag of clothing gone.

"Look over here," Harlan said, as he moved to the far side of the room. The blinds on a narrow vertical window were pulled up and the window cranked open. The screen was lying on the ground outside.

THIRTY-FIVE

The single-engine Cessna slowly climbed from the Little Bears' landing strip. The higher it rose the more Dieter was astounded by the vast areas of the forest below that had burned. "I had no idea how destructive the fires were."

"All that you see is from the big one in '88," Amy said. "A third of the Park's two million acres burned back then."

"Unbelievable."

She piloted out over Yellowstone while Dieter held in his lap the signal detector the Judge had delivered: a TV-type antenna, more than two-feet wide, with a rod attached beneath it for a handle. A thin cable connected the antenna to a hand-held meter in a makeshift aluminum case with headphones attached. He could hold the antenna in one hand and the meter in the other.

"If that contraption picks up a wolf signal, I'll buy you lunch," Amy said, hardly moving her lips as she spoke.

"You're on."

The Judge had given him a lesson on how to use the device. As Dieter dialed across the range the headphones squealed and a needle jumped about on the face of the meter. They rose and fell in sync with weak signals from distant short wave radio and TV broadcasts.

They flew in wide swaths over the Park for twenty minutes before Amy twisted a knob on her instrument panel and called out. "We're approaching the Lamar Valley. Are your electronics working?"

He adjusted his headphones. "Just getting a lot of background noise."

"I'll take us down and keep near the river."

Both focused intently on the ground below as they flew. A herd of pronghorn antelope raced across the rolling fields when Dieter suddenly held an index finger to his lips. He fiddled with the dial. "Can you move lower? I'm picking up something."

"You're just trying to get a free lunch." She did a smooth turn and descended, passing close to the tallest evergreens below.

A signal came in over his headphones and a red light on the meter blinked. He shoved open his window and peered below. "Look! Directly under us."

She eased the aircraft around and banked to the right. He picked up more spikes on the frequency scan. The light blinked faster. "I'm counting eight, maybe nine wolves in single file."

"That's gotta be the Rose Creek pack, just like Dad said."

Spooked by the low-flying aircraft, the wolves loped away into the trees. Dieter laughed and shook the antenna like a trophy. "I told you the Judge knew what he was doing! A genius, that man."

"Amy stretched her neck to look out her window to the rear. "Oh, no."

They were words he didn't like to hear from a pilot.

"We've got a plane coming at us," she said. "Appears to be a Super Cub with colors of the Park Service." She quickly pulled away and climbed. "We don't want to look like we're harassing wildlife. They can get our tail number and investigate us up the wazoo."

Dieter watched as they gained distance on the advancing plane.

"Let's head over to the Gardiner Airport for a while," Amy said. "You settle for a tuna fish sandwich?"

"What will come with it?"

"They make their own special mayo. Don't push me."

*   *   *

While they waited on their food in the terminal sandwich shop, Dieter glanced around the room at a smattering of pilots of other light planes parked in the field near the hangar. Some wore cowboy hats and ate in a slap-dash manner, trading jokes.

When the sandwiches were delivered, Amy picked hers up for a quick bite before yanking from her hip pocket a map and spreading it out on the table. "When we take off, I'll give you on a quick tour of park highlights." She circled areas of interest with a ballpoint pen. "This is the Black Sands Geyser Basin, a natural plumbing system. It actually connects the earth's superhot core to the surface. I'm told that ten thousand thermal features spew up all over the Park. Not only more geysers than any place on earth but the most magnificent hot springs found anywhere. They're boiling throughout the year."

"Where's Old Faithful?"

Amy pointed on the map. "Not very likely we'll see her in action. She only lasts a couple of minutes when she blows." She moved her pen to the area for their search, indicating creeks and small rivers flowing from the Park down into the area around Colter. As she spoke, Dieter marveled at her enthusiasm. The argument at the lake they'd had earlier seemed distant—they were now working as a team. She was in control at the moment and he was comfortable with that. But there was something he had to get off his chest.

"I want you to know," he said, "that I don't blame your dad or the Blackfeet for the wolf problem. They were doing what they believed in."

She swallowed her last bite and wiped her lips. "At least it was what they believed in at the time." She winked and tossed down her napkin. "Let's go exploring."

*   *   *

While they flew, Dieter stared out on the snow that clung to the ragged crown of the Beartooth Mountains to the north. He tracked their progress on Amy's map. After passing Specimen Ridge, she followed the river south along the Grand Canyon of Yellowstone and soared over the rim. The panorama seemed a holy shrine. Ripples of ivory-like stone carved out over eons, the canyon walls tinged red by the morning sun. All of it contrasted with the lime green river meandering through the grandest of canyons.

The altimeter rose to 9100 feet as they headed out across the vast expanse of Hayden Valley at the center of the Park. She dipped the Cessna's wing so he could get a look at a herd of bison swimming across the Yellowstone River. When they crossed the Gibbon River near Paintpot Hill, veils of steam arose from a cluster of geysers that dotted the forest below.

The search began in the Madison Valley near the Park's western boundary along Cougar Creek as they flew north over dense woodlands and across a series of mountain creeks—Maple, Richards, Gneiss, Campanula, Grayling. When they reached the Gallatin River, she took a wide turn and flew south along a path parallel to the one they had flown. Cruising at only five hundred feet, he listened intently for a signal on his headphones. After half an hour of flying the north-south corridors that had been penned on the map, his arm was aching from holding onto the antenna. He placed it down at his feet and at the same instant a beep rang out in his headphones. The needle on the meter began to dance.

"Quick, bring her around!" he shouted and adjusted the dial. He mashed one headphone against his ear as the plane banked. There was now a steady beep with the meter's red light flashing. He stretched to look out the window.

As if sunning itself, a gigantic black wolf lay on a boulder in the middle of a swift stream. The animal appeared undaunted by the roar of the plane.

"What you got?" Amy asked.

"I don't know. I mean, it's a wolf, but look at the *size* of that thing."

She did a clockwise turn and maneuvered back along the river. When the plane approached, the wolf dived in and swam toward shore. After scurrying up the bank, it shook and sprayed water from its dark fur and then darted into a meadow.

"Hold on!" Amy cried out as she pulled back on the stick and shot the nose skyward.

Dieter jerked up.

A towering tree rocketed toward them. He grabbed the sides of his seat with both hands to brace himself and jammed his feet into the floor, mashing the antenna.

The plane grazed the top of a lodge pole pine, sounding as if the underbelly was crushed like a tin can. The single engine sputtered and the entire cabin shook.

THIRTY-SIX

The Cessna had stalled in midair. "Now what?" Dieter asked, trying to hide his panic.

Amy brought the nose down and attempted to restart the engine. An unsettling silence filled the cockpit. "We need to find a place to land," she said in a manner much too relaxed for Dieter.

"Please get the engine running, Amy."

"The prop snagged on the tree."

"Can you get it started?"

"Must've damaged the engine."

"What in the hell does that mean?"

"Keep calm."

Keep calm? The plane rapidly descended toward a blanket of pine trees below.

"There it is!" she cried out. "Salvation asphalt."

He spotted the highway running north of Colter. The plane banked toward it as the road disappeared over a hill. They were approaching the ground too damned fast.

"We'll keep following the highway," she blurted. "It's our best hope. This could be rough."

Isn't that frigging normal for crash landings?

On the other side of the hill the road straightened out. A motorcycle was speeding south, directly at them.

"Here we go," she shouted.

"The motorcycle . . ."

"He'll figure it out. Brace yourself."

The plane glided just above the pavement, then the landing gear slammed into the highway and the brakes squealed. The plane skidded and spun a quarter turn into the heavy brush by the roadside.

"Jump out!" Amy shouted.

He unbuckled and bolted out the door before she finished her order. The startled motorcyclist in jeans and a yellow tank-top jogged toward them. Amy ran around to Dieter's side, holding her head in disbelief as they walked into the field away from the aircraft. "I'm sorry, I'm sorry. It was idiotic of me."

"Don't apologize," he said and hoped that she couldn't pick up the tremor in his voice. "You got us out of it. We're safe."

She flung her arms around his neck while he took hold of the small of her back with both hands and pulled her to him. His cheek brushed hers and he stole a deep breath of her fragrance before she let go.

"Next time," he whispered, "how about if I do the searching and you do the flying?"

"Deal."

*   *   *

Michael Harmon felt out of place after school in the basement of Colter Baptist Church—his first troop meeting as a Boy Scout and he still didn't have a uniform. His disappointment was overshadowed by thoughts of his dad letting him go to the Yellowstone Camporee. That was a big win and big wins were hard to come by.

Megan and another girl her age who wore a frilly skirt instead of shorts, were kept busy by the Scoutmaster's wife during the meeting. Scoutmaster Farmington introduced Michael to the boys of Colter

Troop 173 as they sat on folding chairs in a circle. Michael felt the stares like he was naked or something. They were curious stares except for the scoutmaster's son, one of the older guys who was an overweight smartass. Fat Kenny snickered whenever Michael was around him as if the new kid was too young and dumb to be in the Scouts.

The scoutmaster announced that the first order of business was to get prepared for the Labor Day Camporee coming up that weekend. He said he would be leading an overnight camping trip in the wilderness and the scoutmaster from another troop would lead an all-day canoeing trip. In either case, the boys could sign up for only one event and, for Michael, it was an easy choice.

After the talk, everyone followed the scoutmaster down the wooded path behind the church to the Tranquility Garden picnic area reserved for family get-togethers. Those who were taller and older made a point of moving faster than he could, sometimes brushing an arm or elbow against him whenever they passed. Michael fell behind. When Fat Kenny got close enough, he bumped hard against his shoulder. "Hey, kid," he teased. "The Cubs are back at the church playing with dolls. You're in the wrong Troop."

Michael tried to ignore him, but it wasn't easy. He wanted to bash in his face with a pine branch. When they arrived at the shelter, Mr. Farmington met each boy with a big grin and a pat on the back. Michael was last.

"I'm afraid," the scoutmaster whispered, "that you'll have to walk a little faster if you intend to go hiking this weekend. There's some pretty steep ground in the Park. I think you'd do better on the canoe trip."

Michael took a seat at a back table at the end of the bench beside a redheaded boy no taller than he was and who looked harmless. Mr. Farmington explained how they needed three hikes to earn their *Leave No Trace Awareness* patch. He jabbered about the importance of nature and the environment and about respecting the rights of others to use the outdoors. Even those who weren't born yet. Then he switched to the overnight hike that would begin on Sunday. He spoke about carrying backpacks, setting up tents, wearing the right clothes, and weather forecasts. He reminded them that the hike was only for the boys who had a signed permission slip from a parent.

Michael held up his hand. "I didn't get a slip."

"I gave one to your nanny, Michael. Please ask her about it. Now, how many of you have the list of essential items for the hike?"

As soon as Mr. Farmington said "nanny" the boys around him giggled and his face felt hot. Maybe his dad was right. Maybe he should have stayed with the Cub Scouts another year. On the walk back to the church, Fat Kenny sneaked up on him from behind. "Hey, Mikey! Going home to your nanny?" He spoke loud enough so the boys around him could hear his laugh. "Does your nanny give you milk from her titty?"

More laughter. Michael stopped and stared back at him, curling his hands into fists. Fat Kenny moved in closer and lowered his head, inches from his face. "What's a matter? Are you gonna cry?"

Michael held his breath and walked away. Fat Kenny followed, whispering behind him. "Little boys who've got a nanny should stay out of the woods. It's a scary place. You never know what could—"

Michael collapsed to the ground on his knees. As close as a shadow, Fat Kenny stumbled over him and slammed into the dirt.

"Dammit!" cried the startled boy. He lay on his back while holding his knee in the air with both hands and a look of mortal pain.

With the look of a sergeant, Mr. Farmington marched to the scene and glared down at his son. "Was that foul language coming from your mouth, Kenny?"

"I tripped," he mumbled back. All of the boys stared at Michael.

"Shame on you for that kind of talk, Kenny. If I hear any more of that, you're staying home this weekend. Move it out, boys!"

It had been a risky thing to do. One of Fat Kenny's friends might beat him up later, but it felt good at the moment. The redheaded boy from the picnic table caught up with him. He said his name was Randy Cunningham. "My mom says I won't get to go on the overnighter."

Although he wasn't any taller than Michael, he looked older. "If you can't go, maybe we can hang out at the campground together."

"Who said I wasn't going on the hike?" Michael replied.

"How come you don't got a uniform anyways?"

Michael shrugged his shoulders, like it wasn't important. Then Randy pointed at Fat Kenny limping and they both giggled. Michael had made a friend. Maybe it was going to be a fun weekend after all.

*   *   *

Mrs. Farmington dropped Michael and Megan off at home after the Scout meeting. Michael lumbered toward the cabin as Megan ran ahead. She waited at the side door until he unlocked it, then dashed inside to grab Rusty and wrestle with him on the kitchen floor.

He pulled a gallon jug of milk from the refrigerator. A note was stuck on the door:

> Michael,
>
> I'm sorry but we won't be able to drive up to Bozeman this evening for your uniform. I'll be home in time to fix dinner.
>
> Love,
>
> Dad

Michael ripped the note from the door and wadded it up in his fist. He hurled it onto the kitchen floor and ran into the bedroom where he plopped down on his bed. When Megan strolled into his room, he covered his head with a pillow.

"Remember," she whispered, "you gotta take Rusty out."

"Just get out of my room."

"I don't know what happened, but whatever it was, I didn't do it." She scampered out and gently closed the door behind her, but not before whispering "Rusty" at him one more time.

He threw the pillow to the floor and stood, then walked to the chest of drawers and stooped to open the bottom one. Underneath his winter long johns, he reached for a Boy Scout form:

BOY SCOUT TROOP 173 PERMISSION SLIP AND WAIVER OF CLAIMS

Please read this form. It must be signed and returned to the Gallatin District Scoutmaster before each activity.

Indian Creek Camporee at Yellowstone National Park

Circle ONE only: Overnight / Hike / Canoe Trip

Parent/Guardian for himself/herself and for his/her child or ward by signature herein below waives any and all claims against Boy Scout Troop 173, its leaders and parent volunteers for injury, accident, illness or death occurring during the hike or excursion.

Parent's/Guardian's Signature _____

Date _____

With the folded piece of paper behind his back, he crept toward the kitchen and stopped to peek around the corner. Megan sat on her knees in a chair at the table. With an opened jar and lid beside her elbow, she was painting a slice of bread with a glob of peanut butter. For her, it was more than a snack, it was a party. He tiptoed down the hall and entered his dad's bedroom, where he pushed open the roll-top desk and stared at the mess. Searching through the stacks on top, he was careful to keep every piece of paper in place. When he thought he saw the bank checks, he reached too fast for them and knocked a stack of papers lying near the edge to the floor. He quickly plunged to his hands and knees and collected the scattered papers, hoping they were back in order, more or less. Gently placing the pile on the desk, he twisted and shoved it back and forth into the exact position that he remembered.

He reached for the group of cancelled checks and pulled one out. In one hand he held the check and in the other he picked up the Scout permission slip. He rushed to the window and mashed both pieces of paper against the glass pane, then arranged the check's signature line under the blank line of the permission slip. With a ballpoint pen clutched between his thumb and forefinger and his teeth clamping down on his tongue, he carefully began to trace.

THIRTY-SEVEN

Bantz Montgomery entered Greta McFarland's office, accompanied by Dr. Matthew Wallace from the forensics lab in Oregon.

"Come on in," McFarland ordered.

She'd never looked so bedraggled, Montgomery thought, and he knew why. Word had come in that afternoon about the death of a hiker on the Fawn Pass trail. On the day before, the office received the call from Oregon that Dr. Wallace would be flying in on a government charter with the lab results that McFarland had demanded.

Jack Corey stood in the office by a Yellowstone map on the wall while apparently briefing McFarland. The greetings with Dr. Wallace were quick, then coffee was offered to the special guest but politely refused. The office air hung thick with solemn business as Wallace and Montgomery took their seats and McFarland asked Corey to carry on.

"It was a Grizzly attack," Corey said confidently, pointing to the map. "The hiker's body was located here, not far off the Fawn Pass trail."

"What makes you think a bear did it?" McFarland asked.

"I sent out a team." He nodded toward Montgomery. "Bantz led it."

McFarland squeezed her forehead as Corey spoke. The park superintendent always depended on her to be the go-to person for the media. She'd be the one to take care of the report of a death on a backcountry trail and she needed to do it that weekend. An exhausting turn of events for everyone, but especially for anyone in her position.

"They found fresh scat and tracks where the attack occurred," Corey continued. "Unmistakable Grizzly signs. The body was dragged away and covered with dirt and branches. Typical."

McFarland folded her arms across her chest and gripped her chin with one hand. "Why is that typical?"

"Temporary storage. The bear planned to return to finish off the carcass. Had to hide it from scavengers in the meantime."

Montgomery started to speak, but Corey used his eyes to shut him up.

McFarland asked, "So you would say that this attack had an entirely different signature from the one of the photographer?"

"Precisely."

She turned to face Montgomery directly. "Bantz, what about the other hiker, a Miss Loudermilk, I believe. What did she say happened?"

Montgomery kept his side vision trained on Corey as he spoke. "I wasn't able to get much out of her. She was still sedated and just muttered, really."

"Did she say anything about a wolf?"

"I . . . believe so."

"Who knows what she meant," Corey spoke up. "We had a bear attack on a hiker, Greta. That's always the danger in backcountry."

McFarland lowered her head and massaged her temples. "Good God Almighty, Jack," she said under her breath.

"Sorry?" Corey asked.

Without answering, McFarland turned to the director of the Oregon forensics lab. "Well, Dr. Wallace, I hope you've brought us some data that can help us out here."

"As a matter of fact, we have more than we expected to have by now." He quickly summarized what he and his team had accomplished during the week. They had the attacking animal's saliva from the wounds inflicted on the victims. They had also recovered strands of hair from the fatal neck wound of the photographer and in many cases from the livestock deaths. The lab isolated the DNA from the samples to pin down a single hybrid as the culprit, a cross between the Tosa Inu breed and a North American gray wolf. To complete the investigation, in the previous two days his team analyzed DNA in the stored blood samples from all of the original wolves transported into Yellowstone from Alberta.

"So for us, it was just a matter of matching the foreign trace DNA found in the wounds of the victims," Dr. Wallace said, "with DNA from the stored blood from all of the wolves." Wallace clearly fancied himself as the detective meeting with everyone in the parlor after solving the crime. "And I'm pleased to tell you that we succeeded in getting a perfect match with one of the wolves."

He grabbed a thick folder from his attaché and pulled out of it an eight by ten photo that he passed around the table. It showed a wire cage resting on snow and inside it, an ebony black wolf. Nothing notable about the animal, except for a silver stripe along its chest.

"That's the killer," Dr. Wallace said. "The picture was taken just after capture in Alberta. Wolf number 25M. The male belonged to the Soda Butte pack, the first pack released into the Park."

"It looks like a normal wolf to me," McFarland said.

"According to his records," Wallace replied, "mainly those from the teeth, it was eleven months old when captured. Only a pre-teen in dog age. Yet at one hundred twenty-eight pounds, it was the largest wolf in the pack."

"Why didn't the biologists see a red flag at the time?" McFarland continued.

Dr. Wallace held his open palms out and shrugged. "Other than observing that it was big for its age, there was absolutely nothing unusual. You can see from the picture that its dominant characteristics are those of a wolf. But its genetic makeup leaves no doubt—absolutely none—that 25M is a hybrid."

McFarland peered at Corey. "I take it that you can locate the whereabouts of 25M from the radio transmissions on his collar?"

Corey quickly rifled through the stack of papers he'd brought to the meeting while McFarland tapped an index finger on the table. It took only a minute for Corey to hold up a double-sided sheet of paper that listed every wolf radio-collared and the frequency of its transmitter. "It's right here on the chart." He slid his finger across the paper. "That wolf—25M—transmits at 152.38 megahertz."

"The superintendent wants this taken care of," McFarland quickly responded. "You need to get search and capture underway."

"With all the visitors coming in over a holiday weekend," Corey said, "I've had to pull in a dozen extra rangers. And that's just to direct traffic. We don't have the manpower to—"

"Listen to me carefully, Jack. I am ordering you to track down the wolf this weekend. Even if you and Montgomery have to go it alone."

Looking embarrassed for a colleague, Dr. Wallace averted his eyes.

Take a deep breath, Jack.

Corey sat up straight. "Okay . . . and when we locate this creature, we'll bring in a chopper and get rangers on the ground. I'll page you."

"You can call me directly," McFarland said. "I'll be right here. And remember the regional Boy Scout outing at Indian Creek. I'm told a hundred Scouts or more will be there. What are your plans for that?"

"Nothing out of the ordinary," Corey replied. "The incident happened on the far side of the Big Horn Pass. That's a good fifteen miles or more from their campground. There's no reason to get the Scouts all worked up."

"Is that your only recommendation to the superintendent?"

"We could take other precautions."

"Like?"

"Like closing the Fawn Pass trail."

McFarland leaned back in her chair to think it over before replying. "I'll give the superintendent your advice. It's his decision, but he's out of town. I'll try to reach him."

Montgomery watched amused as it all played out. He'd seen it all in action before. McFarland got what she wanted out of Corey and if anything goes wrong—no matter the size of the problem—she could point the finger at him. And where the hell was the superintendent when it all hit the fan? He'd already gotten out of Dodge for the long weekend.

After the meeting, Montgomery followed Corey into his office.

Corey slammed shut the door and immediately turned and shoved Montgomery against the wall. He pinned back his shoulders and mashed his face into Montgomery's. "For the last time, Bantz, when we're in front of her, let me do the goddamn talking. The next time you pipe up—"

"She asked me a question, Jack."

Corey released his grip and twisted away. "I don't give a shit what she asks you."

"I kept telling you about the wolf tracks—"

"It was a Grizzly kill. Plain and simple."

"But the bear could've smelled the blood and come in *after* the wolf attacked."

"Why the hell are you making such a big deal out of this, Bantz?"

Montgomery waved at the Park map on the wall. "If we don't close off the entire northwest quadrant, I think we should at least give the Scouts a warning."

"You trying to be some kind of hero? Still after my job, you little prick?"

No, he didn't want Corey's job or anything more to do with Yellowstone after the weekend. He wasn't trying to act like a savior for the Scouts, the Park visitors, or for Greta McFarland. He was doing what he was hired to do eight years before. No longer any need to waste his breath. All he had to do was make it through the weekend. He'd had enough. The wild card was Corey.

THIRTY-EIGHT

"Where do you plan to take your overnighter, Mr. Farmington?" Jack Corey asked. He'd agreed to meet up with Leonard Farmington in the afternoon at Yellowstone's Indian Creek campground.

The two men sat on benches at opposite sides of a picnic table. Wearing his tan outfit full of regalia, Farmington had introduced himself as the scoutmaster for the Gallatin District. He'd added that he was also the leader for a Boy Scout troop in Colter. The way he spoke, along with his hand-waving mannerisms, suggested a long history of organizing Scout activities. A trail map lay spread out on the picnic table.

Farmington pointed at the map with a pen engraved with the Boy Scouts of America insignia. "We had our council jamboree here four years ago. Back then, we hiked the Howard Eaton. But this time we plan our overnight hike on the Bighorn Pass. That's our best option, of course, since we're camped so near the trailhead."

"The Bighorn's a popular trail," Corey said. He pointed to the map. "It goes from here all the way over to the western edge at Highway 191. But you should be aware that we did have an unfortunate accident yesterday. Here on the Fawn Pass trail. It runs across the Park north of the Bighorn."

"What kind of accident?"

"A Grizzly mauling. The hiker was killed."

Farmington dropped his jaw and jerked back his head. "Good golly!"

"Now it's nothing really to worry about."

"But we haven't heard or read anything about it."

"It's one reason I wanted to meet with you," Corey said, "and go over the—"

"An actual *Grizzly* mauling?"

"That's why I wanted to review your plans. It was quite sad. A college student hiking with a local girl. She got away unhurt, for the most part."

Farmington couldn't stop shaking his head. He examined the map one more time. "The Fawn Pass trail doesn't look that far away."

"It's pretty far north and west of the campground."

"Do you consider it a safe distance?"

"I don't see it as a threat at all," Corey said. "But keep in mind, we're in a national park. Animals take priority over people here. You do have all the info we provided on campground safety?"

"We know there's always a threat of bears. We'll follow park guidelines, of course. Hang our stored food in the trees and all that."

Corey rose from the table. "By the way, wolves have been spotted in the area."

"We'd love to see a wolf pack! Can you give me any tips?"

"There're no packs where you'll be hiking. But there may be a lone wolf here or there. We've had reports of one on the prowl."

"A wolf on the prowl? Is that something we should be watching out for?"

"Standard precautions, Mr. Farmington. Give any wolves you spot a wide berth. Think of them in the same way you might a Grizzly."

The scoutmaster looked puzzled. "But I've always heard that wolves stay far away from people."

"I don't want to frighten any of the Scouts. Use common sense. Anyway, I'm only talking here about a slim chance of encountering a wolf or a bear. But just to be extra cautious, we're making flyovers in your area this weekend."

Farmington smiled. "That's terrific, Mr. Corey. It's good to know the Park Service is keeping a watch out for us."

"Just doing my job, Mr. Farmington. Just doing my job."

*   *   *

While Montgomery drove toward headquarters, heavy traffic was already building: half of it pickup trucks with camper shells and RVs lashed with bicycles and folding chairs on the rear. They weaved from the middle of the road to the shoulder, hustling along at a top speed of maybe twenty-five. On their bumpers were license plates with pictures of bronco-riding cowboys or skiers and some with mottos proclaiming *Greatest Snow on Earth.*

After he arrived at headquarters there was a note on his desk from "G.M." McFarland wanted to see him as soon as possible. Strange. He'd never been called into her office alone before. But everyone was walking around on eggshells. He had a gut feeling that he knew what it was all about.

When he tapped on her open door she invited him to sit.

"First let me say, Bantz, that Superintendent Gilmer and I are most appreciative of your hard work on the wolf problem."

That's a first. He'd never been thanked by anyone at her level or above for anything he'd ever done. He knew what was coming. It was obvious from her body language at the earlier meeting in her office that she was preparing a change in field strategy.

McFarland hesitated, as if trying to gather the right words. "I'm aware our meeting like this is a bit unusual, but I had a long discussion with the superintendent before leaving you the note."

So this is how they tell you that you've been transferred to another assignment? Or to another national park? Little did she know that she was playing his song.

"I'll confess that I was surprised by your note," he said. "You know, I've put in a good eight years."

Best to play dumb . . . play along with the script.

"Let me stop you right there, Bantz. As you're well aware, we're facing the biggest problem since the fires of '88. The fact that Operation Wolfstock has been corrupted by a killer hybrid wolf is nothing short of a disaster. All of this means those who fought bringing wolves back to Yellowstone were right, Bantz. That includes most of the US Congressmen in the tri-state area, not to mention the powerful lobbies from the cattle industry. In my opinion the Park Service didn't have any idea what it was doing at the time. They were like infants wrestling with a tiger."

She was talking too fast. Her words had the odor of bull crap. "To be honest with you, Miss McFarland, I'm not sure where you're going with this."

"I need your help."

Say what? A red flag flashed in his head. Here she was coming late onto the Yellowstone scene, second-guessing everything that had been done and everyone responsible for it as if she was some kind of expert who would have made everything perfect if only the Park Service had had the wisdom at the time to bring her on board.

"Let me assure you of one thing, Miss McFarland, you can count on Jack Corey to take care of this." He never thought those words would come out of his mouth, but her self-righteousness wrenched it out of him. But why was he defending Jack Corey of all people? Because in the heat of anger he wasn't going to allow a damn bureaucrat who had never stepped foot in the field to get in the last word.

"You sound so certain about Jack." She acted surprised.

"I've known him longer than anyone around. He has a track record of taking on assignments that no one else in the Park Service wanted to touch with a logger's pike."

She pushed her chair away from the desk and crossed her legs, as if to actually begin listening. "Do you mean assignments like the poacher the two of you found last week?"

"Well . . . that's the most recent example."

"Did you know the guy retained a lawyer? He's filing charges. Corey's action was totally out of line, Bantz."

No shock that Corey had failed to let him know about that one. "The point is that Jack can get things done when he puts his mind to it. But maybe that's another story. May I ask what you have planned for me?"

"I'll be straight with you," she answered. "I've been having doubts about Jack taking charge of this search from the beginning."

"If you're thinking I might take over for him, don't count on it. I won't work behind his back."

"I'm not asking that. Jack's had a lot of pressure on him lately. You're aware of that?"

"Are you talking about his family situation?" he asked.

"Well, yes, among other things."

"I think we're getting into territory we should stay out of."

"You're absolutely right, Bantz." She quickly stood and extended her hand. "Thanks for coming in. You have a lot of work ahead of you and I'm keeping you away from it."

He reached for her hand, the first time he'd ever shook it. Her grip was firmer than that of most men.

"I trust," she said, "that you'll keep our little talk confidential?"

"Of course. But one thing you should know. Jack and I will handle it. You can count on it."

THIRTY-NINE

Dieter sat in the living room after the kids had gone to bed. He'd heard the news about the death of a hiker in the Park, but the coverage was confusing. It appeared to have been a Grizzly attack and was under investigation. He'd told the kids nothing about the plane incident, hoping that Michael would not connect with it at school either. The mishap had been a close call. If Amy had flown a few feet lower, it could've been all over for both of them. That thought made him aware once again: there were no godparents for his kids.

Molly and the Judge came to mind, but so did their age. He had a good friend back in Bucks County, Dale McGregor. He'd graduated from high school with Dale, even roomed with him at Penn State when they were freshmen. They'd remained friends over the years. He was an investment banker, but the last time they'd talked he was on his second marriage and gave the impression that one wasn't a thrill ride either. He'd put off thinking about the kids for too long. Tomorrow he needed to talk with Molly. See where she stood on the matter.

A copy of Veterinary Quarterly lay opened in his lap and Rusty was sleeping on the throw rug by his side. He looked down at Rusty and called to him. Abruptly awakened, the dog plunked his paws on his master's leg to get a head rub. Dieter stood and flipped on a Phil Collins CD. While mouthing the words to One More Night, he picked up the TV remote and clicked through the channels. He searched for anything—an old M*A*S*H re-run, a decent movie. Finally he hit the off button and walked into the kitchen. He stopped to stare into the sink at the pile of dirty glassware and dishes.

How many days had those been there? He rinsed a plate and bent down to place it in the dishwasher when something through the window over the sink caught his eye— a fleeting shadow in the distance. He pressed his midriff against the edge of the sink and leaned closer to the window. A three-quarter moon lit up the night.

Perhaps he was too jumpy lately. He opened the cabinet under the sink and grabbed a flashlight, then rushed to the closet and rummaged behind the coats until he found the baseball bat. When he slid open the glass door onto the deck, the only sound was a symphony of tree frogs. Rusty rushed into the backyard clearing while Dieter squeezed the handle of the bat and scanned the woods. Something darted among the trees. Rusty barked and ran toward it.

"Come back, Rusty!" he called out as he followed the dog. Bat in hand, he came upon the path he'd taken many times when walking Rusty and taking the kids on a hike. The dog had disappeared; he had never taken off like that before.

Rusty's unmistakable barking arose again, fifty yards or so ahead. Dieter jogged deeper into the woods, moving off the path toward the bark. He pushed aside tree branches and ran through knee-high grass as tree limbs and thorn bushes scratched his face and arms. He paused to catch his breath.

Rusty was gone. He knew the dog would likely make his way back home, but he couldn't be sure. How would he ever explain this to the kids? It was stupid to let the dog out when something strange was around.

A bark came from the distance, followed by a yelp. Then another bark . . . growling . . . a shriek. Bellowing Rusty's name, he sprinted in the direction of the gut-wrenching sounds as briars tore at his shirt and neck.

His flashlight caught two glowing eyes that grew brighter when he approached. Rusty lay half-buried in a deep thicket by a scrub oak—blood covered his shoulders and belly. Dieter rubbed his hands through the soft coat until he located puncture wounds and abrasions near the throat and upper back. He stripped off his shirt and wrapped it around Rusty's neck and shoulder, tying it firmly to stop the bleeding.

The dog's eyes were open, but his breathing had stopped. Dieter placed his fingertips against the chest near the sternum and picked up a feint heartbeat. He quickly opened Rusty's mouth and pulled his tongue and jaw forward. Closing the dog's mouth again, he cupped his hands over the nose and gently blew into it, twisting his head to watch Rusty's chest rise and fall.

An eternity passed until Rusty began to breathe on his own. Dieter then cuddled all sixty pounds of fur and muscle in his arms and headed for what was his best guess as the direction of the cabin. Everything from that moment on was a blur. He acted only on instinct as he ran, occasionally stopping to lay Rusty down in the weeds and stretch his aching arms. When he finally found the familiar path, he jogged without stopping until he reached the cabin. He carefully placed Rusty upon the woven throw rug on the living room floor and grabbed a clean shirt from the bedroom closet.

After he awakened Michael and Megan, they gathered around their pet. Tears filled Michael's eyes while Megan bawled as Dieter explained that Rusty was attacked by some kind of wild animal, but he would make Rusty okay again. That was a promise. They'd have to come along with him in their pajamas to the clinic. No time to change.

*   *   *

Thank God Amy was at her bungalow in town. After receiving the startling call, she was waiting for them when they arrived at Dieter's clinic. Michael and Megan huddled with her in the reception area as Dieter prepared Rusty for surgery. He hung a bag of Ringer's on a stand beside the table and adjusted the drip, then injected a morphine epidural followed by a brachial plexus nerve block. Palpable hematomas had formed beneath the skin, so he stuck a catheter into a vein then carefully shoved the intubation tube down the trachea and connected the dog to the anesthesia circuit.

After Rusty went under, he cut away the blood-soaked shirt he'd wrapped around him. Puncture wounds on the scalp penetrated into the skull and throat—possibly only the tip of an iceberg of damage. He clipped the fur from around the neck and flushed the wound with sterile saline and surgical scrub. As he sewed up the deep lacerations, he kept palpitating the area. With a sigh of relief, he could find no severed muscles or tendons. Someone on High had to have been looking out for Rusty.

The surgery lasted thirty-five minutes. Afterwards, all stood watching Rusty as he lay sleeping on the table. Packed red cells hung from a clear plastic bag above him and flowed into a vein. A clean bandage was around his neck; his breathing, rapid and shallow. Dieter had no idea how much blood the dog had lost, but it would take at least twenty-four hours to see if he had a fighting chance.

Dieter placed both arms around Michael and Megan and reassured them again that their dog was going to be okay. If it turned out he was wrong, he'd deal with it then, but he couldn't bring himself to leaving any doubts in their minds. Right or wrong, there was no way he was going there.

After the kids reluctantly agreed to return home, Dieter gave them another extended hug while Amy gently squeezed his shoulder. When they were gone, he pulled up two chairs beside the table for a makeshift bed and lay down, trying to remember how long it had been since he'd prayed.

FORTY

The next morning Amy had to knock twice before Dieter made it to the back door of the clinic. She thrust in his face a large coffee and fast-food bag with the aroma of breakfast as she made her way to Rusty's cage. An antibiotic dripped from an IV into a vein in the dog's front leg. She leaned down and stuck two fingers through the wire and wiggled them as she whispered to the dog. Rusty didn't move, but his eyes lit up as he quietly whined. She straightened up and wiped at her eyes.

"Did you get any sleep last night?" she asked.

He brushed back his hair and stifled a yawn. "I'm sure I dozed a few times." He toasted her with his coffee cup. "You didn't have to do this, Amy."

"Rusty is going to make it, isn't he?"

"I did a blood check this morning," Dieter said. "His white count is going down. A lingering infection is my biggest concern. But I just can't tell how much trauma there was to his vitals." He opened the bag and unwrapped the fried egg sandwich. "I'm taking Rusty up to the Livingston vet hospital today. I've already talked with them. They'll keep him this weekend and check him out. Could you take care of the kids after school today?"

"Of course. You look terrible. How do you shower around here anyway?"

"Where there's running water and a sink, you can always make do. How are the kids?"

"They stayed up too late and this morning. Megan couldn't find her art bag again, but we got to school with a minute to spare."

"How late were they up?"

"Maybe past midnight. They were both more upset than I've ever seen them, Dieter. They needed to talk. To talk about what they saw and how they felt."

He paused and took a bite of his breakfast as she sat watching Rusty.

"Have you heard the news yet about the hiker's death?" she suddenly asked.

He spoke as he chewed. "I picked it up on the radio but really didn't know what to make of it. They said it was a Grizzly attack?"

"Pay no damn attention to the radio. They got it totally wrong." She explained that the Judge had called her and given her a rundown on what he'd learned from Molly. She told him that a wolf had stalked the hiker. It charged and brought him down. Brutally killed him on the spot. It was no Grizzly attack."

"How did Molly find out about all of this?"

"The Judge said she'd gone looking for a missing woman—turned out to be one of the Loudermilk women from Duck Creek. Evidently she was hiking with the victim. Molly found her clinging to a branch high up in a tree."

Dieter closed his eyes and rammed his head into the back of his chair.

"Is Michael still going on the Scout Camporee tomorrow?" she asked.

Exactly what he was thinking about. "Believe me, Amy, I've been tossing this around in my head since Michael signed up for it. But I keep thinking how torn up he is over Rusty. And if I called this off on him as well . . ."

"Where's the outing taking place?"

"Center of the Park. Indian Creek campground, between Norris and Mammoth."

"I hope to God the Scouts have cancelled any plans for an overnight hike."

"I have no idea," Dieter replied. "But anyway, I wasn't about to give permission for Michael. He'll find friends to hang around with at the campground. He'll love it."

"How about if I come over early tomorrow to pick up Megan for a trip to the lake? She needs to get away for the weekend. Especially if her brother is going on a fun trip."

"That's perfect. I'll get Rusty up to Livingston by noon."

She walked to Rusty's cage and pressed the tip of her nose against the wire mesh while whispering a long goodbye. Then without fanfare, she walked over to where Dieter sat and tossed her arms around him and squeezed.

After she had gone, he threw the fast food bag into the trash and walked to Rusty's cage and opened it to check again the crimson and yellow stained bandage around his throat. While he massaged the golden head, Rusty whimpered and beat his tail on the floor of the cage.

The veterinary hospital in Livingston was two hours away. Once he got Rusty into expert hands to care for him, he'd rush back to Colter. He needed Josh Pendleton more than ever now.

FORTY-ONE

Dieter watched from the cabin's front window as the van pulled into the driveway promptly at seven a.m. Eager to get going, Michael wore tan corduroy trousers and a light brown shirt under his jacket, his best imitation of a Scout uniform.

But the trousers were too new, they looked too neat. He'd told his dad that the older kids might notice and tease him. Dieter caught him in his underwear in the bedroom wrinkling the trousers and rubbing the legs with the bottom of a dirty shoe to give them a better look.

Michael jogged down the graveled driveway carrying his backpack before Dieter had a chance to give him a hug. He shouted after his son, telling him to be careful and to follow the rules, then waved at Paul Struthers, one of the fathers who'd volunteered for the Camporee. The excited Scouts waved back a mock goodbye through open windows as the van took off.

Amy arrived before Megan awoke to take her to the Little Bears in Lakeview for the Labor Day weekend. She and Dieter sat down with coffee at the kitchen table and he told her about the trip to Livingston and the over-the-top reception by the veterinary staff. He assured her that Rusty was in the best place possible for a quick recovery. For now, he had some important business. He'd see them in a couple of days at the lake house.

"With all that's been happening," Dieter added, "I forgot to ask you about your plane?"

"Dad got it hauled up to Billings for repairs."

"I need to apologize to him. The venture was my idea."

"Don't be crazy. He's just glad neither of us was injured. Or worse. He knew what we were up to . . . even in on the plans. Remember?"

Dieter nodded with a smile. She looked down and fidgeted with her fingers in her lap before raising her head to speak. "It's a heckuva time to bring this up, but I should've told you last night."

His smile dissolved. What was this all about?

"I'll be packing up soon," she said. She stared back at him without blinking.

"Packing up?" Maybe he heard her wrong. He pretended not to understand, but he'd already captured her meaning in the pit of his stomach.

"Not exactly sure when, but I'm packing up that pathetic little Datsun and leaving for the West Coast. Santa Cruz. I've put off telling you for too long."

Planning this for a long time without even giving me a hint?

"I have to confess, I'm surprised," he said.

"Not really, are you?"

"I knew we wouldn't have you around forever, but . . ."

"Molly will have some good leads on where to find another nanny."

"Sure. Yes. I'll talk to her." He sat back in the chair and folded his arms across his chest, nodding to himself to project a fake moxie that he could handle it. Just a minor adjustment in life. No big deal, he lied to himself.

"Your dad told me you were interested in a teaching job upstate."

"I applied for one a while back, but they never got back in touch with me," she said. "The semester's starting sometime in September. They've likely found somebody else."

"Did you call them?"

"Twice in the past week alone. It'll be different out in California by a long shot. After the summer, everybody heads back to work or whatever they do in Santa Cruz. I need to get out there and find a job before the competition heats up."

He'd exhausted ideas on how to react to news that had not only blindsided him but sent his head spinning. "I suppose you're following your dreams."

She stood to leave. "You can say that. Following dreams just like you did in coming to Colter. But I still have one little obstacle remaining before I go."

He shot her a questioning look.

"Convincing my dad it's the right thing to do."

"I have a hunch that won't be easy."

"Hasn't anyone ever told you, Dr. Harmon, that charm always wins out over reason?"

She nodded toward the doorway. Megan stumbled into the room with a hand under her pajama top, scratching her tummy while the other hand wiped sleep from her eyes. Red pillow marks were embossed on one side of her face. She stopped in the middle of the kitchen floor and yawned. "Does anybody around here got any Cocoa Puffs?"

*   *   *

Amy sat waiting for Megan to put on her clothes and wondering why Dieter had to rush away so fast. She helped Megan gather her things while chatting about a picnic they were planning and the horses they'd be riding. Without question she was going to miss both of the kids once in California. They had fun times together during the summer and she never considered her duties for the family a chore. But she had to admit that a feeling of guilt for leaving town was creeping up on her. She needed to sit down with Molly so the two of them could brainstorm how to help Dieter find a good nanny. That was the least she could do before leaving town and she owed it to the kids.

As Megan struggled to hold close a stuffed dog, Amy picked up the miniature pink suitcase and opened the cabin door.

She stopped.

A tall man with a straw hat and a patch of long hair decorating his chin stood on the front porch as if he had been waiting for her. "I didn't mean to startle you, ma'am." He removed his hat, revealing a baldhead and eyes buried by age and scorn.

She grabbed Megan's hand. "What do you want?" She didn't have a gun in her purse or car. Wrong time to remember the warnings her dad had given her over the years. She mentally measured the distance between the porch and her Datsun. How to make a quick getaway with Megan?

"I was looking for Dr. Harmon, ma'am."

"He's coming right behind us. What is it that—"

"But, Amy—" Megan began.

"Now, honey, let's get these things in the car. You're daddy's coming."

"I'll just wait right here for him," the stranger said.

"He's still dressing. May I tell him what this is about?"

"It's about my wife. She's missing."

"Take this, Megan, and go on to the car." Megan looked up at her, scowling, then grappled with the bag of clothes and stuffed dog she held under her arms.

"I didn't catch your name, sir."

"Loudermilk. Joseph Vincent Loudermilk."

Amy swallowed and tried not to let the look on her face give away her shock. She held out her hand. "Amy Little Bear."

He shook it awkwardly. "I believe Dr. Harmon may know something about the whereabouts of my wife."

What is this guy talking about? "I'm afraid you're mistaken, Mr. Loudermilk."

"If you don't mind, ma'am, I'll just wait to ask him myself."

"He doesn't know anything about your wife."

Megan was in the front seat of the car with the window down, straining to hear what was going on.

"Miss, I don't know who you are, but—"

"I'm a friend of the family."

"If you really wanna know, Dr. Harmon took advantage of my wife when he delivered our colt last week. Someone has taken her away, I'm afraid that—"

"Took advantage of your wife?"

"That's correct. I caught them. Now I could either take this to the police or talk with Dr. Harmon."

"Can we go now, Amy," Megan shouted from the car window.

"Just a moment, dear." She turned back to the intruder. "You can take it up with the law, Mr. Loudermilk. But I'm going to have to ask you to leave."

He raised an eyebrow. "And why would you do that?"

"For any reason that I damn well please." She clutched her purse tighter to her chest. Then she relaxed her right leg and shifted her weight imperceptibly over to her left, targeting his testicles.

Without a word, he shoved his hat on and walked to his truck. She followed behind, keeping between him and the Datsun. As she slipped into her car, she spotted two women hunkered down in the open bed of his truck, their faces turned away.

FORTY-TWO

Josh Pendleton shoveled hay with a pitchfork into a feeder. The llamas had gathered inside the open pole barn behind the trailer, jockeying for position. He was calling each by name as if they were his grandkids.

When he spotted Dieter, he put down the pitchfork and ambled over. "You're looking upset, my friend."

"My retriever was attacked, Josh."

"Land o' Goshen! Your Golden? Attacked by what?"

"No idea at the moment. But Rusty's hanging on."

"God forbid, I'm sorry, Doc. How bad was it?"

"Mainly lacerations around his neck." He paused for a moment as Josh shook his head. "Did you hear about the Grizzly attack on the hikers?"

"Was all over the radio."

"From the inside info I have," Dieter said, "it wasn't a Grizzly. It was a wolf."

"How they know that?"

"From the one victim who survived."

Bending down, Josh picked up a stalk of hay and twiddled it between his thumb and forefinger while he contemplated the new piece of evidence.

Before Josh could ask another question, Dieter blurted, "Tell me honestly, do you think there's more than one renegade wolf causing all the havoc in the area?"

"Highly unlikely. Next to impossible is probably a better way of putting it."

Dieter knew that would be his response before he asked it. He was leading Josh down the path he'd already blazed in his mind. "I've looked at a topo map. The distance between my cabin and the site where the attack took place is at least ten miles. Isn't that too big a territory for a single renegade wolf . . . I mean . . ."

"To call home? Come with me, Doc. I'll 'lighten you on some things I've been researching."

Dieter followed as Josh sauntered across the barn, speaking to each llama as he passed. He led the way into an enclosed nursing station in the corner of the open area and flicked on the light. A map was taped to the wall. The region around Colter was recognizable and Dieter stared at the pins with bead heads that covered a narrow swath. One pin stood out with a scrap of red tape attached.

Josh said, "That's where they found the photographer." He pointed at the winding Madison River near Baker's Hole. Each of the other pins located a livestock attack he and Molly had heard about from the neighboring ranchers. Most were never reported, just complained about. The pins scattered along the Park boundary from the Jack Straw Basin south of West Yellowstone north to the Ernest Miller Ridge, a twenty-five mile stretch. Josh inspected the map, waving his finger up and down the western border of Yellowstone. "Look here, Doc. The renegade is working this area. A few miles north of Colter near the border right here would be your cabin." He tapped on the map with his index finger.

"When Amy and I did a flyover," Dieter said, "we spotted a massive black wolf. It was a few miles north of Colter and west of Crowfoot Ridge. If I was reading the map right, it was fairly close to Divide Lake."

"And it's not that far from your place," Josh replied. "It's where Bacon Rind Creek and the Gallatin River meet."

Exactly! All of that was confirmation of what Dieter had already suspected. He turned and paced across the small room and back.

"I'm going looking for it, Josh."

"Looking for *what*?"

"The renegade wolf."

Josh folded his arms across his chest. "And what do you plan to do if you find it?"

"Just want to locate it first. Then consider my options."

"Was you thinking about *shooting* it?"

Dieter looked away without answering. The whole damned affair had gone on too long. The fact was that he'd dedicated his life to caring for animals and believed deeply in that calling. He'd asked himself all night long how could he ever justify twisting that philosophy around, ripping apart the very principle that had guided his life and career. He had to take action and regretted he'd put it off so long.

"That is the craziest thing you've thought of since I've known you," Josh said. "Tell me, Doc. Have you ever spent a single day in the woods hunting?"

"I used to hunt rabbits with my dad."

Josh tossed back his head and laughed. "With a twenty-two, I suppose. It takes more than a popgun to bring down a wolf on the run. You got only one shot and it's got to be fatal."

"I'm fed up with all this, Josh. Fed up living in fear for my kids, my dog. I've even thought about moving back to Pennsylvania. But why? Why should I leave the place I love and want to raise my children because of asses like Jack Corey. He'll never be convinced there's a problem." He then paused before asking the big question. "Will you join me?"

Josh stared back at him as if it were time to knock some sense into a naïve, bred-in-the-city veterinarian. Instead, he shook his head and motioned for Dieter to follow him out of the room.

Dieter wouldn't budge. "I'm going to do this. I made up my mind when I was stitching up Rusty's neck."

Josh kept moving and opened the door as he reached to turn off the light switch.

"I need your help, Josh."

Josh stopped and glared back at Dieter, who stood planted to the floor in the dark. "I can't believe I have to say this to a professional. But have you given any damned thought to what would happen if you got caught?"

"I don't plan on getting caught."

Josh switched the light back on. "You're a stubborn cuss. That's just one level down from a fool. Now the Lord and my llamas know that I'm tryin' to be diplomatic here."

"There are plenty in my past who'd call me something like that . . . or worse."

"You do know, Doctor Vet, that hunting inside the Park can send you up the river? And I ain't talking about the Yellowstone."

Dieter broke into a big smile and said nothing.

"I'm not joking! If I was you, I'd take me serious instead of standing there grinning like a Chessy cat that just swallowed a fat mouse."

"I never thought I'd hear an ol' trapper talk like this. You're acting like you never flirted with breaking the law before."

Josh placed one hand on his hip and lowered his head. He then looked up at Dieter for a long minute while he fiddled with his beard. "I could track down and take out a wolf without leaving a trace."

"I believe that."

"Well, would you believe I'm not as young as I used to be? In my prime I'd plan on a week for something like this. You have to be persistent once you pick up the trail of a wolf. You gotta beat 'em at their own game, one that their ancestors have practiced for ten thousand years."

"So . . . does that mean you'll join me?"

Josh shook his head. "I'm just not up to it, Doc. I can still hike a mile or two—maybe—but the years are taking a toll on my joints." He patted his left knee.

Dieter knew he was expecting too much from his friend, who had already provided him with a mother lode of knowledge. "Of course. Sorry I tried to talk you into this. It was selfish of me."

"Time's short," Josh said. "You better get going 'fore long. The almanac says the big snows should be moving in soon. Easier to track in the snow, but you don't want to risk a blizzard. A lot of high country hikers found that out when they woke up to meet Saint Peter."

FORTY-THREE

Scoutmaster Farmington called out names from the list while the Scouts going on the overnight hike stood with their backpacks on the ground beside them.

Michael had counted thirteen boys gathered at the trailhead, a short walk from Indian Creek campground. Some of them carried hiking sticks made from tree branches. Most of the backpacks looked too heavy. His own was light because he didn't have to carry a pup tent or many supplies. He belonged with the younger kids who'd sleep in the patrol cabin at the end of the hike. Fat Kenny stood nearby, ready to laugh at him as soon as he opened his mouth.

Michael knew that his dad didn't understand he was old enough for all this. He also knew that it was wrong to sign the permission slip for his dad, but there were lots of wrongs to go around.

His dad was wrong for taking him away from his friends in Pennsylvania and he was wrong for bringing Amy into his and Megan's lives. He'd watched the way his dad looked at her and knew what that was all about. Amy wasn't old enough to be his mom. She was more like an older sister. It wasn't fair that his mom was murdered either. If only his dad had only taken the time to go with her downtown that day. He wasn't blaming him but if he had gone with her, maybe he'd still have his mom.

Scoutmaster Farmington flipped though the papers on his clipboard and called out each Scout by name. Michael began thinking through it all again. It was going to be a hike of a few miles at least . . . maybe five. Maybe longer. He could be spending the day instead at Indian Creek, messing around with Randy Cunningham and taking part in archery and games and other stuff. Randy was back there pouting because his parents wouldn't let him go on the hike.

"Michael Harmon?" the scoutmaster called out.

Everyone stared at him. "Yes, sir."

Farmington paused to study the permission slip, spending far too much time. "Your father couldn't be with us this weekend?"

"Yes, sir."

"But he's not here."

"I mean, no, sir."

Fat Kenny held his hand over his mouth, snickering.

Farmington looked back at Michael for a moment, as if he knew what was going on. But then Farmington slid the paper underneath the stack and shouted, "Daniel Throckmorton?"

Michael finally let out his breath. No way he could back out of the hike now. When the last name was called, the Scouts picked up their backpacks and assembled in single file.

*   *   *

The vet at the Livingston hospital had called the night before to say that Rusty had a setback during the day. He had checked his blood count every four hours and had doubled up on the IV antibiotics. Rusty's white cell count was now coming down, a sign the infection was under control.

After Dieter prepared his backpack and laid out his hiking clothes, he rummaged through his old equipment stored in a shed behind the cabin: camping stove, lanterns, cooking utensils, a sleeping bag, air mattress with a hand pump, paring knife, a bundle of plastic storage bags. Glad he'd saved his gear for all those years. Many of the boxes had never been unpacked from the move across country. In one box he found the dart pistol he once used and packed along with it were syringes and vials of old tranquilizing drugs, expired years before— why had he saved those? During one summer in veterinary school, he'd worked for the state on a project to manage black bears in Rothrock State Forest. The project team trapped bears using Aldrich paw snares baited with bacon; tagged them for breeding studies. Even though he only had to shoot bears with drug-loaded darts, he had to become certified for firearms.

He recalled it all quite well—two consecutive weeks away from Fran. He'd leave his old sleeping bag behind. No plans to use that in the wilderness. He flicked through his backpack for the third time, then walked into his bedroom and lifted the mattress to pull out the Ruger .44 Magnum. The grip seemed molded for his own fingers. He lifted the weapon to eye level and rotated the empty chamber. Perfectly balanced. Holding the revolver straight ahead with both hands, he leaned forward and pulled the trigger. The dull snap of the hammer felt rock-solid. He repeated the action, each time taking aim on a different target around his room and pulling the trigger. A box of cartridges was in a dresser drawer covered with underwear. After stuffing the box and revolver into the backpack, he turned on the radio by his bed for the news and weather, but jerked upward when he heard something sounding like a Mack truck pull up outside the cabin.

Opening the front door, he broke into a wide grin. Josh Pendleton stood by a horse trailer latched to the back of his pickup. He shrugged. "What can I say?" He nodded toward the trailer. "Rocko's been looking for adventure."

Unexpected change in plans and perfect timing.

"But . . . what about hiking? Is your knee up for it?"

"Oh, hell yes," Josh replied, flexing his knee. "Made up a ointment with juniper and black pepper and wrapped it up good. It's feeling pretty warm right now."

Josh motioned for Dieter to move closer as he lifted the llama's panniers that had been stuffed with supplies from the floor of the trailer. He opened a pouch and brought out a rusted contraption, holding it up for Dieter to admire. "That's what you call a 'number fourteen'! One of the old reliable traps I've hung onto. I'll wait here while you grab your gear."

Dieter hustled back to the cabin, eager to take advantage of his sudden luck . . . even though he had a different approach in mind.

*   *   *

Josh drove north on Highway 191 along Yellowstone's western border toward the area that he'd earlier pinpointed on his map at the llama ranch. He motioned behind him toward the truck bed where Dieter had tossed the electronics and antenna rig. "So you planning to watch TV on the search?"

Dieter had come close to destroying the antenna when he crushed it with his feet in the plane accident. But when he later twisted the aluminum tubing back into shape, it resembled what the Judge had delivered.

"It's a signal detector," Dieter said.

"Never heard of a signal defector."

"Detector . . . a signal detector. Most of the wolves have transmitters attached to neck collars. They constantly send out electronic signals. Judge Schoonover made up this portable system for me." He explained how he picked up the faint signal from a lone wolf in the flying excursion with Amy.

Throughout the morning they occasionally stopped along the highway to hunt for likely spots to begin the search, walking up streambeds and along cleared paths, scouting for tracks. Josh often found subtle signs of wildlife, whether claw marks on a chunk of bark from a dead log due to a foraging bear or scrapes on an aspen trunk caused by a bull elk rubbing away antler velvet. For a better look at tracks or scat, Josh would awkwardly lower his giant frame to his hands and knees on the ground. One pile of scat was from a cougar. He showed how the cat used its hind feet to mark territory by heaping together leaves, pine straw and twigs before dropping a load on top. Josh spread the mound apart with his pocketknife to reveal bone and hair fragments of the unlucky prey that had been an earlier snack.

They returned to the truck and continued up the highway, repeating the task of pulling off the road and searching. When Josh saw Dieter inspecting the dashboard, he told him that his truck radio stopped working a year before. It turned out to be a blessing; he'd developed a keener ear for engine noise. He said that by listening carefully, he could tell when an oil change was due.

Josh spotted a sign for a trailhead and drove into the dirt parking area. High on a post were the words *Fawn Pass*. As they pulled in, Josh gazed into his rearview mirror. "Hold on just a damn minute. I can't believe this."

A park service truck rolled in behind them. Dieter quickly hid the box and antenna on the floorboard under his legs as the park ranger ambled toward the truck and Josh lowered his window.

"I see you're towing a llama, sir," the ranger said.

"Rocko's his name," Josh replied. "He's one spirited animal. Nothing wrong with that, is there?"

"I take it you plan to do some guiding in the Park?"

"I got a trekking permit, Officer."

"May I see it, sir?"

Josh reached for the wallet in his back pocket. While he fumbled for it, Dieter pushed the antenna further down with a hidden hand. Josh displayed his Park Service permit and the ranger studied it. "Oh, yes, Mr. Pendleton. Pleasure to meet you."

"You know about me?"

"You betcha. Your name's been around." The ranger paused, looked inside the truck, and then back at Josh. "You gentlemen be careful today. A storm's moving in. Could be lightning. Nothing to fool around with in high country."

As the ranger pulled away, Dieter looked at Josh and winked. "What's it like being famous?"

"Wish I could tell you I need a bullwhip to chase the women away."

The trailhead showed footprints of hikers along with vehicle tread marks in soft mud. "ATV tracks," Josh said. "Likely a teenager on a joy ride."

They sauntered a short distance down the trail to explore when Josh suddenly stopped and bent down. He pointed to an obvious animal track—a huge impression of a heel pad and four toes. "Look how sharp the edges are. That track's no more than a day old." He hovered his hand over the print. "A wolf, all right. But just look at its size! Sumbitch."

"Jack Corey told me there wouldn't be any wolves in this area," Dieter replied.

"A print that size ain't from any ordinary wolf."

A rush of adrenaline shot through Dieter as they hurried back to the truck. Josh led Rocko down the ramp from the trailer and hauled out the trekking gear. He spread a pad over the llama's back before tossing the saddle and panniers up and over it. After hooking the front and rear cinches under the animal's belly, he pulled until they were snug. He placed a strap around Rocko's breast and fastened the ends to the saddle, then tied a large coil of rope onto the saddle. ("Could come in handy on the hike.") Dieter helped stuff the panniers with food and gear as Josh made sure the load on each side balanced, then cut off sections of rope to fasten the antenna to the saddle horn and tie the signal meter to the panniers.

Josh stood back to appraise his handiwork. "Rocko, ol' boy, you look like a creature from Mars with that thing growing out of your back." He grabbed him by his muzzle and planted a kiss on his big wet nose, then glanced skyward. "Lots of feathers up there. We'd best get moving."

Dieter nodded and scanned the horizon, wondering again about Michael at the Camporee. Part of him wished he were there with his son, but there would be plenty of times they'd get to go off together exploring the wilderness. For now, he had to take care of the more pressing matter.

Someday, he'd tell Michael all about it.

FORTY-FOUR

When Amy called to check on her, Molly quickly answered the phone: "It was dreadful. I can only imagine how Claire Manning must feel right now."

Amy hadn't heard about the fire that had happened during the night. The offices of the *Gallatin County Weekly Reporter* on the edge of town had burned to the ground.

"You suppose it was arson?" Amy asked.

"It's a newspaper. They could come up with a dozen suspects off the tops of their heads."

"But to burn down the entire operation? It's just a weekly newspaper, for Chrissakes. Who would have a grudge on a newspaper in Colter, Montana?"

"That's what I told the Judge. He just said to leave it to the law. What have you heard about Rusty?"

"Dieter took him up to the vet hospital in Livingston," Amy said. "It's going to be touch and go with the poor thing."

"I get knots in my stomach every time I think about it."

"I'm out at the lake this weekend," Amy said. "Could we do lunch on Tuesday? I've got something I need to talk over with you."

"You can come over now for tea."

"Let's talk over lunch on Tuesday."

"Your call," Molly said. "But before I forget, I had a curious conversation with Ginny Cunningham yesterday."

"I'm afraid I don't know her."

"She's one of the Boy Scout moms. Her Randy is about the same age as Michael. He's at the Park for the big Camporee this weekend, too. I tried to call Dieter to tell him what she'd told me, but couldn't get an answer."

"Not sure where he is this weekend," Amy replied. "He wasn't very open about what he was up to. You heard something I should know about?"

"Ginny told me she was surprised that Michael was going on the backcountry trip. She had a hard time talking her Randy out of it. She felt they're just too young. And with all that's going on with the wolves—"

"Don't worry. Dieter didn't let Michael go."

"But Michael told Randy that he got his dad to sign for permission. He was actually bragging about it."

*   *   *

Mr. Little Bear had insisted on tagging along with Amy to the campground, but she was determined to handle it alone. She had filled him in on the episode with old man Loudermilk and told him to stay at home, be on the lookout. He promised her that if the bastard put a foot on their property, he'd deal with him. She should cross that concern off her list.

When Amy arrived at the Indian Creek campground, the likes of a three-ring circus greeted her. Boy Scouts were scattered around, running, shouting, playing games. She found a scout leader with badges pinned all over his uniform like Christmas ornaments and assumed he might be in charge. After introducing herself, she said she was looking for Michael Harmon.

"Yes, ma'am, we were hoping his dad would be here today."

"He had an unexpected emergency." The words were the first thing to pop into her head.

"That's really too bad. We are short a couple of adults."

"He's a busy man. Can you please help me find Michael?"

"I believe he's on the list for the overnight hike. They've already started on the trail."

"That's not possible. His dad didn't give him permission."

The scout leader sorted through the papers on his clipboard while Amy searched the gaggle of boys.

"I'm sorry, Miss Bear, I—"

"That's, Little Bear."

"Pardon me, Miss Little Bear, while I go inside. I'm sure the list is there." He ducked into a large tent that looked to serve as a makeshift headquarters. Amy twisted her head about to find anyone near the size of Michael. Most of the boys were much taller. When she remembered that Michael didn't have a uniform, that ruled out every kid she saw.

The troop leader emerged from the tent. "Well, what do you know! Michael Harmon is right here." He held the list out for Amy to inspect, pointing to Michael's name.

"I can assure you; that's a mistake. Michael Harmon did *not* have permission to go on any—" She stopped herself as a group of Scouts gathered around. With her hands on her hips, she looked up and took a deep breath.

"We plan these activities well in advance, Miss Little Bear."

She shot back a squinted stare. "Oh, I'm quite confident you do!" She flipped back her hair with both hands and lowered her head. "I'm sorry. Just a little taken aback at the moment."

"Please, Miss. We wouldn't have him on the list if we didn't have a parent signature."

"But . . . he didn't even have a sleeping bag . . . or a tent."

"Not a problem. He didn't need either. They'll camp tonight in a patrol cabin on the other side of the pass. There's a large cleared area for the older Scouts to pitch a tent or sleep under the stars. The Tenderfoots will be bunked in the cabin."

"Okay, okay. I understand. But let me make myself clear. I need to find Michael Harmon."

"I wish you'd registered with us, Miss Little Bear," he said with a firmer voice.

"Registered?"

"As an adult leader."

"Good. I'll do that now."

He drew in his chin. "Not really. You see—"

"Perhaps gender is an issue?"

"Oh, heavens, no!"

"You did say you were short on adults this weekend."

"Of course, but—"

"And here I am, ready and able to help. Eager to get started, in fact." For the first time, she smiled.

He quickly explained that wasn't the way things were done in Scouting. She didn't apply and wasn't cleared by the district as an adult leader. There was paperwork . . . and an interview.

"May I have a word with you alone?" Amy asked.

They moved to the shelter of a tree and she spoke more softly. "I believe there's a lone wolf roaming the Park. It attacked and killed a hiker yesterday. It's somewhere between here and the border near Colter."

The troop leader glared at her as if she had just walked out of an asylum. "Miss Little Bear, we know about the Grizzly incident on the Fawn Pass trail."

"Who told you it was a Grizzly?"

"Our regional scoutmaster was briefed first thing this morning."

"Briefed? By who?"

"The Park's chief ranger."

"Chief Corey?"

"You know him?"

"He didn't have you *cancel* the hike?"

"You don't need to get upset, Miss Little Bear. He told us to take normal precautions. He's making flyovers throughout the weekend for our protection."

"But this is the largest wilderness area in the lower forty-eight!" She lowered her voice. "How the . . . how do you think they'll protect you? I can't believe you didn't cancel the hike."

"If it wasn't safe, why would Yellowstone's chief ranger give us the go-ahead?"

Seething inside, she tried to look calm. "Do you have a map?"

The troop leader shuffled back into his canvas headquarters while she paced outside it. After a minute, he stuck his head through the tent opening and invited her in to see a trail map spread out on a folding table. They explored it together, beginning with the Bighorn Pass trail out of the campground. The first few miles followed Panther Creek, then it broke through the Bighorn Pass between the Three Rivers and Bannock Peak. From the Bighorn Pass, the trail turned northward to follow the Gallatin River.

Amy traced along with her index finger and paused. A few miles beyond the pass, a spur of the Big Horn connected with the Fawn Pass, the very trail where the attack on the hikers was reported. It linked directly with the trail Michael and the other Scouts were hiking. She leaned with both hands on the table and shook her head back and forth as she stared at the map.

He asked if she were okay. She lifted her head and thought for a moment before speaking. "How long have they been gone on their hike?"

He looked at his watch and pursed his lips. "A couple of hours. But I hope you don't plan to catch up with them. They're at least four miles ahead of you by now."

She lifted the tent flap and looked back at him. "I've always liked giving guys a head start."

FORTY-FIVE

"The weather should blow through today," Bantz Montgomery said. "Probably best we put off the search till tomorrow."

"Remember Mother Superior's orders," Corey replied.

"But if the weather's not cooperating, Jack?"

"McFarland said we begin *today*."

The problem was Montgomery's latest observation at Gardiner: high winds and overcast skies with a ceiling of twenty-five hundred feet. Visibility, three and a half miles and dwindling.

In Corey's office they plotted out a course while Montgomery wondered if McFarland had reached the superintendent for a decision on closing the Fawn Pass trail. A short-wave scanner on a table by the wall crackled with walkie-talkie chatter among rangers spread throughout the Park. There were too many speeders and that wasn't going to be tolerated during Labor Day weekend. A teenager who had stepped into the edge of a hot spring and scalded his foot was rushed to the emergency clinic at Lake Lodge. They already had two DUI arrests, one for possession. A collision involving three vehicles reported near the Tetons exit. No serious injuries.

Montgomery paid little attention to the scanner. He'd been thinking it through most of the night, how to say what he should've said long before now. But he knew that even mentioning Greta McFarland's name would set him off.

"I've got something to level with you, Jack."

Corey spoke while staying focused on the map. "We're always straight with each other."

"When you were at Indian Creek with the Scouts, McFarland called me into her office."

Corey looked up with a scowl.

"She was pushing on me, Jack."

"What the hell are you talking about?"

"She expressed doubts about you being in charge."

Corey slowly leaned back in his chair. "Me? In charge of what? The Park?"

"No . . . the hunt for the hybrid."

"That asshole is trying to go around everybody in the chain. What did you tell her?"

"I said that I wanted no part of going behind your back. If anybody could handle this, it's you. I told her to relax. We'd take care of it."

Corey folded his hands behind his head and smiled. "Did you know she's screwing the superintendent?"

Montgomery didn't want to go there or anywhere close. "Never heard that one."

"The beautiful Black Princess fucking her old white married boss. How do you think she got the job in the first place? The bitch has been aiming for me ever since she arrived."

Montgomery pretended to be searching the map. How easy it was for McFarland to push Corey's buttons. A hatred so utterly deep it always shuts down his mind. On the other hand, Corey hated his ex as much as McFarland. Truth was, the chief park ranger hated many people while holding a strong dislike for most. Maybe the real problem was that Corey hated himself above everyone else.

Through the static on the shortwave they both heard the same word: *llama*.

Corey nudged him to go turn up the volume. A ranger was reporting to the dispatcher that he'd stopped to question a driver hauling a horse trailer with a llama inside. Corey grabbed for the phone and called Comm Central, ordering the clerk to have the ranger call him.

In less than thirty seconds the phone rang and Corey snatched the receiver. "What were their names? . . . The ones with the llama, dammit . . . Did he have a permit? . . . What did they say they were doing? . . . Where? . . . Not necessary . . . Thanks."

Corey hung up then rose out of his seat and barked. "Let's get to the airport!"

"There's no light craft flying now, Jack."

Corey seized Montgomery's wrist and buried his fingernails into his flesh until it turned white. He pronounced each word with a military cadence as he spoke. "Radio to Gardiner. Tell them to get a chopper ready."

*   *   *

While Montgomery prepared for the trip, Corey dashed home. He entered the side door and brushed past the kitchen table, where a large brown envelope lay unopened with a return address of the Livingston law offices of Higgins, Markley, and Jones. He charged up the stairs, two steps at a time, yanked off his clothes in the bedroom, and pulled another uniform wrapped in plastic out of the closet. It was freshly starched and pressed. Extra starch. He put on the tan shirt with the NPS logo and buttoned it up, then sat on the bed with his trousers and rubbed his forefinger and thumb along the crease. He walked back to the closet and scanned the floor. Where were his goddamn hiking boots?

He rushed to the garage and searched the shelves, looking among the tools and rags on top of and under the workbench. He knocked over a used can of paint and the lid fell off. Black enamel spread like lava over the floor. At the garage door he spotted the boots and kicked them up against the wall before picking them up. When he returned to the bedroom, he pulled on each boot, tying the leather laces with a double-knot. There would be a lot of hiking. In the back corner of the closet, he lugged out his scoped .30/.30, then opened the bottom dresser drawer and grabbed a box of shells, stuffing a handful into each pocket.

What if one of them had a weapon? People were known to shoot rangers.

Like what happened to Willie Petruski with Idaho Fish and Wildlife three years before. Willie tried to arrest two hunters who were stalking elk a week before the season opened. They shot Willie through the heart. Corey attended the funeral, along with over fifty rangers from all over the West. Only time in his life he ever cried.

Next to the box of ammo was a souvenir from his tour of duty in Nam, a Ka-Bar fighting knife encased in a sheath with an emblem of the US Marine Corps. He gripped the knife and twisted it about to study its features. Parkerized finish, with a razor edge. He dragged the blade along a forefinger, just delicately enough to draw blood.

In front of the full-length mirror, he carefully positioned his ranger hat. Bringing both hands up, he readjusted it, tilting it a half an inch to the right, a finger's width forward. He gazed at his image.

What had happened to the dream? Where did it all begin to fall apart?

It didn't matter. What mattered was respect. People had to learn that you can't go around making fools of others, least of all making a fool of him. Some people just didn't understand that simple moral principle. He jerked back his knee and with a swift kick shattered the mirror. Slivers of glass sprayed out over the bedroom carpet. Too much time had been wasted; had to get back to the airport.

There was urgent work to do for the Park.

FORTY-SIX

Montgomery fingered his mustache as he sat at the controls of a blue and white Bell 206 Jet Ranger. While the engine was warming he studied the sky and checked his watch one more time.

He held licenses to fly a variety of light fixed-wing aircraft as well as the smaller choppers. All of it was thanks to skills learned in the US Army.

But he had now grown sick of it all. Babysitting his boss to make sure he met his obligations was taking a toll—plus a daily Valium and forty milligrams of Prilosec. The glove box in his truck held a bottle of a hundred Tums but less than a dozen were left. The worst part of the job was covering for a guy whose biggest problem was fanatical hatred for so many he imagined were trying to do him in. McFarland was catching on and that was going to lead to nothing good.

When Corey sauntered toward the helipad Montgomery couldn't believe what he saw—a rifle strapped over Corey's shoulder. No ranger, absolutely no one, was authorized to use those scoped rifles stored under lock and key by the superintendent. Corey must have snatched one without notifying anybody. A gust of wind blew off his hat and sent it rolling across the chopper pad.

Montgomery jumped from his seat and chased it down. When he handed it over, he noticed a glob of dried blood on Corey's shirt collar and the back of his neck was scratched raw.

"Thank you, ranger," Corey said, as if speaking to someone he didn't recognize. "Ready to fly?"

Over the whirl of the chopper blades, Montgomery could only read his lips. "Winds are gusting to thirty knots," he shouted back. "And they're calling for heavy precip."

Corey walked toward the chopper, opened the passenger door and climbed in. Montgomery followed and peered in before the door closed. "Jack, we don't have the weather going for us right now. Maybe later?"

"Let's get moving," Corey said. He spoke with an eerie calmness. "On the double."

"Sorry, but I can't go up for any recon this afternoon."

"I don't want you to do any recon, shithead. I just want you to take me out over the western border. Take a quick look and we can return. Let's get flying. That's an order."

While Corey entered through the passenger side, Montgomery placed his hand against the cabin door and stared down at the ground. He had the right to refuse orders from anyone when inclement weather loomed.

Corey pounded on the window.

Montgomery yanked open the door and hopped into his seat behind the controls. He put on the headset and checked gauges on the panel, then spoke into the mic. "Gardiner traffic, this is N7785. National Park Service. Lifting off southwest helipad, exiting traffic pattern to the south. Monitoring one twenty-one five, Gardiner."

Firmly gripping the collective and the stick, he lifted off. Corey sat strapped in, composed and staring straight ahead as if in a trance. Montgomery glimpsed around at the rifle propped up behind the seat. Hopefully, the damn safety was on.

They flew south to Sheepeater Cliff, then turned west to pick up Indian Creek and follow it between Antler Peak and Dome Mountain, staying clear of the 10,000-foot peaks. He was already shifting about in the wind and didn't need any sudden downdrafts. Keeping south of

Echo Peak, he veered to the northwest until he spotted Grayling Creek south of Crowfoot Ridge, then followed the creek toward the Park border at Highway 191, maintaining a heading of due north.

Corey pressed his forehead against the window. Montgomery tightened his grip on the stick and fought the winds blasting across the Gallatin Range.

"Circle back," Corey said in a low monotone.

When Montgomery brought the chopper around, Corey pointed down at a parking area off the highway. A pickup was parked with a horse trailer attached.

"Let's explore those trails," Corey mumbled, barely audible. Montgomery flew low over the treetops for a better view. Not sure which trail was which, he covered several miles along two of them. The third trail followed the Gallatin River, the largest stream in the area.

They both spotted the figures by the Gallatin at the same time. Two hikers were pulling a pack animal and running for cover.

"Good job, ranger!" Corey said. "Take me downstream and find somewhere to land."

"You want me to land?"

"What did I just say?"

"I have to get you back to headquarters, Jack. You're my responsibility."

"I said, set this thing down. Now."

Montgomery dropped the craft into a narrow clearing close to the riverbank. As soon as they touched down, Corey released his strap and jumped out the open door. He reached behind the passenger's seat and grabbed the rifle, then strapped it over his shoulder and looked back at Montgomery. "Thanks for the ride. I can handle it from here."

Montgomery pulled off his headset. "What the hell do you mean?"

"Give me two hours. Then meet me back here." Corey turned and jogged away.

Montgomery jumped down from the chopper and gave chase. "Hey, Boss! Please . . ." He grabbed him from behind by the arm.

Corey pivoted around—his face contorted and his fist cocked behind his head—and threw a roundhouse punch straight into Montgomery's jaw.

The force of the blow knocked him onto the ground and shook off Corey's hat, sending it tumbling with the wind toward the bank and flying into the river.

"Damn you!" Corey shouted. He turned to watch his hat float away while massaging the knuckles of his right hand. "Now see what you did, asshole."

Montgomery rubbed the side of his face and tested the movement of his lower jaw. Then he marched toward his boss and rammed his nose into his face. "Look, Jack. Don't you ever place a hand on me again or I'll bash your—"

Corey's underhand punch was direct to the solar plexus. Montgomery reached for his stomach and collapsed. Before he could catch his breath, Corey straddled him like a bronco and squeezed his throat with both hands. Montgomery grabbed Corey's wrists and shoved, staring into a vacant gaze as if looking into the eyes of a corpse. With all the strength he could gather he hurled Corey back into the dirt and then lay exhausted, struggling to breathe. When he looked up, Corey was aiming the rifle between his eyes.

"Go ahead; do it!" Montgomery screamed. "Shoot me, Jack. Shoot the only guy who's willing to take up for you no matter the stupid crazy things you do. Try counting the number of people who'll stand by you when times get tough. Go ahead and shoot. I don't give a goddamn anymore."

Corey stood fixed like a statue except for his heaving chest.

"What's the matter, Jack? You some kind of chicken shit?"

Corey lowered the rifle to his side. "I'm not going to shoot you, idiot. I just want you to shut up. I want everybody to shut up. I know what I'm doing."

"You don't need me around anymore then. I've had it with being your 'yes' man, Jack. You're dead wrong this time."

Corey sneered. "Wrong about what?"

"Don't you see the wolves didn't work out? There's at least one killer on the loose, maybe more."

Corey stared straight through him without responding.

"Listen to me," Montgomery said. "Hundreds of hikers and fishermen are in the backcountry this weekend. We don't have a single warning posted. And you let the Boy Scout campout go on as planned! Do you have any idea what'll happen if there's an attack on a kid?"

"You don't have to yell. I can hear you."

"I know you can *hear* me. But do you understand what I'm trying to tell you?"

"Exactly what is it you're trying to tell me, shithead. What's your goddamn bottom line?"

"Operation Wolfstock failed, Jack. We didn't take into account the possibility of bringing a *hybrid* into the Park—a renegade killer. We screwed up big time."

Corey's face turned from anger to disgust. "Get out of here, Montgomery. Fly your chopper away and don't come back. Don't ever come back. You're a fucking waste, just like the others."

Montgomery massaged his jaw. He'd been there with Corey too many times over the years. When the chief park ranger got into one of his outbursts, it was as if he had submerged himself inside a steel cocoon to fend off the rest of the world. He should follow Corey's orders and fly away, but his gut told him to ignore his boss' ranting. The man needed help or else he was going to do something tragically stupid. Something that Montgomery would likely have to pay for, like so damn many times before. Only this time could be so much worse.

"I'm flying over to West Yellowstone, Jack. I'll fuel up there and wait out the squall. Keep your radio open." He looked down to see if Corey's walkie-talkie was still fastened on his belt.

Corey moved quickly away, his rifle strapped over his shoulder.

When Montgomery brought the chopper down at the West Yellowstone airstrip, he hurried into the cover of the hangar and radioed to the ranger on duty at headquarters. He told him he'd dropped off his boss by the Gallatin River.

Yes, it must have been along the Bighorn Pass trail. Of course it was a dumb thing to do, but who the hell could tell Jack Corey that? Once the front passes over and the winds settle down, he'd go back for him. Yes, Corey had his walkie-talkie on.

"We have at least three hours of daylight," Montgomery said. "That should be—"

He was interrupted by the ranger on the other end.

"No," Montgomery shouted. "Who's on call? . . . Where's the superintendent? . . . Do *not* call Greta McFarland . . . There's no emergency, dammit. I'll give you a call back in another hour with a weather report. Remember, there's no need to bring McFarland in—"

The other radio shut off before he finished.

FORTY-SEVEN

Dieter and Josh trudged down a path meandering through the pines beside a rushing stream. Josh's limp, an old trapper's gait, contrasted with Rocko's bearing, Dieter thought as he followed directly behind the llama and marveled at how lightly the grand animal stepped along. His footpads were as soft as a kitten's, barely leaving a mark. He wished for Rusty by his side. At times, he glanced at the metal box tied onto Rocko's pannier just below the antenna mounted on the saddle horn. The red light on the top of the box never gave a hint of flashing. He wasn't sure of the device's range or even if it was working.

Whenever they neared water, Rocko grew nervous and moved with caution. Josh said llamas were scared silly around a stream or river, a fear born of wisdom since they couldn't judge the depth and weren't swimmers. They'd hiked at least two miles before they stopped to rest on a flat boulder. Clouds whipped across the sky as blue jays and ravens cackled in the trees.

Dieter took measure of Josh. What was it that drew the old trapper to him? Who else could have lured him into a freezing storage bin used for a corpse? Josh knew nature and wildlife more than anyone he'd ever met. Always looking for adventure, he was old enough to be his father. But he was different from his own dad in every way. For one, he was sober. Although he lived alone he never claimed to be lonely. Many could only dream of the life Josh lived. When he wasn't fishing or hunting for his dinner, he was tending to the llamas he loved or sitting in his front yard contemplating his world by day or watching a moonrise by night. Whatever the tie binding Dieter and Josh, it was growing tighter each day.

A bull elk bugled in the distance. A narrower trail split off the main one. Overgrown with weeds and clearly not well-traveled, it was more a path than a trail. Walking down it a short distance, fresh wolf tracks appeared.

"He's going for the river, Doc. This is just a short spur leading south to the Gallatin. That's where we'll hit another trail down from Bighorn Pass."

"Does it go all the way across the Park?"

"Not that far. But if you take it east, it follows the river up through the Bighorn Pass to the center of the Park. If you head west, you go back to Highway 191 where we came from. The renegade could be making just one big circle."

"But if he took the trail through the pass, where would he end up?"

"Indian Creek. There's a campground at the—"

"My God, Josh, Indian Creek is where Michael and the Boy Scouts are this weekend." Dieter brushed a hand through his hair and took a deep breath. His gut was right about keeping Michael away from the Camporee. Or maybe he was too protective. Maybe Amy was right. He was hovering too much over the kids. That's something that Fran would never have accused him. She did the hovering for both.

"It's a good fifteen mile from here, Doc."

"But it's a distance a wolf can easily cover, isn't it?"

Josh paused. "Don't get all shook up yet. It won't take long until we reach the river. Then we'll see from his tracks where he's headed."

Josh and Rocko led the way along the narrow weed-choked trail. In one stretch, the wolf tracks disappeared for fifty yards before Josh picked them up again. At the Bighorn Pass trail the Gallatin ran swift and clear. Rocko moved cautiously to the riverbank to lap water. As

Josh watched over the llama he remarked that upstream above the falls the river flowed wider and deeper.

"A waterfall?" Dieter asked.

"You'd be surprised how often you run into those natural beauties in the backcountry."

Dieter had already prepared himself for the news before Josh examined the tracks. The wolf was headed upstream, toward Indian Creek. When they came across scat just off the trail, Josh leaned down and stretched his hand out to linger above the pile. He looked up. "Warm."

Dieter glimpsed at the meter hanging from Rocko's pannier.

"Keep an eye out. A wolf can smell you a mile away," Josh said. "Can hear you coming from twice that. Especially with low cloud cover."

"You mean like now?"

"Like now. His senses make him the ultimate hunter. No animal on earth can match it."

The chopping hum of rotors arose like a thunderstorm.

"Take cover!" Dieter shouted. Josh grabbed Rocko's lead and they moved under a pair of cottonwood trees as the helicopter passed overhead. It flew low enough to reveal the NPS emblem on the tail section. When it was gone, Dieter looked skyward. "Corey told me they do regular sorties to monitor the wolf packs. But they do that with small planes. If they're making flyovers in choppers, something must be going on."

FORTY-EIGHT

From his bedroom window on the second floor, Joseph Vincent Loudermilk watched the patrol car crawling along the highway. He suspected it would turn out like this. But he had his supplies ready, his canvas duffel bag packed and by the bed.

Charlene, the little runaway twat, had probably been found. She wasn't even able to do that right. She'd spill everything, making him out to be Satan himself.

She never understood the ways of the Lord. God knows he tried to teach her. He had the Sermon on the Mount memorized. How many men in Montana could say that? He delivered it to her how many times? Word for word, just as written by the hand of God in the King James Version of the Book of Matthew.

The law didn't understand the ways of the Lord neither, but what else would you expect? He was a God-fearing man. He'd never done nothing to his wives or children that wasn't right, wasn't part of his duties. He always had the Lord's approval before he ever laid a hand on any of them.

If that little twat had listened to him, obeyed him, learned from him, she would've been a better woman, a better mother and wife. She would've had the chance to meet the Lord Jesus Christ in person in the Latter Days. She gave all that up. Why would any woman of sound mind give up that chance?

He crept downstairs and hid by the fancy draperies hanging from the picture window in the living room. Sliding between the wall and a drape, he inched his head along the wall until one eye caught the view out the window. The deputy sheriff's car was parked off to the side of the road, a hundred yards down from the gate and almost out of sight.

He moved from behind the drapes and yelled for Enos and Jeremiah. Round up the younger kids, he calmly told them. Go into the living room and sit in a circle. Just sit there and stay quiet. They carried out his orders quickly, efficiently. Good boys. Well-trained. They understood.

He rushed into a back bedroom and grabbed an extra blanket from the closet, then stuffed it into his duffel bag. Spotting a small rope on the closet floor, he added it to his cache.

Outside, he carried the bag over his shoulder, an arm slung through one strap. He sneaked beyond the barn and through the trees, getting as close as possible to the gate without being seen from the road, then stooped behind the bushes. He could barely make out the figure down the road of the deputy slouched in his seat.

An elbow protruded out the open window. The deputy appeared to be talking into his two-way radio.

The rusted pickup with Katherine Belle and Marilee stopped at the gate. He ducked down into the bushes and slowly pushed his head up to watch. Marilee opened the passenger door and moved toward the gate, holding onto a ring of keys.

The patrol car pulled in beside the truck and surprised both women.

Katherine Belle turned her head away and as soon as the gate opened, she drove through and stopped.

The deputy walked to the truck and tapped on the window. "Sorry to bother you, Miss," he shouted, "but I need to talk with you."

"You'll have to come back, Officer," Katherine Belle said, "when my husband's here." She glared at him like he was an intruder trying to grab her. Joseph Vincent only heard every other word, but from his vantage point he could read her lips.

"Ma'am, I need to interview a Mr. Joseph Loudermilk. I just have a few questions."

She smiled and switched to her sweeter voice. "I'm afraid he's gone away for a spell."

"I'm sorry, Miss . . . ?"

"Mrs. Loudermilk. I am Katherine Belle Loudermilk."

"Ma'am, I have good reason to believe your husband is at home."

"You were misinformed, sir."

"If you don't mind, I'll get in my car and follow you to the house."

"I'd be obliged if you returned later. Your timing is most inconvenient."

"Sorry, ma'am. Either I talk to Mr. Loudermilk now, or I'll have to bring him in."

"Suit yourself. My sister will lock the gate."

"I would prefer if she wouldn't lock it while I'm here, ma'am."

Joseph Vincent picked up the duffel bag and ran for the barn. Katherine Belle was the reincarnation of Judas Iscariot. She'd pay like none of the others ever paid before. He rushed down the path of Divine Revelation behind the barn until he lost sight of the house. He'd stay away for a while, because it would all blow over in time.

He brought along plenty of snack food and could snare rabbits and find berries and plants to eat. An ample supply of water seeped into the Divine Chamber, the ideal spot to commune with the Almighty. Jesus prayed in the desert for forty days and forty nights. He could do that, too. Then he'd go find the harlot, Charlene. Or God would return her to him. Either way, the Lord would administer the blood atonement.

Panting, he climbed to the top of the hill and stopped at a clump of bushes. He paused for a moment to look back down the path and then ducked into a dense grove of quaking aspen. He used one arm to push away the limbs that kept snapping back into his face. The cool damp air from the gaping hole in the earth hit him like a winter breeze and he smiled. The cave was his lair, the Chamber of Divine Revelation. The opening was large enough that he only had to lean down to enter. Inside, he stood with three feet of clearance.

A strange feeling suddenly overcame him, a sense that he wasn't alone. Something was there. Deep within the darkness, that something moved toward him.

Then a voice straight from Hell echoed from the Chamber walls.

"Hello, Poppy."

FORTY-NINE

The roar of the waterfall grew louder as they hiked. The first to catch sight of it, Dieter shouted. "Will you look at that!"

"Hancock Falls," Josh replied. "Named after one of the early Yellowstone explorers. Must be an eighty-foot drop."

The imposing falls plummeted down onto massive boulders spread about in the narrow fast-flowing river before them, not more than thirty yards wide. Dead trees that had drifted over the brim lay scattered in a churning pool. What the falls lacked in width it made up for in height and sheer volume of flow.

Josh spotted more tracks and bent down to examine them, then pointed toward the river. "They lead to that flat rock on the water's edge. Take a look at how those larger rocks line up. He's crossed to the other side."

"No way we can wade that," Dieter replied.

"Let's hike up above the falls and look for easier places to cross."

"Do you think he'll still be following the river?"

"You can put money on it. Who knows what drove him to cross at this point. Less he senses a path to get around the falls. On upstream he could just as well come back to this side."

Dieter gazed above the waterfall where a cloud of steam rose high into the air behind distant trees. When Josh saw where Dieter was staring he said, "You've got to watch out for the scattered hot springs in these parts. We're not that far from the geysers and thermal springs around Mammoth."

Beneath skies of a dingy charcoal gray, the switchback to the top of the falls looked steep and challenging. A cold steady wind arose from the west and brought in a light rain. Josh held Rocko at a stop and grabbed the rope hooked around the saddle. He tied one end to a ring on the strap around Rocko's breast and stuck his arm through the remaining coil. "I'll lead Rocko up the path if you can stay at his rear. You might have to push him at times."

Dieter nodded and took a position behind Rocko as they began the trek along the switchback. Progress was slow. Josh's heavy breathing could be heard above the rumble of the falls while he pulled on the rope and grunted with Dieter shoving on Rocko's rear. When finally reaching the top of the falls, they followed the river upstream several hundred yards to a clearing.

"That's a patrol cabin up ahead," Josh said. "It's used often by park rangers." The tiny log cabin was in the open field between the woods and the river. Josh rubbed his knee and mumbled about the need for a break.

While Dieter collected water from the stream, Josh rummaged through Rocko's panniers, careful not to bump his head against the antenna on the saddle horn. He dug out a small camp stove and dented steel coffee pot followed by two ham sandwiches and a fresh egg from a cool pack.

Dieter sat cross-legged near the bank and watched his partner perform. The flat top of a boulder served to hold the stove. After bringing the water to a boil, Josh tossed into the pot a handful of ground coffee with a pinch of salt and waited. When the brew simmered, he cracked the egg on a rock, tossed away the yolk and white, and dropped the crushed shell into the pot to filter the grounds. It wasn't long before he poured rich black coffee into two tin cups. While Dieter sipped the hot brew, he knew that he had to stop fretting. Michael would be safe with Leonard Farmington and Paul Struthers.

The Scouts and the renegade wolf were miles apart and chances of any encounter were one in a million. He patted the inside of his jacket and took comfort in the feel of hard steel. Given the chance, he'd accomplish his mission quickly, humanely. Fortunately, in the wilderness a carcass wasn't going to last long before it would be devoured by foragers. He owed the undertaking to his clients and kids . . . and to Rusty.

Ambling over to Rocko, he stopped and stroked his wet fur. After untying the antenna from the saddle and the meter linked to it, he turned to Josh, who was relaxing with his back against a boulder. "I'm going to do some exploring," Dieter said.

He held the antenna above his shoulder, grasped tightly the meter's handle with his other hand and began walking along the trail.

*   *   *

The troop had paused next to the Gallatin River. Some of the Scouts lay in the grass while others snooped along the bank. Most sat in small groups, eating snacks and drinking cold sodas. The ones taking turns at the spotting scope searched mountain slopes to be first to catch a glimpse of a bighorn sheep or even better, a Grizzly.

Michael jerked up when a boy standing behind the scope shouted that he'd found something. Others ran to crowd around it, shoving to be the next to look. Scoutmaster Farmington rushed toward the group and called out, "What you got, Rowen?"

"Looks like a small bear. A black bear!"

Farmington struggled with the scope. Someone pointed to a dark spot moving across the hillside, but Michael couldn't see it. Mr. Struthers held his binoculars to his face. "I'm not so sure. It's moving much too fast for a bear."

"I can't pick it up with this thing," Farmington complained, moving his head away from the spotting scope. Everyone stared at the hillside.

"I've lost track of it now," Mr. Struthers said. The scoutmaster then motioned for him and the pair huddled away from the boys.

Michael sat on the ground near them, positioning himself to listen in on the conversation. The scoutmaster had opened a large folded map—he called it a "topo"—and said they were less than two miles from the camping area near the waterfalls. Michael looked forward to sleeping in a cabin with other Tenderfoots. He was tired, hungry and wet, just like everybody else.

"Okay, Scouts," Farmington called out. "Come on over."

They bunched around their leader as he explained the need to keep together in a tight group until they reached the camping area, which wasn't far. While they hiked they should talk as loud as they wanted. Sing, if they wished. Whistle. Any kind of noisemaking would be okay.

The scoutmaster said that after getting into dry clothes and getting a good night's sleep, they could look forward to a fun hike back to the Camporee tomorrow under sunny skies. In a steady drizzle, the boys took off laughing and arguing over what marching song to sing.

While Michael walked, the Scouts passed him by one by one, just like they did on the hike at the church. It was a lot easier for them to pass by him this time because he was more tired than he'd ever been in his life. Everyone was moving too fast, trying to keep up with the leader. Michael kept falling behind until someone would look back and call out to him. Then he'd walk faster, but it was now happening more often.

He wanted to go home. When he stumbled over a rock for the third time, he lay flat for a moment and then rolled into a sitting position. The Scout ahead of him disappeared over the rim of the hill.

"Hey!" Michael shouted, but not loud enough. "Hey!" he repeated, louder.

No answer.

Maybe they didn't want to hear him. But they'd be mad when they discovered he wasn't around. That would slow them down, for sure.

They'd have to come all the way back for him, but he didn't care about causing a problem anymore. Serve them right.

Larger drops of rain began to fall, stinging his face and splattering like pellets of hail in the puddles around him. He shivered. A dead log lay in weeds beside a shallow place where there might be enough room for shelter.

He crawled down into a low spot, pressed his shoulder against the log, and curled up with his face mashed against rotting bark, drawing in the musty stench with each breath. As he pulled the jacket collar up around his neck, he slid his hands inside the sleeves, yawned and leaned against his pack.

Hunger gnawed at his stomach as he squeezed shut his eyes.

FIFTY

The chopper climbed straight up and sped away, leaving behind the silence that Jack Corey had craved. He stood for a long moment, a smile across his face, then sauntered to the rushing river and stooped to examine tracks near the bank—clear prints of hard-leather boots. Hiking boots plus a hoofed animal that left behind soft impressions like a lamb on wet sand. But he knew llama tracks when he saw them. Yanking the walkie-talkie off his belt, he heaved it into the river.

He opened and checked the rifle chamber. The best strategy was to approach from a distance and call out. The bastards would be carrying weapons and he'd have to tell them to put them down. No tricks and no sudden movements or he would shoot them on the spot.

The superintendent depended on him to enforce the letter of the law. He was already counting on a big bonus for discovering the low-life poacher who'd killed the wolf over at Red Lodge. No doubt he'd get an even bigger bonus for this mission. Of course, the superintendent would try to make a big deal about it. He could see the look there'd be then on the face of Greta McFarland, the Black Princess whore.

He cradled the rifle in the bend of his left elbow while he rambled alongside the river and searched for a place to cross to put the river between him and them. One spot in fast water was shallow enough but ran too swift in narrow pockets. Couldn't take the chance. Another place was more promising.

He stepped from the bank onto a rock that was well above the surface and then found two more within easy stretch. There was no choice but to plant a foot down into the rapid flow while he held his rifle high overhead. He sought out a foothold sandwiched between two rocks as water slapped above his knees.

His waterlogged trousers rubbed against his thighs and freezing water squished inside his boots. Focusing on the gravel bottom, he slogged along until he finally arrived at the edge of the bank where he jumped up onto the field grass.

An hour passed before he stopped to rest under a large pine. He placed the rifle barrel against the trunk and unzipped his jacket, swallowing to lubricate his dry throat. All that cold rushing water and so few ever saw it. Why the hell should they? They were too occupied waiting on Old Faithful to erupt while they sat on log benches fixated on their wristwatches. No need to worry about warnings that he'd given so many backcountry hikers, warnings about the possibility of giardia in the streams. This pure mountain water was direct from a lake at ten thousand feet.

Alert, he moved toward the bank. When he reached the river, he bent down and scooped up water with the palm of his hand. He quickly looked about before slapping a few chilled drops into his mouth. Lowering his head again, he dipped his cupped palm into the water and slurped up more as he twisted his head about to search and listen. His eyes darting back and forth, he rapidly scooped water again and again until his thirst was quenched.

He stood and grabbed his rifle.

Keep moving.

The mellow rumble of a waterfall in the distance egged him on. When he arrived at its base, his first thought was that of another wonder of the backcountry he'd never known existed. If only he had the time to sit and marvel at it, to draw near it and bathe in its spray. The path around it looked steep, but he scrambled along it until he reached the top of the falls. Out of breath, he glared at the sight before him. The Gallatin River—a mighty surge of clear, deep water—plunged over the rim.

A whiff of sulfur fumes caught him by surprise. Then he spotted the cascade of steaming water that bubbled from a crevice in the rocky ground and meandered like a scalding slime down the bank to the river.

Voices.

Crouching down, he waddled through the junipers. The long neck of a grazing llama appeared through a gap in the trees. He stooped behind a boulder and cautiously raised his head. It was them all right.

He needed to alert headquarters and reached for the walkie-talkie on his belt, first one side, then the other. Not there.

Dammit to hell!

He released the rifle's safety. Careful not to make the slightest sound, he rested the barrel on top of a boulder, held his breath and glared at the quivering image of outlaws in the rifle's scope. A warning shot, that was all . . . just a warning shot.

*   *   *

After the rain let up, Dieter walked the trail. He held the antenna high and tried to keep one eye on the meter while watching the ground for rocks and puddles of mud. When his arm grew tired, he switched hands. At that same moment the red light on the meter flickered.

He stopped and reoriented the antenna. The light flickered again and this time the needle on the meter's face surged to the right.

A signal pickup?

He smacked the metal box against his hip and flipped the switch on and off when a thundering bang pierced the stillness.

A pine bough shattered above his head. Before he could react, a second shot rang out. He tossed the equipment into the weeds and ran in Josh's direction. When another bullet ricocheted off a rock to his right, he dropped to the ground and lay flat on his stomach. Yet another shot and Josh cried out.

Dieter wormed his way toward him.

Josh had fallen. He held onto his leg and squirmed as Rocko pranced around his master, hovering over him. Blood drenched Josh's trouser leg, just below his waist. Dieter grabbed his partner's jacket and attempted to drag him toward the safety of scrub oak. Rocko jammed his snout between Dieter's face and Josh, the sight and smell of blood throwing the llama into a frenzy. While Dieter struggled he felt the llama's breath on his neck as the animal let out a low-pitched hum. With both hands under Josh's arms, Dieter tugged, readjusted and tugged more, repeating the maneuver until he finally dragged Josh into cover. He sliced open the leg of Josh's trousers with a pocketknife. Blood was gushing from his thigh—a bullet had ripped through it.

"Lie still," Dieter whispered. "We'll get out of this."

He grabbed a thin stick from the ground and broke it in half, then removed his belt and secured it around Josh's thigh just above the wound with the stick wedged between flesh and belt. As he twisted the jerry-rigged tourniquet, the bleeding gradually stopped. Josh stared back at him, his teeth clenched in agony. Rocko crouched on the other side, licking at Josh's ashen face. Dieter reached inside his jacket and pulled out his .44 Magnum. His head down he slowly made his way across a bed of pine straw on his belly until he could peek through the underbrush and search for the sniper.

*   *   *

Corey balanced himself on one knee and lowered the rifle to his side. Tree branches thrashed in the wind and he could no longer see Joshua Pendleton or the vet across the river. He stood and scrambled in the direction he'd fired. Puffs of steam soared high above a stand of trees. He ducked under the pine and moved closer.

A hot spring appeared—no more than fifteen feet in diameter and surrounded by a limestone crust. The white mineral spiraled deep into clear green water and now and then a bubble scampered to the top and burst free. Wedged within a narrow crevice far beneath the slowly boiling surface lay the blanched skeleton of a large mammal completely intact.

Alarmed by a rustling of bushes, he twisted around. A pair of amber eyes peered from the head of a massive black body on four legs standing in the white haze rising from the hot spring. He jerked the butt of the rifle to his shoulder and took aim through the steam, only to lose sight of the piercing eyes. He inched forward.

The glowing eyes beamed again, larger than before. He raised the rifle and pulled the trigger.

Click. The cartridge had jammed in the chamber.

The amber eyes moved toward him.

He slammed the rifle to the ground and grabbed the fighting knife from its sheath hooked to his belt. Standing at the edge of the spring, he crouched low, his shield hand stretched out in front. The other hand squeezed the handle of the weapon like an axe.

He was back in the jungle, inside the DMZ with the 147th Brigade. Just him, and the quick and agile VC soldier.

The gook had run out of ammo, too.

Corey felt no remorse when his dagger penetrated the victim's rib cage. He twisted the weapon into the gook's lungs and watched him gurgle up blood as he struggled to cry out. The kid didn't look older than fourteen. Dumb shit should've known better than to take on a United States Marine.

Steam from the hot spring suddenly swirled around him and the stench of sulfur burned like a flame inside his nose. He spat out the foul taste of acid and then slung his knife into the dirt. His fingers couldn't function to unbutton his collar, so he ripped open his shirt with both hands. Sweat streamed down his face and neck and gathered at his collarbone before dripping off his chin.

He yanked the knife from the ground and slashed at the air, darting, weaving.

The wolf charged and lunged for his head.

Corey dived to earth.

The creature overshot him and crashed into the weeds, spinning around. He rose up on his hands and knees and waved the knife in wide circles, motioning with his free hand toward the fierce beast.

C'mon! Come to Daddy.

When the wolf charged again, he rolled away at the last instant and thrust his knife at the animal's belly. It yowled when it hit the dirt. The tip of the blade had ripped into its hindquarters.

Corey jumped to his feet, but reeled around too quickly. He slipped and stumbled backwards into the hot spring.

The stinging deep within felt as if someone had set fire to his gut. The scorching heat of the boiling water paralyzed his legs. He struggled to breathe the putrid air as the water rose to his chest. He reached out and ploughed his fingernails into the dirt to lug his body out of the spring.

The juniper shrub he flailed at was just out of reach. When the tips of his fingers brushed a root, he lurched with his hand until he could grab hold. He dragged his chest and stomach over the jagged rim as his bones scraped against the inside of his flesh. A layer of parched skin peeled off at the mineralized edge of the spring, leaving behind a ghostlike sheath of his scalded arm—the perfect likeness of his wrist and fingers.

No longer having the strength nor will to hold on, he slowly slid back into the water, unable to scream, only sob. A dark outline of the wolf appeared through the haze. The creature sat calmly, watching him submerge through amber eyes.

He sank beneath the surface, astonished by the perfect clarity of the water. But the brilliant colors of the mineral walls began to blur and the image faded into cinder gray before vanishing into black. He gasped for breath and swallowed the superheated water that seared his gullet on its way down.

FIFTY-ONE

Michael awoke from what sounded like gunfire in the distance. He sat up, shivering.

The rain had stopped. A dense fog loomed over the path and trees. The wet cold soaked through his pants and clung to his damp skin.

Where was everyone? Why did they leave him behind?

He jumped to his feet and shouted for Mr. Farmington. Then for Mr. Struthers.

Anybody?

Famished, he wandered into the trees and searched for berries or anything with color growing from the bushes. A patch of blue and white wildflowers—curly ones— reared up from the ground. He bent down and sniffed, then took a big whiff. He plucked one and licked at it with the tip of his tongue. Holding the flower in his fist, he stretched his lips wide, bit into the bloom and chewed on it with his back teeth. He quickly spat it all out and wiped his lips and tongue with the sleeve of his jacket.

Then he remembered. He dropped to his knees, zipped open his backpack, and searched through the trash until he found a package of Juicy Fruit gum. He scraped at the wrapper with his fingernails until he could open the package and pull out a stick. After fumbling to unwrap it, he shoved it into his mouth. Unwrapping two more, he crammed them in as well.

With arms looped through his backpack, he turned to find the way back to the hiking path and search for the others. Then he remembered what Mr. Farmington warned at the troop meeting.

If you ever get lost, stay put. Never wander away.

The middle of the trail seemed the best place to squat. When he pursed his lips to whistle, nothing but a stream of spit blew out from his gum-packed jaws.

A song came into his head, the one he'd learned in Mr. Struther's car on the way to the campground. He made believe he was in the backseat again and he sang out. "Do your ears hang low . . ."

He tossed out each word as if he might be embarrassed for someone to hear. "Do they wobble to and fro . . ."

He paused. Something was moving far down the trail. But he couldn't be sure.

"Can you tie them in a knot . . ."

He stopped chewing for a moment to listen. Afraid to move or breathe, he carefully turned his head about and scanned the trees.

"Can you tie . . . them in a bow?"

Something was moving his way. He jumped up and ducked into the weeds.

First, a loud hissing and then flapping wings shattered the cool air. A fat grouse flopped on the ground in a blaring fuss, guarding her nest. He pedaled backward and gave the bird all the space it demanded until he suddenly tripped and fell into the wet weeds.

"Michael!" a voice called out. "Is that you, Michael?"

A rain-drenched Amy was running toward him. He lowered his head to his chest so she couldn't see him cry.

*   *   *

Dieter lay still, studying the scene. He crawled back to Josh's side. "How you doing, partner?"

Under the shelter of thick pine Josh was dry but pale. He took a deep breath and slowly exhaled. "Let's get the hell out of here," Josh said. He struggled to sit up.

"Hold on." Dieter grabbed him and lowered him back to the ground. He had to go for help, but he was at least two hours away from the truck. How could he leave Josh alone? On the other hand, how long could he wait it out?

A throng of ravens fluttered in overhead. The antenna and meter that he'd pitched to the ground caught his eye. The red light was slowly blinking.

Rocko jolted up. Dieter threw a hand over the llama's back. "Get down, boy," he whispered. Rocko cuddled beside Josh and braced, the llama's ears swiveling and pointing. The red light on the meter flashed faster.

Dieter crawled back to the underbrush and reached inside his jacket for the .44 Magnum.

A colossal wolf with a coat of burnished black and traces of silver on its mane loped along the opposite bank. It held its head high as if onto a scent. A leather collar surrounded its neck and a patch of blood mysteriously stained its hindquarters. The wolf hobbled in their direction and waded through the shallow water where it perched on a rock to survey the area. It picked up its hind leg to lick the wound.

Dieter lay flat and squeezed the revolver with both quivering hands. He rammed the butt of the gun into the mud and as he remembered Cory's warning: *If a ranger of mine catches anyone even looking like he's hunting wolves . . . the full force of the law . . . slamming down like a sledge hammer?*

Not that Corey's threats mattered. Why the hell should they?

Never had Dieter imagined that he would find himself in this position: about to shoot a defenseless animal. Death had to be quick and painless. That was only right.

The wolf leaped onto another rock, but quickly slipped into the rushing water. Kicking with all fours, it found a smaller rock to climb on and then took a final leap onto the graveled shoreline. Once more it stretched its muzzle around to lick at blood before turning in Dieter's direction.

Holding tight to the revolver, he slowly rose to his feet and began to creep toward the wolf, which retreated toward the steep embankment. Dieter lifted the revolver with extended arms and took aim at its head as a drizzly rain returned.

The wolf cowered—its tail and ears drooping—and flaunted a paw in the air.

Dieter focused on its eyes. He pictured the vacant image in Rusty's eyes that horrible night, then dropped the revolver to his side.

The wolf moved to the water and lowered its head to leap. The river ran swift and deep at the top of the falls.

"No! Stop!"

Dieter sprinted for the bank and heaved the revolver at the wolf. The weapon flew over the animal's head and splashed into the river as Dieter yelled again.

The wolf leapt into the river. The freezing water seemed to energize the animal and it paddled to keep its head above water—drifting swiftly downstream all the while.

Dieter raced along the bank, keeping pace with the wolf while the rain picked up force and hammered at his face. As he watched, the animal was caught in the eddy downstream from a boulder.

The wolf struggled against the roiling undertow, but it was clear in an instant that the current was too strong.

Dieter stooped to grab a dead tree limb and dragged it with him as he waded into the river. A voice behind him shouted, but he couldn't make out the words.

The frigid water hit him like a fist in the stomach, the violent flow tugging at his legs. He tried to reach the drowning creature with the tree limb, but he was too far away.

He took a step toward the flailing wolf, and then another. Each movement brought a new battle to keep his footing against the relentless current. His legs and feet were becoming numb from the cold, but he inched forward and tried to stretch his overextended muscles enough to reach the floundering animal with the limb.

A stone must have rolled under his boot heel. His right foot slid to the side and he tried to recover his balance. Both feet gave way and he went down.

The river snatched him like a piece of litter caught in a storm drain. He thrashed about with his arms and legs and tried his damnedest to imitate what others did whenever he watched them swim.

The Gallatin hauled him hopelessly downstream. Again shouting erupted from the shore, but he couldn't make out who was calling to him. He tumbled in somersaults and swallowed the river in gulps before slamming his ribcage into a log wedged between two boulders.

Blindly grabbing onto the log with both hands, he sputtered and coughed while he jerked himself above the surface.

The wolf had somehow gotten free of the eddy, but it was still at the mercy of the rushing water. It paddled feebly against the power of the river.

Dieter could only watch in agony as the majestic animal vanished over the rim of the falls.

Both arms clutching desperately to the log, Dieter was only seconds from the same fate. The frigid water turned the muscles of his neck and shoulders to stone. The shoreline appeared only as a haze, far removed from reality.

The shivering stopped. A surprising calm overtook him as he realized he was rapidly losing the strength to hold on. A preposterous way to die, really.

His thoughts turned to Michael and Megan, the many plans he'd made for them as he grew older and they grew up. *I'm sorry, Fran. I'm sorry I let you down.* And what would Josh think of his stupid blundering?

Would Fran be there to greet him?

It had been a lousy day for hunting.

A strange object flew directly at his head and splashed water into his face when it hit the surface. He flailed at it and attempted to push it away.

*   *   *

His wounded leg throbbing with each step, Josh led Rocko along the shore through the blowing rain, yelling at Dieter. His foolish partner couldn't get out of the rapid current on his own. He stopped and pulled out the rope from beneath Rocko's panniers. Creating several long loops with the rope, he could only hope it would be long enough to reach. He tied the end into a lasso, raised it over his head, and twirled. When he tossed the loop across the river, pain shot through his thigh like the stab of a dull knife.

The lasso splattered into the water nowhere close to the log. He dragged the rope back across the surface and cussed between heavy breaths. He made up more loops—larger ones this time. When he heaved the lasso into the air, he yelled out through the damned excruciating pain like a cowboy on a bronco.

FIFTY-TWO

How in God's name could the youngest Scout be left behind?

The thought kept bombarding Amy's brain while she trampled in the rain alongside Michael. How was she going to explain all this to Dieter? She and Michael hurried to catch up with the Scouts. She held her thin jacket collar tightly around her neck, but it wasn't the rain creeping down between her shoulder blades that bothered her. She was fuming about the stupid strategic mistake the scoutmaster had made.

When they met up with the Scouts backtracking on the trail and nearby woods, they were calling out Michael's name. Scoutmaster Farmington was shocked to see Amy although more than thrilled at the sight of Michael. As if the boy was Jesus returning, she thought.

She felt like announcing to him the First Principle of Hiking—*don't lose anybody!*

The scoutmaster's apologies were weak but abundant. The Scouts, drenched from the rain, trudged back toward the camping area at the waterfalls.

*   *   *

"We're almost there," Farmington barked for the third time. They had hiked in the frigging rain for an hour and the scoutmaster no longer had credibility on the topic of how far they had left to go. Amy walked

270

in the center of a single file of exhausted Scouts while Farmington hung back at the rear. Paul Struthers—introduced to her as a volunteer father—was in the lead when they came on an open field by the river that ran wide and deep. Farmington announced that the patrol cabin was just ahead.

Something was wrong.

It was hard to make out the image through the downpour. When she got closer, the figure of a man emerged, crouching on the bank. He was gripping a rope that coiled around his arms and chest like a python and was leaning back, straining, as if playing tug-of-war with someone in the river.

Josh Pendleton?

She jogged toward him, but began to run as soon as she spotted his blood-soaked trousers and the panic in his strawberry face. An agitated llama stood by his side. In the middle of the river a man was half-submerged with a loop of rope around his chest. He was about to lose hold of a log stuck between large boulders jutting above the surface. Through the sheets of rain she couldn't see the face of the drowning victim but knew who it had to be. Glancing at Michael and then back to the river, she gazed in fright at how close the brim of a gargantuan waterfall was to Dieter, who struggled on the other end of the rope.

Josh was planted like a Ponderosa pine on the bank. A llama— poised to attack anyone who approached—stood guard.

Farmington made the first move toward Josh. The llama snorted and lowered its head, its nostrils flared and ears pinned back. When he took another step, the excited animal charged and rammed him in the groin, sending him on the run back through the mud.

Michael slipped between the Scouts to the front and moved toward the llama. "Hello, guy! Hey, boy!" He spoke softly, holding out his hand. The llama arched its head and thrust out its tongue, tasting the tips of the boy's outstretched fingers. It licked his hand and wrist and worked its way up his arm. Michael reached up and displayed a fist stuffed with Juicy Fruit gum, still in wrappers.

"Can you take him up to the trees?" Amy shouted.

Michael grabbed the llama's lead and moved away, whispering to it as he patted its neck. He doesn't recognize his dad out in the river, Amy thought. Mr. Struthers rushed to Josh's side and covered his head and shoulders with his own plastic poncho to shelter him from the downpour. He then uncoiled the rope from around Josh then twisted it about his own waist as he dug in with the heels of his boots to anchor himself in the mud.

The scoutmaster and four of the older boys ran down to the bank to help Struthers pull. They grabbed onto the rope and tugged in an attempt to pull in the slack in the rope that had bowed against the force of the current. Together, they tugged, backpedaled, tugged. When one fell to the ground, he tripped over another. Three more Scouts joined in to help.

Amy watched in terror as the river swelled above Dieter's neck and beat at his face, pinning him against the boulder. She shook her head in exasperation, realizing that the Scouts somehow had to overcome the ungodly drag of the rope against the current. Otherwise there was no chance in hell to haul him in.

The Scouts huddled on the bank in single file, each holding tightly with rope-burned palms and fingers to the rescue line while the older ones moved into the rushing river. Those in back squatted into the mud. Farmington was in front, up to his waist in water. He turned toward Amy on shore and yelled. "We can't keep going! It's too dangerous."

Jesus, no!

Michael ran down to the edge of the river, suddenly aware it was his dad out there, drowning.

Amy shouted back at Farmington. "Hold on, Leonard. Give me just one more minute." She seized Michael by his jacket before he waded out. She clamped her arms around him and carried him back to shore, flopping down with him behind the group. "I want you to help with the rope, Michael. When I tell everyone to pull, give it all the muscle you have. Do you understand?"

He was panting, wildly staring back at her through streaks of rain. When he nodded, she rubbed his wet hair and rushed back to the river's edge, where she waved toward Dieter with both arms high above her head. Uncertain if he could see her, she folded her arms around her chest and threw her hands out away from her body with her fingers spread open.

She repeated her action with exaggerated gestures, grabbing her chest, tossing her hands out harder, faster. Let go, she thought, mouthing the words.

Let go of the log!

She flung out her arms, back to her chest and out again, hoping and praying he could see her through the rain.

"Let go, Dieter," she cried above the roar of the falls, gesturing again and again. "Let go . . . let go! For God's sake, let go!"

He waved back. Holding onto the rope with both hands, Dieter dived upstream against the current. The river surged into his face as he reared back his head.

A younger boy at the front of the group fell into the water and Mr. Farmington grabbed him from behind. The other Scouts slipped in the mud, but still clung to the rope, refusing to turn loose.

"Pull, men," Amy yelled. "Pull like crazy. Head for the trees behind you and pull!"

Calling encouragement to one another, they shuffled back away from the river and toward the trees, everyone in sync like one monster gear.

Dieter was losing the battle, drifting toward the waterfall. Amy gasped and cupped her hands to her mouth. The force of the current towed the Scouts along the bank until Dieter swung on an arc out over the falls with his legs flailing in midair.

He came hurling back. His chest smacked the water and his head narrowly missed another boulder that jutted above the surface.

The Scouts rushed for the trees, hauling Dieter through the river. He slid into shore and slammed his face into the gravel, gradually skidding to a halt. When the Scouts braked, they rolled into a human ball, cheering and yelling.

Dieter lay buried in the mud. A rumble roared in from above and river water sprayed into the air like a small tornado.

*   *   *

The noise pierced Dieter's skull. His wet clothes flapped in a torrent of wind. Voices. Commotion.

Someone was shaking him, shouting. He wallowed in the warm mud, completely spent. A blurred figure of a man with a handlebar mustache checked his breathing and pulse. "He's okay. Just scratched up a bit."

Amy crouched over Dieter and squeezed his face with the soft hands of a nun . . . or an angel. Michael lay with his arms around Dieter's waist and his head glued to his dad's belly.

Too exhausted to move, Dieter could only watch rescuers bring out stretchers from the helicopter and rush to get both him and Josh inside the craft. After hooking up an IV to Josh onboard, the rescuers stripped away Dieter's soaked clothes and boots and slipped him into a jump suit. They wrapped him in a blanket and applied a heat pack under his neck before locking him in next to a window.

He pressed his face against the glass as they lifted off. The Scouts stood back, ducking and holding hands up to shield their faces from the whirlwind. Amy and Michael waved. Dieter was too numb and too weak to wave back.

When the chopper paused in midair, Dieter stared down on the string of jagged boulders at the base of the waterfall. A flock of ravens had gathered on the bank, feasting on a large black carcass.

FIFTY-THREE

"Where are we anyway?" Josh asked.

"Bozeman Deaconess," Dieter replied. "You just got out of surgery. The bullet smashed up your thigh pretty bad. Just plain luck the main artery wasn't hit."

Josh's left leg was wrapped in a bandage from crotch to knee and his foot rested on two stacked pillows. "Who the hell was trying to knock us off?"

"Would you believe Jack Corey?"

"Not only do I believe it, I would have bet on it."

"They found him floating in a hot spring—more or less poached."

Josh coughed and reached for his glass of water on a bedside tray. "Sometimes the Lord acts in mysterious ways," he muttered. "You should've taken that wolf out with your revolver, you know. Would've saved everybody a lot of trouble."

Dieter moved closer and placed his head down to Josh's ear as he whispered. "What revolver you talking about, partner?"

Both men smiled.

While Dieter had waited during the surgery that morning, a visitor from Yellowstone Headquarters arrived—Greta McFarland. She apologized that the superintendent couldn't accompany her. He was called to Washington on urgent business.

275

No doubt he was.

The conversation was awkward. Of course, they were concerned about both his and Mr. Pendleton's wellbeing. Of course, the National Park Service would cover all medical expenses. They also knew the details regarding the bravery of the Boy Scouts and intended to provide special Yellowstone Park Awards to each for their acts of heroism. Of course.

She spoke only in vague generalities about Jack Corey. His sudden and unexplained transformation shocked everybody, she said, adding nothing about a renegade wolf. Dieter made a quick decision not to bring up either topic.

Two days later, Dieter drove Amy, Michael, and Megan the twenty-four mile trip to Livingston and the veterinary hospital. Rusty was ready to be checked out. When they first spotted their precious pet in his cage, he wagged his tail and whimpered. He wasn't able to bark. The throat wound was going to need a couple of more weeks to heal, but a complete recovery was expected.

That evening they drove back through the center of the Park toward Colter. Rusty was well drugged, lying on a blanket in the backseat, his head on Michael's lap and his tail in Megan's. Because the pair claimed starvation, Dieter stopped at the Yellowstone Lake Lodge for a buffet dinner.

After the kids had stuffed themselves, they wanted to explore the gift shop. Amy watched as they pranced away, then turned to Dieter. "I thought you might want to know that I've changed my mind."

"About?"

"Moving."

"You're staying in Colter?"

"Nope, I'm headed upstate to Browning."

"But what about the beaches of the West Coast? Wine and sunsets?"

"That can wait. My people need me more than California can use me. I finally got the call. I'm starting my teaching career on the Reservation."

Dieter smiled to himself as he pictured the lively discussions that must have played out with her dad. He would long remember the Little Bear family.

"I'll miss the kids," she said. "I feel like they're mine, too." She folded her arms on the table, leaned forward and lightly gripped his forearm. "I suppose, if you really want to know, I just might miss you as well."

They held their stare for a brief moment and he recalled the sinking of his stomach when he saw the pine tree flying at them from her plane and, afterwards, the fleeting moment his cheek brushed hers.

When he started to speak, she interrupted. "Things are changing around Colter, Dieter."

"Aren't they everywhere?"

"When I stopped by Molly and the Judge's place this morning, she told me the latest. She didn't want us to be alarmed by learning it from TV. There's been a murder. An honest-to-God murder this time."

He lowered his voice. "What are you talking about?"

"I'm talking about Joseph Vincent Loudermilk."

"Joseph Loudermilk? What happened?"

"Stabbed to death. Undetermined number of times. He was found on his farm inside a cave, of all places. The details sound pretty gruesome."

"How . . . gruesome?"

"His eyeballs were carved out and stuffed into his mouth."

Dieter tossed back his head and looked away for a moment as he tried to grapple with the news. "Do they know who did it?"

"All I can tell you is that Molly hesitated for a long time when I asked. Then she said they didn't have a clue."

He fidgeted in his chair while she played with her spoon.

When Michael and Megan returned to the table, Dieter thought it a good time for a walk. They strolled down the path from the lodge as a full moon climbed above the silhouette of the Absaroka Mountains surrounding Yellowstone Lake. His mind drifted as they stared out over the wilderness and the vast body of water at the heart of Yellowstone. Amy was right. Although he'd barely settled in Colter, many changes had already taken place. He'd made many friends for life. His thoughts turned to the one image that flashed through his mind often since his ordeal on the Gallatin—Michael with his arms tightly hugging his waist, his head on Dieter's belly as he lay in the mud.

He suddenly stopped and cupped his hand to his ear, motioning for the others to listen. Above the clamor of waves slapping the rocks along the shore came the howls of a wolf pack echoing across the lake.

It was like a song, Dieter thought. The song of wolves, thriving once again where their ancestors had roamed free a century before.

He held his stare out over the water.

AFTERWORD

The tragedy recorded here was not the first of its kind. Abbé Pierre Pourcher, from the French village of Saint-Martin de Boubaux, compiled historical accounts of the Beast of Gévaudan, a creature responsible for killing at least sixty-four people in the Cevennes Mountains of southern France between 1764 and 1767. After hunting parties failed to find and destroy the animal, an elderly villager by the name of Antoine de Bauterne finally succeeded in tracking down and shooting it. The animal was quickly identified by its unique color and size: a hybrid wolf.

Yellowstone Park's superintendent resigned three days after that Labor Day in 1997. The following week, Acting Director Greta McFarland appointed Bantz Montgomery as the new chief park ranger. He remained in that position for five years before taking an early retirement and moving to a cabin on Huckleberry Gulch north of the Park. Greta McFarland lives in the suburbs of Washington, DC. She retired as a staffer for the National Park Service in the office of the Secretary of the Interior.

Charlene Loudermilk was never seen again. The remaining Loudermilk clan departed Colter a month after her disappearance; their whereabouts are currently unknown. The Schoonovers—Molly and the Judge—still get together with Josh Pendleton on his ranch near Colter. On occasional summer evenings, they share the sunset and a shot of single malt Scotch. Amy Little Bear resides on the Blackfeet Reservation in Browning, Montana, where she teaches Native American History at the Alternative High School.

Dieter Harmon's son Michael is on the veterinary science faculty at Montana State University in Bozeman. Dieter's daughter, Megan, owns and operates an art studio in West Yellowstone. Among her favorite pastimes is backpacking at every opportunity on Yellowstone trails with her dad. Occasionally, they are accompanied by Amy Little Bear. There aren't as many opportunities as Dieter would like because of his thriving reputation as a veterinarian throughout the Madison and Gallatin River regions. Rusty led a healthy, active life until his death at the ripe old age of fourteen.

The restoration of the North American gray wolf to Yellowstone National Park is complete. The latest survey revealed over one hundred wolves in eleven packs and with nine breeding pairs.

The Park contains over 900 miles of hiking trails, hosting thousands of backpackers each summer. In response to recent inquiries the U.S. Department of the Interior stated, "There is no credible evidence that hybrid wolves exist within the Greater Yellowstone Basin."

Anonymous sources confirm that surveillance continues.

ABOUT THE AUTHOR

James Marshall Smith is an award-winning author and scientist with a research career that has spanned multiple disciplines from biophysics to terrorism response. His work has taken him around the globe, providing source material for intriguing characters and alluring insight to his fiction. His first novel, *Silent Source*, was described by the San Francisco Book Review as a "stunning debut." The Manhattan Book Review praised him as the "master of suspense" and compared his fiction to the writing of James Patterson.

Hybrid was a short-list finalist for the Faulkner-Wisdom Award and a finalist for the Colorado Gold Novel Contest.

James lives in Georgia with his wife June and their bossy Maltese, Georgie. You can find him online at JamesMarshallSmith.com.

CUTTING-EDGE NAVAL THRILLERS
BY
JEFF EDWARDS

www.braveshipbooks.com

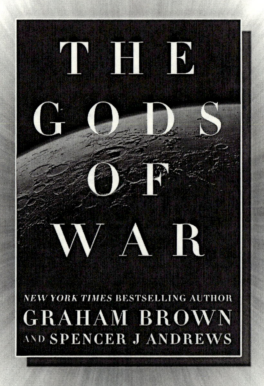

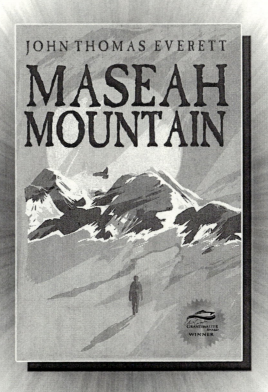

**THE THOUSAND YEAR REICH MAY BE
ONLY BEGINNING...**

ALLAN LEVERONE

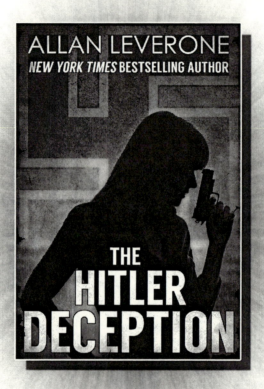

A Tracie Tanner Thriller

www.braveshipbooks.com

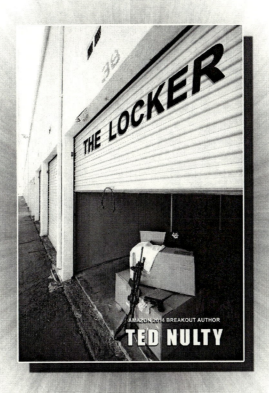

CPSIA information can be obtained
at www.ICGtesting.com
Printed in the USA
LVOW11*1522080418
572692LV00003B/31/P